NO GREATER BORN

NO GREATER BORN

DOROTHY R. PAPE

Thomas Nelson Publishers
Nashville • Camden • New York

Published in Nashville, Tennessee, by Thomas Nelson, Inc. and distributed in Canada by Lawson Falle, Ltd., Cambridge, Ontario.

Printed in the United States of America.

Library of Congress Cataloging in Publication Data

Pape, Dorothy R., 1913–
  No greater born.

  Bibliography: p.
  1. John, the Baptist, Saint—Fiction.   2. Jesus
Christ—Fiction.   I. Title.
PS3566.A6135N6   1984   813'.54   84-20617
ISBN 0-8407-5881-2

Contents

PART THREE—THE FULFILLMENT

Preface

The idea for this book came as I read the early chapters of the fourth Gospel one morning and realized afresh the dramatic and tragic qualities of John the Baptist's life. The discovery of the Dead Sea Scrolls and the Qumran community ruins, together with certain of John's characteristics and the lack of any other likely place for a child to be brought up in the Judean desert, make it seem probable he spent his youth there. As far as I'm aware, this is the first attempt at a "popular" portrayal of Qumran, and perhaps it may create wider interest in that intriguing community, still the subject of much scholarly concern.

Every Bible verse about John the Baptist is woven into this story, plus some necessarily imaginative reconstruction based on personal visits to Israel and considerable reading of authorities acknowledged in the bibliography. For example, a Philippino monk in the village of Ain Karim, where John was supposedly born, alerted me to the tradition of the attempt on John's life as a baby.

Commentators provide a variety of interpretations for the many problems relating to John. Are the locusts he ate insects (allowable food under Levitical law), or, as our Arab guide insisted, the long pods of the carob tree which are lined with a sweet-tasting gelatinous substance? These are known as St. John's Bread and are thought to be the "husks" the prodigal son coveted.

Views vary, too, on the exact meaning of John's baptism and on what Jesus meant when he said, "I say to you, among those born of women there is not a greater prophet than John the Baptist; but he who is least in the kingdom of God is greater than he" (Luke 7:28).

Did John ever speak to Jesus again after his baptism? The Bible is silent about this, and also about the mystery of why John never joined forces with him.

Was Salome the sister of Jesus' mother, and James and John therefore his cousins, and so related to John the Baptist? Alfred Edersheim claims so in *The Life and Times of Jesus the Messiah,* and a comparison of John 19:25 and Mark 15:40 strongly suggests this.

Was it Antipas' birthday celebration at which the other Salome danced, as most English translations say, or should it be the anniversary of his accession since birthdays were a private matter and not an occasion for public festivity? Was Salome's dance designed to stimulate her stepfather's sexual desire, as opera and film writers, plus most theologians, like to suggest? Indeed it is surprising with what detail many nineteenth century divines dwell on this, and also Mary Magdalene's past, although the Bible gives no hint of this in either case.

Was John beheaded at Machaerus or Sebaste? The only evidence for the former is that the historian Josephus records it there; but he wrote 40 years after the event, which Antipas tried to keep secret, and other details of Josephus' have been found inaccurate. Tourists can no longer go to Machaerus, but a guide in that area said recently most authorities now think John was beheaded at Sebaste. An ancient-looking iron trap door beneath the old ruins of St. John the Baptist Church in Sebaste has long been claimed as covering the burial place of John's head, while his body was taken by his disciples to Damascus. Certainly Machaerus was not a propitious place for Antipas to celebrate that particular year because it was near the territory of King Aretas, father of his first wife whom he had just divorced.

I had always imagined that John's baptism was only for men, since no mention is made of women receiving it. Dr. Wesley H. Brown of the Institute for Advanced Theological Studies in Jerusalem informs me, however, that it is generally believed now that women were included. It is also thought that it was a self-administered rite in the presence of John, similar to the current practice then of proselyte baptism. I am very grateful to him and others who have personally shared some of the most recent findings.

Finally, I believe there is real need for an increased awareness today of John's message and method. John, I believe, would have had little time for those who claim on some pollster's survey to be "born again" but who live the working week no better than the next man. John demanded a repentance leading to a dramatic change in wrong living and in relationships with both God and man. His preaching was backed one hundred percent by his own consistent lifestyle, with its patent self-sacrifice and integrity.

PART
ONE

Elizabeth

1

His Name is John

"They're coming! They're just around the bend!" Sarah cried as she ran excitedly into the inner room. She was the daughter of the neighboring priest, Phineas, and had been helping Elizabeth since the birth of her baby eight days before.

Elizabeth gently disconnected the infant from her breast and rearranged her gown. Then clutching him to her protectively, she slowly moved through the middle section of the house where Sarah's mother was busy preparing the food. She went into the large outer room where several women neighbors were already gathered. They were talking in low, yet excited voices. As soon as they saw Elizabeth, they pressed forward for a peep at the baby. They murmured joyful congratulations, but they quieted abruptly when they heard the sound of men's voices, and drew back discreetly against the wall.

The short, stocky figure of Elizabeth's husband, Zachariah, appeared in the doorway, and he ceremoniously motioned those behind him to enter.

Leading the group was Jannai, ruler of the synagogue in Ain Karim, the picturesque village in the Judean hills in which a number of priests of the Abijah course made their home. Jannai was closely followed by other leading men of the synagogue, and more friends and neighbors.

Without a glance at the women, Jannai strode up to the small table on which was spread a linen sheet. From the folds of his robe he produced a small package.

"Bring the child here." He motioned to Zachariah, and Elizabeth stepped beside her husband and moved to the table. With trembling fingers and conflicting feelings, she removed some of the swaddling bands from her baby. Her heart shrank at the thought of pain soon to be inflicted. Yet she was also nearly bursting with joy that at last she was a mother. She had produced a son who, in turn, would have the great honor of becoming a priest of Israel. Someday he would officiate in the worship of God, like his father.

"Blessed be the Lord our God, who has sanctified us by His precepts, and given us circumcision," intoned Jannai.

Deftly he severed the foreskin, and a sharp little cry came from the bundle on the table. As soon as the bandage was applied Elizabeth gathered him up and soothed him to silence.

"Bring the wine," ordered Jannai, and then he proceeded with the naming of the child.

"God, the God of our fathers, raise up this child to his father and mother, and let his name be called in Israel Zachariah, the son of Zachariah."

"Oh no!" protested Elizabeth quickly. "He must be called John."

Jannai gave her an indignant stare at this unorthodox interruption.

"None of your relatives bear that name," he retorted impatiently. "What foolish idea is this?"

"She's just a stupid old woman. The bearing of a child at this age has probably been too much for her," muttered one of the elders. "Take no notice of her."

"If only Zachariah himself could speak," fumed Jannai, turning around impatiently. "Is there no other responsible male relative present?"

Just then he noticed a look of great anxiety on Zachariah's face, and his hand motioned frantically to a shelf along one of the walls.

"There's the writing tablet. He wants to write something!" exclaimed one of the other men.

"Good! Bring it over here and let us get this business completed."

Jannai swept aside the cloth as the waxed writing tablet was brought, while someone else moved a stool to the table so that Zachariah could sit and write more easily. The men bent over his shoulders and watched as Zachariah picked up the reed pen and carefully scratched out his message.

JOHN IS HIS NAME.

"Look at that!" exclaimed Jannai in disgust, and the others began to express their surprise, too. But they were suddenly arrested by an exclamation and look of heavenly joy on Zachariah's face.

"Glory, glory to God in the highest, who only does wonderous things," burst from his lips now. "Yes, his name is John, this child is indeed 'Jehovah's Gift' to us. He was promised to me in the temple as I offered incense at the altar nine months ago, and this is the name the Lord gave through his angel. Listen, my friends, while I tell you what happened."

"Yes, tell us," the synagogue leaders said eagerly, and sat down on the benches while the women stood against the walls.

"An angel of the Lord appeared to tell me my wife was about to conceive. He said the child would not only bring *us* great joy, but many others, also. He is to be a Nazarite from birth, and will turn many sons of Israel to the Lord our God. He is to prepare a people ready for the Lord."

"Remarkable!"

"To think this should happen to someone in our village!"

"It is really a miracle Elizabeth should have a child after all these years. What is it all going to mean?"

"From his very conception he was to be filled with God's Spirit," Zachariah continued. "The angel said. . ."

"You mean we are to have another *prophet?*" an elder interrupted. "After four hundred years of silence, God will speak to his people again?"

"So it seems."

"But why did you become deaf and dumb, Zachariah?"

Zachariah was embarrassed. "It was because I couldn't believe the angel, at first. I asked for some sign that what he had told me would really happen. So he said I would become dumb until all was fulfilled."

"Well, we will certainly keep a watchful eye on this child in the synagogue when he is older. Meanwhile . . ." Jannai half turned

17

in Elizabeth's direction, but was careful not to let his eyes rest on her, "be sure you give him the best of care . . . and obey your husband."

He turned again to address the company. "Now, let us commit this remarkable child to the Holy One."

At the end of the prayer Sarah and her mother brought in the food they had prepared. There was a buzz of conversation as they all continued to discuss the extraordinary news they had just heard.

After the meal Jannai motioned to the other men to leave. With due formality and respect, Zachariah accompanied them on their way. All were overjoyed at his ability to speak and hear again.

The women were more relaxed after the men's departure. But realizing this was an exhausting occasion for Elizabeth, only eight days after the birth, they, too, soon began to leave. Once more they expressed good wishes, inwardly marveling at the good fortune which had come so late to Elizabeth. They had previously regarded her a little contemptuously for being unable to bear a child.

As the women departed, only one sour note was sounded, in a whisper Elizabeth was uncertain she was meant to hear. It came from Abigail, wife of Zachariah's cousin and fellow-priest, Zoma, speaking to their married daughter.

"I just don't believe all Zachariah told us! Drawing the lot to offer incense and having Elizabeth get pregnant has unhinged his mind a bit. As for her, her breasts must be as wrinkled as a grandmother's! She'll never be able to nurse the baby. Mark my word, he'll be dead in a few weeks!"

Fear and anger gripped Elizabeth for a moment, but she pretended not to have heard. She turned to say good-bye to another guest.

At last all had gone, except Sarah and her mother. Suddenly realizing how tired she was, Elizabeth took John back to the inner room and lay down. Her eyes gazed contentedly on the little head as it nuzzled her breast. She marveled anew at the miracle of his birth. Abigail's prediction showed no sign of being fulfilled yet. How thankful she was for Zachariah's continued love and faithfulness to her. He could have divorced her after ten years of childlessness, as many men would have done.

She longed for his return now, so that they could talk again for the first time in nine months! Those had been difficult days indeed. She was thankful that she had been born into a priest's family, so she had been taught to read and write. Thus she and her husband had at least been able to communicate on the small writing tablet.

She would never forget that day he had returned from the temple, speechless and deaf. Nor would she forget what had taken place that night in the little upper guest room at her brother's house in Jerusalem. As was the custom, as many people as possible from the village accompanied the priests to Jerusalem for their course of duty twice a year, as well as for the three great feasts. The priests had to stay in rooms at the temple because the rules of purity forbade sexual relations throughout their week of duty. During this time Elizabeth was able to stay with her younger brother, Hilkiah, and his wife Hannah, who lived in the Ophel district near the temple.

The absence of children had enabled Elizabeth to accompany her husband regularly, and incidentally had led to a closer fellowship with him than was common. She had welcomed each occasion for going to Jerusalem and used every opportunity for worship and sacrifice possible for a woman. Ever since she could remember, she had had a deep reverence for God. Her sheltered life offered few opportunities for great temptations, but she had consciously tried to please first her parents, then her husband. Still, she had been denied the child for which she constantly prayed. She had always heard that bearing children was the very reason for woman's existence. But after passing her fortieth birthday, she had given up hope.

Then had come that strange evening when, his week's course at the temple completed, Zachariah had hurried into her brother's house, his eyes shining with a strange excitement, his hands gesticulating wildly. He signaled for the writing tablet and had written, "My lot to burn incense. Vision of angel with message from God. Struck dumb for a time."

That night, after a frustratingly silent evening, Zachariah had signaled they should retire early to the upper room. He spent longer than usual in prayer. Afterward, to her great surprise, for one rabbinic school decreed there should be no sexual activity in the Holy City, they had had a very special time of lovemaking.

The journey home the next day on their donkeys had been a strange, silent one. As soon as they were in the house, however, Zachariah had seized the writing tablet and written, "God has promised us a son. John is to be his name."

She had stared in disbelief at first, thinking his experience had unbalanced his mind. Guessing her thoughts, he had added, "Angel made me dumb as sign this will come true."

At that, she remembered the previous night's experience, and her wildly beating heart nearly sent her reeling to the floor. Zachariah placed his strong arm around her and led her to the couch to recover, his face wreathed in smiles.

Soon she knew she was pregnant. In spite of her fever of joyful excitement, she had decided not to tell the neighbors, but to keep at home as much as possible to prevent any danger of miscarriage.

Physically they had been difficult days, but nothing could spoil her inner joy. Then in the sixth month there had been the unexpected visit of her young relative, Mary, from Nazareth. How she longed to be able to tell Zachariah more about that!

Now she could hear him at the outer door and her heart beat faster as he came in and sat down on the edge of the bed beside her and John. The bed had been another of his acts of thoughtfulness. Most people in their village slept on the floor, but Zachariah had realized a raised bed might be easier for her in her condition.

He was bending over their child now with an eager, loving look, stroking the dark hair.

"Our very own John, God's great gift. At last I can tell you all about it."

"Yes! What really happened there in the temple, Zachariah?"

"Well, our course of priests gathered as usual in the early morning for the lots to be drawn for offering the incense. As I watched, there came the stone with my name on it—the first time in all these years of service!"

"Not many in our village have had it, have they?"

"No. I could see Zoma was jealous, so I chose him to get the glowing coal off the altar and carry it in the silver fire pan. Phineas carried the incense bowl. I prepared in great excitement, and at last I was alone. I said the prayer, then held out the fire to ignite the incense. As I lifted my eyes I saw an angel!"

"Weren't you scared?"

"I certainly was! But he said at once, 'Stop being afraid, Zachariah, your prayer has been heard. Your wife, Elizabeth, will bear you a son, and you shall name him John.'"

"The angel even said *my* name?" Elizabeth could hardly believe such an honor possible.

"Yes, and he added the baby will be 'great before the Lord.' Think of that! And filled with the Spirit from his very conception."

"I really believe that," Elizabeth interrupted excitedly. "I tried to tell you how he had jumped within me when Mary arrived with her wonderful news that she was to bear our Savior, the king who is to have David's throne. So our little John is to prepare the way for him? Somehow it makes me a little scared of him, if he's to be such an important person!"

"There's no need to be afraid. The angel said so, remember? It just means God is specially caring for him and plans to do great things through him when he is grown. The angel even said he would go forth 'in the spirit and power of Elijah.'"

"Elijah!" Elizabeth's tone was full of awe. "You hadn't mentioned that before."

"Yes. Do you grasp the full significance of those words, Elizabeth? They are from the last of our sacred writings, the prophecy of Malachi. 'Behold, I will send you Elijah the prophet before the coming of the great and dreadful day of the Lord. And he will turn the hearts of the fathers to the children, and the hearts of the children to the fathers.' John's birth is the fulfilment of that prophecy of long ago! As one of our guests remarked, he will be the first prophet for four hundred years."

"Turn the hearts of the fathers to the children?" Elizabeth sounded puzzled. "Surely fathers instinctively love their children." She held little John up to burp him, and pressed him more closely to her.

"One would think so, especially at this age." Zachariah reached over and patted John's head. "But we have only to look around to see many families at odds among themselves. King Herod recently had two sons slain for allegedly plotting against him. And that was done at the instigation of another son! Many other fathers live in fear of their sons killing them to gain their inheritance more quickly. The times are evil, with little family solidarity—

multiple wives, and quarreling half-brothers. Where will it all end?"

Elizabeth gave a little shudder. "Well, that will be a great thing for our little John to accomplish. What else did the angel say?"

"He's to convert the rebellious to the ways of the wise and righteous to make ready a people for the Lord."

"What a wonderful, but difficult task! How can just one man influence so many, when almost our whole nation is corrupt and ungodly?"

"I believe times have never been more evil, or our people further from God. Yet throughout our history God has chosen, time and again, to use one man to bring the nation back to himself. Remember Moses, Josiah, Ezra . . ."

"But they were from great families in royal courts, while ours is such a humble home."

"But a godly one, Elizabeth. For generations our ancestors have sought to serve God. Our own fathers were righteous men. The Lord in his grace has kept us from much of the corruption of the world."

"I suppose that's true." She saw the baby was asleep now, and placed him carefully on the bed beside her. Zachariah quickly seized her hand and squeezed it.

"It *is* true. I've *seen* the angel Gabriel! He said he had a message from God and here is the very proof of its truth lying on the bed before our eyes. God will accomplish His purposes, have no doubt about that."

"I've been thinking about his being a Nazarite, too, Zachariah. It's not going to be easy in this village with its fine vines! What a good thing you decided to work as a potter, rather than a vine-dresser, when you're not on duty at the temple. At least we don't have grapes growing near the house."

"Yes, but I think it was when I refused to go into partnership with Zoma as a vine grower that he first began to dislike us."

"But why?"

"For the same reason that causes so many family squabbles. He thought he would inherit our portion because we had no children. Anyway, now Zoma has joined the Pharisees. He is in so well with them, that he has nothing to worry about. And with his brother-in-law, Ishmael, having an administrative job at the temple, Zoma will probably be able to get in there, too, before long."

"I hope so. The village will really be a happier place without Zoma and his wife." Elizabeth nearly told her husband of Abigail's words earlier, but thought better of it. "But about John being a Nazarite—it's really going to be hard to keep him away from the wine and grapes when they are the chief product of this village. We shall surely need God's wisdom and help!"

Elizabeth lay awake a long time that night. She determined she must try to find out all she could about Elijah. Once she was strong enough to go out again, she would beg the keeper of the scrolls at the synagogue to let her look at them. Then she remembered hearing he didn't believe in women being given access to knowledge. It would be better to ask Zachariah to borrow them, and she would study them in secret in their inner room.

Finally she fell into an uneasy sleep and dreamed that John was grown up and preaching to great crowds in the temple courtyard, while for some unaccountable reason Zoma and his wife Abigail were trying to incite the people to stone him.

2

A Prophecy and
a Presentiment

A month passed, and soon it would be the fortieth day after the birth. Then Elizabeth could go to the temple to make her offering and be pronounced clean again by the priest. How she looked forward to that day, and how willingly she and Zachariah would offer the pair of doves for this precious gift God had given them! At first she had wished it had been during Zachariah's course of duty so he could help perform the ceremony. Then she concluded it was much better that he could be free to be with her the whole day.

At last the day dawned on which they were to make the journey to Jerusalem. How different were the needed preparations when traveling with a baby! They would have to go more slowly, too, and stop to feed him. They would also need rest somewhere when the sun was hottest overhead, for no shade was available on the back of a donkey.

As they plodded along, she thought over the meaning of the purification ceremony. She had often been in the Court of Women at the beautiful new temple when other mothers were there on account of their newborn babies. She had longed then that she, too, might have the experience. Now it was to be a reality. She and Zachariah would offer this firstborn so joyfully to God, for indeed little John was already his in a special way. She wished they could have afforded a lamb, but they had no flock of their own. The lambs provided at the temple were sold at a highly inflated price. The surplus profit went into the private purse of the high priest—or so most people surmised.

And why did she need to be pronounced clean again? How could bearing a son, which was supposed to be the very thing women were created for, make her unclean? Was it something to do with the subsequent loss of blood? All women were considered unclean during the menstrual cycle and they couldn't go to the synagogue during those times. But when women had no control over such natural things, why must they be penalized for them? Well, she wouldn't worry about that today. She'd just be thankful she had a child to bring—a child who was destined to accomplish so much for the Lord.

Baby John was restless as the day grew hot. The tight swaddling bands, which gave a great sense of security, left little space for air to circulate. However, the travelers were able to rest at an inn they knew well. John slept within the coolness of its thick stone walls.

Finally they arrived at her brother Hilkiah's house. He and his wife, Hannah, welcomed them joyfully. It was the first time they had seen Elizabeth since her visit nearly eleven months before.

The following morning they all walked to the temple, through the Beautiful Gate, and up into the Court of Women. On one side of this was the imposing Nicanor Gate, which led into the court of Israel, where only Jewish men were allowed. Beyond this was the temple building itself. In this was the Holy Place where Zachariah had offered the incense, and beyond that was the Holy of Holies. Only the High Priest could enter there and even then only once a year, on the Day of Atonement.

At the fifteen semicircular steps to the Nicanor Gate, the rites of purification were held for lepers and women after childbirth. Here, also, women suspected of adultery had to drink "the water of bitterness" that would prove whether or not they were guilty. Elizabeth was glad there was not such a woman there today, for it was a painful process. Nor, these days, were there many lepers who believed they were healed, though Elizabeth had seen an occasional one anxiously seeking a favorable verdict from the priest. It struck her now as a little odd that bearing a child seemed to be placed in the same category as leprosy and adultery.

There was just one new mother ahead of them, so they did not have long to wait. After the two turtle doves had been duly received and slaughtered, the priest on duty said the appropriate prayers and declared Elizabeth purified. With joy surging through her, she was about to turn away when she noticed Zachariah trembling all over, his eyes turned heavenward.

Suddenly he began to speak in a loud, clear voice, strangely unlike his own.

> Praise to the God of Israel!
> For he has turned to his people Israel,
> saved them and set them free;
> and has raised up a deliverer of victorious power
> from the house of his servant David.
>
> So he promised: age after age he proclaimed
> by the lips of his prophets,
> that he would deliver us from our enemies,
> out of the hand of all who hate us;
> that he would deal mercifully with our fathers,
> calling to mind his solemn covenant.
>
> Such was the oath he swore to our father Abraham,
> to rescue us from enemy hands,
> and grant us, free from fear, to worship him
> with a holy worship, with uprightness of heart,
> in his presence, our whole life long.

By this time a crowd had gathered, but Zachariah seemed unaware. His eyes now gazed off in the distance toward Bethlehem. Then they turned to little John, asleep again in Elizabeth's arms. He took a deep breath, and continued in the same voice as before.

> And you, little one, will be called prophet of the Highest;
> for you will go in advance of the Lord to prepare his way,
> to bring to his people a knowledge of salvation
> by remission of their sins
> through the tender mercies of our God,
> by which the light of dawn will beam on us from on high,
> to shine on those sitting in darkness
> and in the shadow of death,
> to direct our feet into the path of peace.

A PROPHECY AND A PRESENTIMENT

Zachariah's voice died away, and he stood with closed eyes for a few moments. Elizabeth had been hanging on every word, trying to plumb the depths of their meaning. Now she was suddenly embarrassed by the crowd as it pressed around the infant and asked, "Who are you? What sort of child is this?"

"What was that about a deliverer from the house of David?" asked a man in a louder voice.

Zachariah suddenly came to himself, and in his ordinary voice began to answer some of the questions. Then two temple guards pushed their way through the crowd, demanding to know what all the disturbance was about.

"It's just one of the country priests. He's been standing here prophesying," answered another man.

"He told us a deliverer is coming from the house of David," said another with a mocking laugh as he turned to walk away.

"What's that?" demanded the senior guard, as he pushed his way to the center of the throng to find an elderly couple standing there with a baby.

Hilkiah quickly moved over to the guards, and they recognized him at once as one of the permanent staff of priests at the temple.

"What's going on here?" they asked him.

"It's just my sister, come for her purification rite. As you see, the parents are no longer young, and this birth has seemed like a miracle after waiting so many years."

"But why the crowd?"

"The father believes God has given them the child for a special ministry and he just received a prophetic utterance. It was really praise to God for the gift of the child and a prayer of hope that he will eventually turn many to God."

"Well, you'd better move on now. See, other mothers are waiting."

Indeed, there were several. Elizabeth hastily whispered to Zachariah, "Let us go, but I hope you can remember every word you have just spoken."

They spent the remainder of the day quietly at Hilkiah's house, Hannah taking a special interest in John because her four children were all grown. Zachariah, who hadn't been able to speak on his last visit, now told them more about what had happened when he offered the incense. They could only marvel and wonder what the future would hold for a child who was such an obvious gift from God.

"But I would keep quiet about his future, if I were you, especially in Jerusalem. Nearly everyone here is power-hungry. Any potential rival is someone to get rid of in a hurry," Hilkiah warned them.

Elizabeth opened her eyes wide. "You mean they—they don't *want* God to send a deliverer in these evil days?"

"Many hope to be that deliverer so they can get power and multiply their wealth. The religious leaders here are just as corrupt as Herod. All try to play the others off with the Romans to their own advantage."

"But how can they worship God every day and yet be like that inside?" Elizabeth asked.

"Their worship is nothing but a formal routine, while their eyes are on all the money changing hands at the various booths. Our religion is at its lowest ebb in history. The Sadducees care about *nothing* but money, political power, and status. The Pharisees seek to control the ordinary people, binding them under endless rules and regulations that most of the Pharisees don't keep themselves. I'm so thankful that I accepted Herod's offer to become one of the stonemasons for building the sanctuary of the temple. It is an inspiring job. At least we have to give King Herod credit for that. And because of that, I have escaped all the inner politics and temptations."

"It certainly is a wonderful structure. How long will it be before it is finished?"

"Probably another couple of decades before all the outer courts and walls Herod has in mind are finished."

"I've heard there's one religious group, the Essenes, that doesn't use the temple. Is that right?" asked Elizabeth.

"Yes, it's true. They appear to be almost the only ones who are really living devout lives. But they tend to shut themselves off from ordinary folk and avoid the temple as evil, except for paying their tax. And I'm not sure if that isolation is right or wrong," Hilkiah answered.

"We're really concerned about it, because our son Eleazer is thinking of joining them," added Hannah. "We just don't know what to think."

"What about Jason? Is he interested too?"

"No, I don't think so. Being married into the family of Euthinos, with the hereditary right to supply the incense for the temple, he's pretty well entrenched. And since that service is not connected with any fraud to worshippers, as in the sale of sacrifices, I think he's fairly satisfied. I'd say your little John is going to have a tremendous task, though, if he's going to change all the evils that go on here!"

Back in Ain Karim, baby John seemed no worse for the journey. On the other hand, Elizabeth felt very tired. But she was determined that one thing must be settled before anything else.

"Zachariah," she urged after their simple supper, "that prophecy—can you remember it again? We must write it down."

Zachariah closed his eyes. "Yes, yes, I think I can. In a sense it has been on my mind ever since I became dumb and began to search the Scriptures for details of the Coming One. It just suddenly all came out, there in the temple yesterday."

"Our little writing tablet is no use for that. We ought to have some parchment. Oh, Zachariah, do you think we can afford it? It's so important we should have a record of it to show the child when he is older."

"That's true. Somehow we must get some parchment. I believe we have an order for two specially large waterpots. I'll work on those tomorrow and that will bring us a little extra income."

After a couple of days rest with the help of Sarah, Elizabeth was ready to tackle the ordinary household duties again. There was no denying, though, that she found life considerably harder now than in former days, especially drawing the extra water needed from the well—it was nearly one hundred paces from the house. The job would be easier once the winter rains came, filling the cistern in their courtyard again.

The village was still talking about this miracle baby. Interest revived after John's dedication trip to Jerusalem, although neither father nor mother mentioned Zachariah's prophetic utterance. Various neighbors came to visit, bringing little gifts. Even Abigail arrived carrying a bottle of wine. Perhaps she had heard that Elizabeth was no longer drinking it, since little John was to be a Nazarite for life.

Abigail expressed surprise that the baby looked so healthy and had obviously grown since the day of his circumcision.

"I don't know how you do it with those small breasts," she said, her sharp eyes appraising Elizabeth's figure. "I only hope you can keep it up. This wine will be good for you." She placed it conspicuously on the table and waited until Elizabeth had murmured her thanks.

"There's something I think I should warn you about, Elizabeth. Our neighbor, Perez, returned from Jerusalem yesterday with a message from my brother Ishmael. He's on the temple staff now, you know."

"Yes, of course I know."

"He says that Zachariah caused some kind of commotion when you were at the temple for the purification. Is that right?"

"*He* didn't cause the commotion. People just gathered around because he started prophesying about our son."

"No one prophesies these days. God has sent no one to our nation for hundreds of years. He's just left us to the Romans and Herod. What we need is another Judas Maccabees! But your son will never be that. Children of old parents usually grow up little runts or mentally deficient, so don't set your heart on anything like that. All this excitement has turned Zachariah's head."

"That's not true!" Elizabeth protested vehemently. "An angel *did* appear to him there at the altar. He promised us this child. He promised that God would make him a blessing to many, turning the rebellious to righteousness."

Abigail looked completely unconvinced. "My brother said Zachariah uttered something about a deliverer arising from the house of David. Is that right?"

"Yes," admitted Elizabeth.

"Well, the word is getting around the temple. Nobody there is wanting a savior from that quarter, I can tell you. They're getting along very well with both Rome and Herod at the moment. So I thought I'd better come and warn you. Just forget about all those fanciful ideas of Zachariah's."

"How can we, when it is *God* who has spoken about them?"

Abigail shrugged. "So you are living in the same fantasy world as your husband. You'd better be more sensible and down to earth if you are to have any hope of raising that boy. I'm just saying this for your own good." With that, she stalked out of the house.

Elizabeth breathed a sigh of relief as Abigail disappeared, but she found she couldn't overcome the uneasy feeling aroused by Abigail's words. How she wished Zachariah were home.

A PROPHECY AND A PRESENTIMENT

At last she heard the courtyard gate shut. The pottery work-shop and kiln were beside Abiel's house on the other side of the village, so at least Elizabeth didn't have all the cleaning involved in that. But sometimes she felt it would be good to have her husband within earshot, especially since John's arrival.

Her husband came in looking tired but pleased. "I've finished the waterpots, and Abiel has advanced some money for the parchment. I'll go buy it tomorrow."

He looked so pleased that Elizabeth didn't have the heart to tell him of Abigail's visit until after supper. He looked a little anxious as he heard of the repercussions in Jerusalem.

"These days you can't trust anyone, it seems. But God has spoken to us. We can trust him and know that he will fulfill his word. But it may not be without difficulties—or even danger," he added in a suddenly lowered voice.

3

Of Tyranny and Traitors

Soon the interest of the village people shifted with the furor and preparation for the national census ordered by the Roman Emperor, Caesar Augustus. Some declared it threatened greatly increased taxation. Others feared it meant the Jewish people would no longer enjoy their present privileges under the Romans—namely the freedom to carry on all the requirements of their religion, which also involved exemption from conscription into the Roman armies. But King Herod was firmly behind the Emperor and there was nothing anyone could do to prevent the census.

For nearly every family in Ain Karim it meant making room for absent male relatives and their families who must return there to register. Zachariah and Elizabeth had been born there, but Zachariah had no immediate living relatives. Elizabeth's younger brother, Hilkiah, and his wife would be coming, with their two sons, Jason and Eleazer, plus Jason's three children. It would be a tight fit, but it was only for two nights. Elizabeth planned to put the women and children in the inner room and the men in the living room. Their house was, in fact, bigger than most in the village, many of which had only one room. Long ago, when times had been easier, Zachariah's father had added the kitchen and sleeping room to form three sides around a central court.

Elizabeth was indeed glad of this opportunity to return the hospitality she and Zachariah had enjoyed so frequently at her brother's home in Jerusalem. Since Hilkiah had moved there sixteen years ago to become a priest stonemason for Herod's proposed new temple, he had had little time to come and visit.

Fortunately, the coming invasion of relatives meant there was an increased demand for pottery products, and Zachariah was very busy. This would help them since the pay of country priests was pitifully low. Some of the chief priests in Jerusalem were even seizing the offerings and hides of sacrificial animals that were due the officiating priests on the days they served.

"I keep wondering how my relative, Mary, is getting on," Elizabeth said to Zachariah one evening a few days before the census. "It has been a long while since we heard of her safe return to Nazareth. It must be getting near her time. How good it was that Joseph accepted her and married her earlier than planned."

"Yes. People would find her story even stranger than ours," Zachariah responded with a smile. "Being from the house of David, I suppose they'll have to travel all the way to Bethlehem."

"They seem far from royalty now, I must say. Mary's father, too, is of David's line, of course, though another branch. It's always easy for the daughters of priests to make a good marriage, but theirs apparently wasn't much of a financial success. Yet God has chosen *her*, out of all the possible young women of countless generations, to be the one to bear this Savior."

"Let us hope the child is already safely born. It's at least a three day journey for them to Bethlehem."

"Yes. I found the half-day's travel to Jerusalem bad enough. I wonder if they'll have time to visit us! Those were such wonderful weeks we spent together when she came to tell me the great news Gabriel had given her."

"I doubt that Joseph will want to spend more time away from work. And he'll know that everyone has many visitors at such a time. Don't build your hopes too high, Elizabeth. God will bring these two babies together in his own good time."

At last the day came when all the guests were due. Ain Karim had never had so many people and animals in its streets. When Elizabeth went to draw water from the well she found a long line of donkeys and a few horses which belonged to the more wealthy. Carrying her pitcher home on her head she found it difficult to make her way along the narrow cobbled street.

It was late evening when her own guests arrived, for it had taken longer than expected to travel the crowded highway and get attention for a party of six adults and three children in the busy inns.

After their first greetings and general admiration expressed over six-month-old John, Hilkiah began to tell of their experiences on the road, managing to make their ordeal sound quite humorous.

"And at least there were too many people about to fear robbers," added Hannah. "That is always my greatest concern. Nowhere seems safe these days."

"Perhaps it's because I'm not often out after dark," continued Hilkiah, "but it seemed to me there was an exceptionally bright star shining. It was south of the Holy City, just a little southeast of here, in fact."

"Over Bethlehem then?" Zachariah suggested.

"Yes, I suppose it would be about there."

Zachariah and Elizabeth exchanged glances.

"Do you think there could possibly be any connection with Mary and her child?" Elizabeth asked in a half whisper.

"Possibly. God uses various signs as it pleases him. I remember a prophecy about a star. In the fourth book of Torah, Balaam prophesied something like: 'A star shall come out of Jacob, a scepter shall rise out of Israel.' Those things are often thought of as symbols of royalty. So it's just possible there could be a connection," Zachariah added with a smile at his wife.

"I wonder if the star's still there. Shall we go up on the roof and see?" Elizabeth asked eagerly.

Zachariah agreed and led the way, their guests following a little awkwardly on their still cramped legs from the long donkey ride. Elizabeth dutifully came last, trying to hide her impatience.

"Yes, there it is," she heard Hilkiah say. "Do you see? Over there."

"That's the direction of Bethlehem, all right. It does seem unusually bright." Zachariah then turned to help Elizabeth up the last step, and gave her arm a little squeeze.

They all stood gazing silently for a while, then began to shiver as the cool night breeze hit them.

"I suppose we had better go down again," said Elizabeth reluctantly. "I know how tired you must all be. But it really is unusually low and bright, and—why look! A whole patch in the sky over there seems bright now!"

"What can it be?" The others were all at a loss to explain the phenomenon.

"Well, I suppose we shall hear something about it from the astrologers in Jerusalem," Hilkiah said finally. "I think I've had enough star-gazing for one night. It's getting really cold."

After the tiresome business of registering for the census was completed the next day, Elizabeth served a roast lamb in honor of her guests. Although they hadn't been able to afford one as their temple offering, Zachariah's partner had obtained two lambs a few weeks earlier and had been fattening them for this time of needed hospitality. Baby John was the center of attention and even late into the evening everyone seemed reluctant to settle down for the night.

Morning came too soon for Elizabeth, and she hurriedly prepared breakfast of fish and bread for her guests, who were anxious to make an early start.

"And don't forget to let us know anything you find out about that star," were Elizabeth's parting words.

"Yes, I certainly will," promised Hilkiah.

Elizabeth hoped each day they might receive some news of Mary and Joseph, but none came. Perhaps they planned to stay with some of his relatives in Bethlehem until it was time for her purification. They might then go to Jerusalem by way of Ain Karim, although it would be somewhat out of their way. When the fortieth day after the census passed, however, Elizabeth had to give up hope of seeing Mary and her new baby. Perhaps Joseph hadn't wanted her to have too much to do with her own relatives. Some husbands were like that. How fortunate she had been with Zachariah. He had always been very friendly with her brother. But then he was with everyone. Her heart glowed with love and appreciation, and she decided to make his favorite honey bread for supper.

He had been away all week with his fellow priests for their course in Jerusalem and would be returning this evening. Most priests found that the exclusively meat diet during their week of duty upset their digestion and having to work all the time in the temple with bare feet often gave them a chill, so the honey bread would be a special treat.

Elizabeth was excited about something she had to show her husband, too. Zachariah had some time ago carefully copied out on the precious parchment Gabriel's message, and the prophecy he had uttered in the temple. Since then Elizabeth had secretly been making a beautiful bright blue cover for the scroll, embroidered with white lilies. This week, while Zachariah had been away, she had completed it. She knew he would be pleased.

John had become an ever-increasing joy to them as he learned to sit up, take notice of things, and respond to their smiles. But Elizabeth was finding his growing weight a real burden. *How will I manage as he gets older, especially during those times when Zachariah is on duty in Jerusalem?* she wondered. *I've managed so far, though, and I must trust God for the future.*

She got out the bowl and necessary ingredients and was soon mixing the dough for the honey bread. She made it into ten flat rounds and placed them on the hot stones around the fire in the center of the kitchen floor.

Shortly after she had turned the half-baked breads, she heard hoofs in the courtyard. It was early for Zachariah and for a brief moment she wondered if it could be Mary. But before she could reach the outer door she was amazed to see her brother, Hilkiah, stride in.

"Why—" she began as she hurried to greet him, but he held her hands tightly, his breath coming in quick gasps.

"Hush! There's not a moment to lose! Get your warmest cloak, a sheepskin blanket, some food, and little John. We must leave at once!"

"But Hilkiah!" She stood before him, feeling she must know more before she could follow his crazy directions.

"Elizabeth, believe me! Herod's soldiers are on their way to kill John. They could be here at any moment!"

He dragged her through the kitchen to the far room and started rolling up the sleeping baby in his coverings.

Elizabeth felt paralyzed with horror, but managed to seize the heavy double skeepskin from the bed as she pleaded, "*Why*, Hilkiah? He *couldn't* want to kill a child!"

"Hasn't he killed his favorite wife, then her two sons, and isn't he about to kill another?" Hilkiah almost spat out the words as he snatched the sheepskin from her and began to roll it up.

"I'll tell you more as we travel, but get what you can carry for yourself and John and come quickly!"

Elizabeth dazedly stuffed a few things into a cloth bag, and tied it to her waist. Then her eyes fell on the precious scroll, and she carefully tucked it into the top of her robe.

In the kitchen Hilkiah found a small sack, snatched up the hot bread, then poured a little water on the fire. He noticed some dried fruit hanging on the wall and dropped that in the sack also, then hurried back to Elizabeth. He thrust John into her arms, swung the sheepskin roll on his shoulder, and pulled her after him, picking up the food sack as he passed.

"But Zachariah—" began Elizabeth, hesitating by the fire as she saw no bread was left for him.

"We can't wait to write a message—and it's better he doesn't know where you are. Quick, up on my donkey. Cover your head with your hood and try to hide the baby. Pray no one will see us. Do not speak, until we are beyond the houses."

He led the donkey up the lane above them, rather than down toward the well and the street leading to the main trail going east to Jerusalem. Soon they were beyond the few houses situated on the hill and Hilkiah felt it was safe to speak.

"Well, it all began with that bright star we saw. Do you remember?"

"Of course. But how—"

"Apparently some astrologers in Persia noted the appearance of this unfamiliar star. They believed it heralded the birth of a new king."

"So it *was* for Mary's son?" Elizabeth whispered, but her brother ignored her question.

"They saw the star move gradually westward and decided to follow it, bringing gifts for this new king. It led them right to our country. They went to Jerusalem expecting to find the baby in the royal palace there. King Herod happened to be in residence when they arrived, although he has been spending much of his time in Jericho since he's been so sick."

Hilkiah could sense Elizabeth shifting impatiently on the donkey and tried to come quickly to the point.

"The wise men requested an audience with him and asked, 'Where is the newborn king of the Jews? For we saw his star in the east, and we have come to worship him.' That really threw Herod into a fright, thinking he was going to lose his kingdom. He had the wise men entertained in a side room while he hastily sent for the chief priests and demanded, 'Where is the Messiah to be born?' They answered it was in Bethlehem of Judea."

"So that is why Mary *had* to be in Bethlehem?"

"Herod was frantic then, but he called the wise men in again and asked when they had first seen the star. Then he sent them on to Bethlehem to find the child. But he told them to come back and tell him where the child was, so he could go and worship him, too."

"King *Herod* go and worship Mary's child?"

"That's what he said. But of course his one idea was to destroy the child. For some reason the wise men didn't go back to Jerusalem and when they failed to appear, Herod went mad." Hilkiah paused, wondering how best to break the next news.

"But what has he done?"

"First he ordered a company of soldiers to go to Bethlehem and kill every boy child under two years of age."

Mary gave a quick gasp of horror.

"Then that former neighbor of yours, Zoma's brother-in-law, Ishmael, told Herod a remarkable child had recently been born in Ain Karim to the priest, Zachariah—and that he'd been shouting some prophecy about it in the temple. Herod immediately gave Ishmael a reward and ordered another squad of soldiers to come here and slay John."

"No!" Elizabeth gasped in horror.

"That's why it's better Zachariah doesn't know where you are now."

"But how did you find out all this and get ahead of the soldiers?"

"Jason overheard Ishmael talking to one of the other priests. The rest was soon known all over the temple area. He brought me the news as soon as he could. The soldiers were a little ahead of me, but they stopped at an inn. They have to have plenty of drink under their belts for a job like this, I guess. So I was able to get ahead of them."

Elizabeth shuddered. "Hilkiah, you've put your own life in danger, too. But that Ishmael! How *could* he be such a traitor to his family, his course of the priesthood, and our whole village! It's—it's unbelievable."

"These days men are willing to sacrifice anything, including their children and parents, for their own advancement. There seems to be no natural affection any more. Perhaps Ishmael had something against your family?"

"I can only think it's because our property would have gone to them if John hadn't been born."

"Ah, that explains it!"

Elizabeth now suddenly remembered the soldiers were going to Bethlehem, too.

"Poor Mary and her baby! I wonder what's happened to them."

"Set your heart at rest about them. God has all things in control. I was going to tell you about her. She and Joseph and the baby, whom they have named Jesus, as the angel Gabriel told them, spent the night with us on their way back to Nazareth."

"Oh did they? How wonderful! What is the baby like?"

"Well, just a baby, as far as I could see," answered Hilkiah with a smile. "Mary told us of the visit of the wise men just the day before they left, and they had brought some very expensive gifts for Jesus."

"Really?"

"It was all God's doing. Mary and her family were to have spent a second night with us. But soon after we were all asleep, Joseph was awakened by God in a dream and warned that Herod would soon seek the child's life. God told him they were to flee at once to Egypt. The gold and valuable spices the wise men had given was more than enough to pay their travel expenses, and they were gone a whole day ahead of Herod's discovery that the wise men were not coming back to him."

"But Egypt! That's so far away! Oh!—where are you taking *me*, Hilkiah?" Elizabeth asked in sudden fear.

"I remembered that cave I used to visit as a boy, where David was supposed to have hidden from Saul. Do you remember my telling you about it? It's five or six miles up the valley, and there's water there. It's a wild, overgrown place now, and the soldiers aren't likely to go searching far outside the village. You should be safe if you stay hidden there."

"How—how long do you think we will have to hide?" Elizabeth tried to keep her fear from showing in her voice.

"It's hard to tell. Maybe even two weeks." Elizabeth shivered. "If possible, I'll try to get you out before, of course. I can't return to Ain Karim now, or I'd be under suspicion immediately. So I plan to return through Emmaus and will leave word with Hannah's nephew, Cleopas, about where you are. Then I'll have to hurry back to Jerusalem before I am missed there."

The path was becoming rough now and in the growing darkness it was difficult to pick their way. The donkey, who had been driven hard all day, was showing signs of weariness. Hilkiah, too, was obviously tiring under the heavy, awkward sheepskin bundle.

"There's a bit of grass here. Should we stop and let the donkey feed a little?" suggested Elizabeth. "There are no houses in sight. It should be safe."

Hilkiah reluctantly agreed. He took little John from her and laid him down in the grass, then helped her from the saddle. For the first time on this desperate journey John began to cry, so Elizabeth sat on the sheepskins and let him nurse.

"*Pray* the milk supply won't dry up," she pleaded, looking anxiously at her brother.

"Certainly we will. But don't be afraid. God has a plan for this little life, and he will not let Herod or anyone else thwart it. Be sure of that."

4

The Cave

After a short rest Hilkiah hastened them on again. This time they remained quiet, busy with their own thoughts and too weary to speak. Only Hilkiah's words of guidance and encouragement to the donkey broke the silence.

At last he stopped the animal at a place where the path was about to enter a dense wood stretching above and below it.

"The cave is near here, less than a mile, if I remember right. I'm afraid we'll have to walk the rest of the way because some of the tree branches are low. It's very steep, too. I'll leave the donkey and the sheepskin here and come back for them after I've carried little John to the cave for you. Do you think you can manage?"

Elizabeth's heart had sunk at this news, but she nodded her head and set out close behind her brother, watching his every step. How he found his way was a mystery to her, for she couldn't discern any path in the darkness. She was only aware they were descending steeply. Every few steps Hilkiah turned to give her a hand, having tied the bag of food around his waist.

After what seemed an endless time, he suddenly stopped.

"Praise to the Almighty, the Holy One! Here it is."

Elizabeth found herself facing a high slab of dark rock with no evident opening. But Hilkiah led the way to the far end where a projecting angle had hidden the narrow entrance.

"It will be warm and dry in here. It's much bigger than you'd imagine. And, most important, there's fresh water seeping through the rock in one place far to the rear. So you won't need to come out into the open at all."

As he spoke, Hilkiah's eyes seemed to be searching the ground around the entrance, then he held John out to her.

"Take him a moment, while I go inside and look around."

Neither of them put into words the fear uppermost in their minds. Lions or other wild beasts could have made the cave their lair, or a group of robbers could have taken advantage of its shelter.

With ears strained, and eyes scanning the eerie shadows of the surrounding woods under the star-lit sky, Elizabeth waited, perspiring in spite of the cool night breeze now sweeping up the valley. Sometimes she thought she caught a glimmer of eyes peering at her among the trees. She felt a sudden, desperate urge to call out to Hilkiah, but she knew it would be foolish. She marveled that little John seemed so content and had hardly cried throughout the difficult journey. Surely this must be the work of the Spirit within him.

At last her brother reappeared.

"Everything seems all right. Come in and find a suitable place for John to sleep, then I'll go for the sheepskins."

At first it seemed to Elizabeth that everything was pitch-black inside. As Hilkiah took her hand she wondered how he could possibly find his way around. All she could tell was that they seemed to be on sandy soil.

"Look back to the cave entrance to get your bearings. You see it isn't completely dark outside. Here's a ledge of rock that makes a good seat. Stay there until I return with the sheepskin, then we'll fix up your bed."

With that Hilkiah was gone. Elizabeth gingerly lowered herself on the rock and began swaying gently back and forth as John at last began to whimper. Just as she felt her arms could bear his weight no longer, she sensed he was asleep, and laid him down between her feet. She feared that if she put him on the ledge he might roll off. She had no idea how far it extended.

It seemed even more frightening then, without the warmth of his little body against hers, and with everything so quiet. She half-wished he would begin to cry again! That would at least give her something to think about and perhaps it would frighten away smaller animals, too. But what about the larger ones that were said to exist still in the area?

She shuddered and felt she couldn't possibly stay in this place.

As soon as Hilkiah returned she would beg him to take her to Emmaus. But he had been so good, planned so carefully, and risked his own life for her sake and the baby's.

Now she could hear twigs snapping, and what she fervently hoped was the sound of his footsteps. A dark shape appeared against the night sky in the entrance. With a gasp of relief she recognized Hilkiah.

"Here I am," he said cheerfully. "I hope it didn't seem long. I forgot to leave the food bag before, too. In the morning you should hang it up somewhere, so it won't attract mice. Keep it under the sheepskin with you now. Your life may depend on it, you know. As I said, there's water back there, and I brought the cup from my saddlebag."

"Oh, what a good thing you remembered that!"

"Shall I get you a drink now? I think I can find it once my eyes get used to the darkness again."

Remembering John's needs, Elizabeth thankfully accepted the offer. Soon Hilkiah returned and held out the cup. She was surprised and thankful at the sweetness of the water. It was as good as that at Ain Karim.

"Now let's fold the sheepskins in half. This way you'll have some over you and some beneath. With John beside you it'll be cosy as can be. Now I must go. I must be far from here by daylight."

"Yes, yes, and thank you so much for everything, Hilkiah." Elizabeth could hardly believe the words came from her own lips. Somehow she managed to keep the tears out of her eyes for a moment.

Hilkiah held up his hand in a solemn blessing.

"God bless you and keep you. May the light of his countenance be upon you, and give you his peace." Then he was gone.

Elizabeth lay motionless, listening until the sound of his footsteps died away. Aware she was now completely alone, such a weakness overwhelmed her that she suddenly felt faint. Only the touch of John's warm body forced her to cling to consciousness. But gradually, as the time passed without incident, her terror subsided. The words of Hilkiah's blessing came back to her. "The light of his countenance be upon you, and give you his peace." Intuitively she realized she was alone with God in a way she had never experienced before. His face was turned to her, an unknown, humble woman to whom he had entrusted a babe with a momentous future. The thought brought a strange peace to her agitated spirit and stilled her trembling limbs at last.

The next thing she knew was the hungry cry of her baby and the early morning sunlight streaming in through the cave entrance. She rubbed her eyes, conscious of a strangely ominous feeling she couldn't immediately comprehend. Quickly she pulled John up to her breast, her heart overwhelmed with thanksgiving for the safety and sleep they had enjoyed throughout the night. In spite of the great shock she had sustained, her supply of milk seemed little diminished. As John was feeding she realized she herself was very hungry, for she had had no supper the previous night.

When the baby was satisfied Elizabeth sat up amid the sheepskins and looked behind her. She was amazed at the extent of the cave, for it stretched back at least one hundred paces, where it then narrowed and appeared as if it might extend further in two directions.

She was torn between the desire to explore the cave and to look outside and take her bearings there. But most of all she longed to appease her now ravenous hunger.

She decided to drink the remaining half cup of water first, and then explore the cave while the sun was still low and shining directly into it. *I must look for the source of the water, especially,* she thought. She hesitated a moment, wondering whether to take John along or leave him on the sheepskin. She could move more quickly, and carry the water more easily without him, yet she feared to leave him for a moment in this strange place.

Telling herself not to be foolish, she finally edged away from John. When he made no complaint, she set off quickly along the right side of the cave. Soon her ears caught the sound of dripping water, but it seemed to come from around the farthest bend.

She expected it to be dark there, but a small ray of daylight came thorough a fissure in the rock above. Water could be seen seeping from the wall of the cave and then disappearing through a narrow cleft at its base into unknown depths below.

Elizabeth held her cup against the wall, impatient to get back to her son. Eventually it was full and she held her hands there, doing her best to approximate the rules of purity before eating. Then she hurried back, not stopping to explore any of the small recesses on the opposite side. As soon as she came into view of the main cave, she saw that John had managed to roll himself off the sheepskin.

As she hurried nearer, she saw he had discovered the food bag and taken everything out, placing it in the sand. Carefully putting the cup down on the ledge, Elizabeth rushed over to rescue the food and was just in time to see him pick up a raisin and lift it toward his mouth.

"No, no!" she cried, snatching it from his little fingers. "John must *never* eat that!"

A Nazarite from birth was what the angel had said he was to be, and here he had almost broken the vow made for him before he was a year old. *He must never touch a raisin, even here,* she determined, thinking of the strict instructions given by Moses in the Law.

By the time she had shaken the sand off the honey breads, they didn't seem quite so appetizing. Elizabeth put nine of them back in the bag, and contemplated the tenth for a moment. Should she eat it all now or divide it, eating the other half in the late afternoon? Perhaps that way, with plenty of water in between, she would not feel quite so hungry. She counted out the dried figs, dates, and raisins. If she were to stretch them over ten days she could have two figs, two dates, and five raisins each day. With a honey bread that would certainly keep her alive, but what about her milk supply? And what if no one came to rescue her after ten days?

There was no point in worrying about it now, she decided. Hilkiah would certainly do his best. She should be thankful she had made this specially nourishing bread for Zachariah. Surely it must have been the Lord who directed in this. How she wished Zachariah were here to share the food and ask the blessing.

Suddenly she was reminded of something the early morning sunshine had driven from her mind. She had been dreaming that Zachariah was in great danger. Well, it was only natural to dream such a thing after all the stress she had been through. But what *would* Zachariah be doing now? What had he done last night when he returned and found the house empty? Or when the soldiers arrived at the door? She shivered at the thought, then resolutely closed her eyes and said aloud the prayer of thanksgiving for the food, which the Pharisees taught that only men of the house should say.

Slowly she ate half the honey bread, pausing between each

bite. She felt satisfied and decided to leave the fruit until later, when John was having his morning nap. Now she could play with him to her heart's content—having no household chores to do.

She picked him up and walked slowly down the opposite side of the cave, peering into the different little recesses to see if there were any signs of man or animal having been there. In one, a faint familiar odor made her stop abruptly and bend down to look.

Yes, there was crumbling evidence of something having relieved itself there without taking the trouble to cover it over. With distaste, Elizabeth pushed the sand with her foot in an attempt to bury it, for she feared John might crawl down there sometime. Even now he was struggling to be free, but she walked back with him several steps before putting him down to crawl, something he had recently learned to enjoy.

Once relieved of his weight, Elizabeth suddenly realized that a large animal or person had been in the cave quite recently, maybe not more than a week ago. And they might well return! Of course, that was the possibility she had feared last night, but now the certainty of knowing someone *had* been there was more disquieting than ever. She just mustn't think about it. Perhaps it was only a young goat herdsman looking for one of his lost charges. She bent down to help John scoop up the sand into little heaps. Soon they were laughing together as he joyfully let the sand trickle through his fingers. For the moment some of Elizabeth's fears were forgotten.

Then she remembered she still hadn't looked outside. Hilkiah had warned her not to go out, but the sun was higher now, and the entrance in shadow, so she would just stand there and see what it was like.

Leaving John playing with the sand, she went slowly to the cave entrance, slipping on her grey outer cloak, which she thought would blend in well with the color of the rock.

A beautiful sight met her eyes. The woods surrounding the cave were a mixture of oak and cyprus, and descended steeply in front of her to the stream, which ran through the long, deep valley. The hillsides opposite were also wooded, from the stream up to a little above the level of the cave, but higher up there were terraced fields that stretched away almost as far as Ain Karim. That was why she must not go out, for she might be visible to anyone looking carefully from the cultivated area opposite.

As she peered around to the right she knew the winding valley would eventually pass beneath her village on the opposite bank. How she longed to be back there! But it would be impossible for her to carry John that distance, even if she knew it were safe there.

Hearing John squeal with a new note of excitement, she hastily turned back into the cave. In his hand was something that sparkled. Hurrying toward him she exclaimed in astonishment. He was holding a bracelet that looked to her to be made of gold and sapphires. Beside him was the round lid of a small earthenware pot. As she moved closer she saw the rim of the pot, which John must have found as he scooped away in the sand.

Trembling, Elizabeth put in her hand and brought out more jewels, then some silver coins.

Now a new horror seized her. Whoever had left these, probably stolen goods, would return for them. But when? Hastily she put everything back in the jar, replaced the lid, and covered it with sand again.

"Oh Lord, deliver us from the hands of evil men!" she prayed in the words of a familiar psalm. This reminded her that its writer, David, had hidden in this very cave when King Saul was seeking to kill him. She glanced up at the rock walls, wondering what stories they could tell of David and others who had found shelter there. God had protected David in the face of fearful odds, and he had fulfilled his promise that David should be the new king of Israel. And God would protect her John, too, she told herself, as she settled him for his nap.

Then she remembered the parchment she had stuffed inside her gown as they had hastily left the house. She had early memorized its contents, but she had felt instinctively that it must go wherever John went.

As soon as John was asleep she unrolled it and sat on the rocky ledge a short distance from him. There she slowly read aloud the first stanzas of Zachariah's prophecy concerning Mary's son.

Such was the oath he swore to our father Abraham to rescue us from enemy hands, and grant us, free from fear, to worship him with a holy worship. . . .

That was what she needed now, freedom from fear. And God had also promised rescue from enemy hands. She hurried on to the part she liked best, about John.

And you, little one, will be called prophet of the Highest, for you will go in advance of the Lord to prepare his way. . . .

What a wonderful title. "Prophet of the Highest," especially when there had been no prophet for four hundred years.

And what strange work he had to do.

And lead his people to salvation through knowledge of him, by the forgiveness of their sins.

This part was always a puzzle to Elizabeth. The only way she knew of for the forgiveness of sins was the prescribed animal sacrifices at the temple. Why would John need to tell people about this? The religious leaders weren't likely to let people forget it. That was how they got all their money. It was certainly strange; but the next lines were beautiful.

In the tender compassion of our God the morning sun from heaven will rise upon us,
to shine on those who live in darkness, under the cloud of death and to guide our feet into the way of peace.

Our God of tender compassion for those in darkness—she must remember that when night came on. She read the whole parchment through again to be sure she remembered it correctly, then decided that each day in the cave she would repeat it in John's hearing, with the hope it would become part of his very life and thought.

With thanksgiving she next ate a fig and two raisins, her mouth filling with saliva at the sweetness. After that she drank two cups of water to stay the pangs of hunger a little, until she could eat the rest of her bread in the evening.

The remainder of the day passed without incident, and as soon as it became dark she lay down beside John and slept soundly.

That was the general pattern of the next four days: playing with John, reciting the parchment, and then trying to repeat other passages of Scripture she had learned as a child or heard in the synagogue. She was begining to lose a little weight now and often felt hungry, although not so badly as she had feared. On the fourth day John did not seem quite satisfied, however, and she decided to give him a small piece of bread she had chewed first to soften. That seemed to quiet him, but it left her a little hungrier.

THE CAVE

On the fifth day rain came, and they didn't see the sun all day. Elizabeth accordingly thought there was no danger of anyone being on the hillside opposite. When she had put John down to sleep, she went to the cave entrance to enjoy the rare sight of clouds moving across the sky.

As she turned her eyes from the clouds and dropped them to the valley and then the hill beneath her, she suddenly saw the head of a man.

He was clutching the bushes to help him climb the steep slope, and he was heading straight for the cave.

Elizabeth stayed only long enough to be sure it was not Cleopas, then fled inside to little John.

5

The Intruder

Elizabeth shook uncontrollably as she knelt to pick up the sleeping baby. It seemed her worst fears were soon to be realized. There was no doubt that the approaching figure was intent on coming to the cave. But was he one of Herod's men, or a robber coming to retrieve the buried jewels?

Either prospect could mean death to her and the child. Her first instinct was to seize John and retreat to the farthest recess of the cave in the desperate hope they might remain undiscovered. This thought was immediately followed by the realization she could not carry the baby, sheepskins, and food bag all at the same time. On seeing any sign of habitation she knew the intruder would at once search the cave.

"Oh, God in heaven, what shall I do?" she breathed in anguish.

Little John looked so peaceful, she hesitated to pick him up and instead suddenly found herself removing two of the breads and a handful of dates from the sack. She then rushed to a small hole she had noticed in the rock wall to the rear of the cave and deposited the food there.

Quickly she returned to the baby. Perhaps she could hide him, too. At least he might escape notice and live until Hilkiah managed to send help. As gently as she could, she eased him up into her arms, her eyes on the entrance and her ears now strained to catch any sound of approaching footsteps.

She heard nothing, but just as she stood up, the cave entrance became partially darkened. The next moment a figure appeared, slowly edging his way into the cave. He held a curved knife menacingly in his right hand.

Elizabeth drew in a sharp breath of fear and involuntarily gave John a tight squeeze, causing him to give an indignant cry at being so soon awakened from his sleep.

The man froze, evidently trying to get his eyes accustomed to the semi-darkness of the cave, his knife still raised.

Elizabeth, too, remained motionless with shock, her eyes riveted on the intruder, trying to determine who or what he was.

He appeared to be about twenty years of age, and was of slender build. His longish curly black hair and beard were dripping with rain water, as was the goat's hair blanket thrown over his shoulders. His robe was hoisted up into his girdle, revealing legs and sandals covered with mud. If he was one of Herod's men, Elizabeth surmised he would not be alone. As the seconds passed and no one else appeared, she came to the conclusion he was most likely a robber. But with that knife so near, it wasn't much consolation.

The tense silence grew embarrassing, and Elizabeth suspected he was probably waiting to see if there were others in the cave before he either attacked or fled. His miserable appearance unexpectedly began to move her to pity.

"Come in out of the rain. At least it is dry here, though we have no fire," she calmly said. At the sound of her voice John began to cry in earnest. She sank down on the sheepskin to settle the baby and also hide her trembling limbs. But she dared not to let her eyes leave the intruder.

She could see he was now a little irresolute, and the hand with the dagger was lowered slightly. This gave her confidence and she even managed to smile.

"Do come in and make yourself comfortable," she invited again. "Or perhaps this is really your cave, and we are trespassing?"

"Who are you?" demanded the youth, ignoring her question.

Elizabeth hesitated, then felt an inner conviction that it would be best to tell the truth boldly. Besides, she realized she probably would not make a convincing liar.

"My name is Elizabeth. I am hiding from King Herod, who is seeking to kill this baby."

The words had an electrifying effect on the young man. He stuffed the dagger in his belt, shook the rain from his blanket, then strode over and sat down on the sand near Elizabeth.

"We have a common enemy, then," he snarled, a bitter hatred shining in his dark eyes. He was silent a moment, as he tried to squeeze the raindrops from his hair.

"My name is Barabbas," he said at last. "That devil Herod has slaughtered all my family—my father, mother, elder brother, his wife and child, and my younger brother and sister. Curse him, curse him!" He smashed his fists into the sand as he spoke.

"I'm so sorry," murmured Elizabeth.

"I alone managed to escape, and now I have to live the life of an outlaw. I'm on my way to join a group that operates in the hills south of here, around Hebron. But just outside Ain Karim I nearly stumbled into a group of Herod's men. It was a narrow escape!"

"Do you know what they are there for?" Elizabeth added anxiously.

"I heard they had killed some babies there and in Bethlehem. Herod ordered his men back again because they had missed one baby."

Elizabeth began to sob and couldn't speak for a moment. "My poor neighbors!" she said at last. "I am from Ain Karim, and this—this is the child Herod wanted to kill."

"Why on earth? What wrong could he possibly have done at that age?" A speculative gleam came into his eyes. "Or is he one of that devil's bastards and a possible future pretender to the throne? Are you the nurse? Perhaps we could make a deal and get a good ransom for him?"

Elizabeth was speechless, her heart wrenched at the horrible and callous suggestion, and she was distraught anew at this fresh source of danger for John. Then she remembered he was God's special child and once again managed to control her fear.

"No, this is my son." She smiled at his look of disbelief. "It is true. It is almost a miracle. My husband, who is a priest, was offering incense in the temple when the angel Gabriel appeared to him and told him our prayers of many years were to be answered. And when he didn't believe it, the angel said that he would not be able to speak again until after the baby's birth. And that is just what happened."

"Hmm. A pretty good story, at least. And what's the baby to become, king of Judah?" he asked with a laugh.

"Oh, no," Elizabeth hastened to explain, "he is to be the forerunner of the Messiah. Look, here is the prophecy, just as it was given to my husband," and she pulled out the scroll from its beautiful blue, embroidered covering and unrolled it for him to see.

"I'll take your word for it. I'm not much of a reader," he said. "But that's certainly a beautiful cover you have for it."

"Thank you, I made it myself," Elizabeth said, pleased that he had noticed it. "It seemed such a very special thing that *our* son is to be the one who will prepare men's hearts for the Messiah, who was born just a short time ago in Bethlehem. Herod heard about it from some wise men and assumed they meant a future king had been born. So he ordered all the babies to be killed to be sure of destroying the child."

"So what happens to the prophecy?"

"Thanks to God's intervention it still stands. My brother was able to warn me in time. He brought me here before Herod's men arrived. He told me the babe who is to be the Messiah escaped, too. God warned the parents in a dream. How great is the Holy One!"

"God didn't seem able to do anything to save my family," sneered Barabbas, "and I can't see that any Messiah is going to help me. I have to take care of myself. I trust no one."

"Please don't say that," begged Elizabeth. "No one can live without God. The whole history of our nation is the story of God's provision . . . and man's rejection of him."

"All our religious leaders are a bunch of hypocrites. I have no time for them. What I need is food! I've had nothing to eat all day, and I'm famished. Do you have anything here?"

Elizabeth suppressed a sigh and reached for the food bag. It was a little early for her second meal, but she was hungry. She could well imagine how the young man felt with an empty stomach.

"There is this," she said slowly, displaying the three-and-half remaining loaves. "This is our fifth day here. I have been eating half of one of these, morning and evening. Here, you can have this," and she held out one of the precious breads and three dates.

Barabbas snatched it from her and began devouring it. She feared it would be gone in five or six mouthfuls, and he might then demand the rest of her supply.

"Wait a minute," she pleaded, "let us give thanks to the Holy One first. It is he who supplied this for us. Will you pronounce the blessing?"

Barabbas hesitated a moment, then perfunctorily recited the familiar words.

"Thank you, and I find it helps to lessen hunger if you eat as slowly as possible," Elizabeth added with a smile. "I know how hungry you must be. There is water in the cave, though, and that helps to satisfy one a little."

She hesitated then, fearing that if she offered to get the water the intruder would eat the remaining food while she was out of sight.

"I have just one cup here," she continued, getting up and lifting it from the ledge. "It will soon be dark. I must feed the baby now. Would you like to go for a drink and then kindly bring back a cupful for me?"

"Where do you get it?"

Elizabeth was glad to hear this question. Perhaps it meant he had never been in the cave before.

"The water flows out of the rock at the rear of the cave to the right. There is still some daylight, so you will be able to see from a crack in the roof."

He seized the cup a little roughly and moved down the cave. Elizabeth was thankful he had gone, for getting water was certainly not a man's job. *But since he is an outlaw, he must be used to taking care of himself,* she reflected.

As soon as he was out of sight, she put back the two remaining loaves in the bag. She rolled it up and put it aside, praying that the young man would not ask for any more. Then she anxiously put the baby to her breast, and little John was sucking hungrily when Barabbas returned with the water.

"Well, I wouldn't have believed it possible!" he exclaimed, as he eyed them both. "You look old enough to be a grandmother."

"Yes, I told you it was a miracle birth," said Elizabeth gently. "The Lord in his lovingkindness took away my barrenness. I am indeed the most fortunate of women—if only we can successfully escape from here." She was trying desperately to keep his thoughts from food and from any evil designs on herself and John. "They say King Herod is nearly on his deathbed. Do you know if that is true?"

"Yes, I hear he's just a stinking mass of flesh, with worms coming out of his private parts! The doctors can't do a thing for him," Barabbas declared with fierce satisfaction.

"And yet, in spite of all that, he can still plan murder!"

"Yes, he plans to kill his own son, Antipater. But to kill the entire infant population of towns and villages! A devil incarnate, that's what he is."

Seeing his mind had been successfully diverted from food, Elizabeth decided to ask a question that had been troubling her ever since the intruder's arrival.

"Tell me, Barabbas, how did you know about this cave?" She tried to sound as casual as possible, but waited breathlessly for his answer.

"Oh, one of the outlaws who used to live in this area suggested I come this way. He said David used to hide here when King Saul chased him. As I was running from Herod's soldiers I came through the field opposite and saw this great rock across the valley. So I went straight down and waded across the stream which will soon be a river with all this rain."

Elizabeth secretly breathed a sigh of relief. So he probably didn't know about the jewels. Or had this other man asked him to come this way to pick them up? She still could not be sure. And how long was he proposing to stay in the cave?

She finished burping little John, then put him down to crawl for his last exercise before bedtime. She took care to put him as far as possible from where the treasure was buried.

"Would you mind keeping an eye on him while I go get some more water before it is dark? I have to drink plenty for the baby's sake. I'll bring you some more, too."

Without waiting for an answer, she hurried to the rear of the cave and eagerly drank two cupfuls of the water. What a comforting feeling of fullness it gave! After filling the cup a third time, she hurried back to the outer cave.

She found Barabbas kneeling on the ground beside John, helping him with his favorite occupation of scooping up handfuls of sand. They were within a couple of feet of where the jar was buried! Was he trying to find the treasure, she wondered.

"He's a cute little fellow, all right. Knows what he wants to do, too." Barabbas stood up with a suddenly dejected air.

"I might have had a son myself by now," he continued, "but for that devil of a king. My father was in the midst of negotiating my engagement when the trouble came. But no father now is going to betroth his daughter to an outlaw! I suppose my only hope will be to capture a girl who is traveling and murder her escorts. I've seen other outlaws who get wives that way." Again he clenched his fists, only to drop them in a gesture of despair.

"It's very hard, I know, but God can find a way of escape for you, as I believe he will for us—if you'll just trust him, Barabbas," Elizabeth said earnestly.

The young man only swung around and strode to the cave opening. After a moment he returned.

"It's stopped raining," he announced, "I think I'll be on my way."

"But—but don't you need some rest first?" Elizabeth was torn between thankfulness that her unwelcome visitor was apparently about to depart without harming them and a motherly concern for this young man bereft of all his family.

"It's best to travel at night. I had some sleep this morning . . . but I need some more food."

The words did not seem to be spoken threateningly, yet Elizabeth saw him adjusting the curved dagger in his belt. Was it meant to be a threat, she wondered, or just an automatic preparation for resuming his journey. What should she do?

As he stood expectantly, she reached for the sack and took out one of the remaining breads.

"Here, you shall have one, but I must keep the other," she said, trying to sound like a mother talking to her son. "Do you have money to buy anything?"

"Not until I've robbed someone."

"Oh, don't do that!" Elizabeth pleaded. She had been so concerned with the robber, she hadn't noticed little John crawling behind her back.

"Hey, what's that you've got?" she heard Barabbas say as he swooped down to take something from John's hand.

She turned and to her horror saw John had uncovered the pot of jewels again.

"Is this stuff yours?" Barabbas asked sharply.

"No. I told you my husband is a country priest. We have never been rich. Someone must have hidden it here."

"Well, it's not going to stay here! What incredible luck!" The young man quickly stuffed the pouch in his belt with the money and put as much of the jewelry as he could into a small leather bag tied around his waist under his robe. Then he swung his goat-skin blanket over his shoulders.

"We'll leave a little for the owner, or whoever stole it. They may be in as great a need as I. Will you take some in payment for the bread?"

"I couldn't do that!" Elizabeth shuddered.

"Please yourself. And thank you for the hospitality. May the fates be kind to you and your son. Perhaps I can do you a good turn one day."

"Thank you. Take care and the Lord go with you."

The young man half shook his head. "No one is going to care for me except myself. Farewell." And with that he was gone.

6

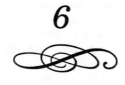

Rescue and
a Grim Revelation

Elizabeth sank down onto the sheepskin, weak with the sudden reaction after the tension of the last few hours.

Her first feeling was of intense thankfulness to the Lord for preserving her and little John from so great a potential danger. Truly he must have restrained this fierce and embittered young outlaw from doing them any harm. As the time passed, however, Elizabeth almost smiled at herself as she began to realize she was almost regretting the departure of the young man. After being entirely alone for five days it had been a welcome relief to have an adult to talk to—even a robber. As she thought of his story she was again filled with compassion for him and prayed that God would have mercy upon him.

It was now almost dark. She shook out the sheepskin and folded it again to prepare for their night's sleep. She remembered the breads she had hidden, too, and returned them to the food sack in the hope they would keep a little fresher, though by now they were very dry. She was thankful now that she had thought of hiding them because she was sure Barabbas would have demanded more if he had known she had it. *Three more days supply*, she thought. *Will help arrive in time?*

As darkness obscured the cave entrance, Elizabeth lay down, but sleep was slow in coming. She thought back to what the young man had said about Herod's soldiers returning and wondered if they were still in the area, intent on finding her and the baby. And what was happening to Zachariah all this time? Surely he would have returned to Ain Karim, but perhaps Hilkiah had been able to get word to him of what had happened to her. Then the soldiers would probably torture him to try and make him say where they were. She shuddered. Torture was a routine method with Herod for getting information, but often the victims made up stories accusing others in order to get relief from their agony.

"Oh, God, give Zachariah courage," she prayed. "Thank you for caring for us up to now and continue your lovingkindness through this night also." And with the prayer barely out of her lips she fell asleep.

She thought she had probably slept late when she was awakened by little John's hungry cry, but it was still very overcast, so she had no means of knowing the time. As she put him to her breast, she suddenly remembered that today must be the Sabbath. It had been, in fact, since yesterday's sunset, but her unexpected guest had put it completely out of her mind.

She smiled to herself as she thought of the many regulations governing the Sabbath and how easy it would be to keep them here in the cave. Every day so far had been like the Sabbath. She had no possibility of walking any distance, she had nothing to cook, wash, or keep clean, no grain to grind; nor a mirror she must not look into.

She would make the day different somehow, though, she decided. How could she best please God in these circumstances? Perhaps not play with John in the sand? And yet that seemed so innocent, and it was necessary to keep a close watch on him.

Suppose she made it a day of fast for herself? That way she would have supplies for an extra day. Yet the honey breads were getting stale and it was so important to keep up her strength and her milk supply.

One thing she could be pretty certain of was that there would be no casual visitors because the cave was more than a Sabbath day's journey from any dwelling place. And it was not really a likely place for Herod's soldiers to come because there was mud everywhere. The hillsides would be very slippery after all the rain.

Finally she decided that when she had eaten her own breakfast she would sing all the psalms she could remember.

She was surprised at how many there were, and how well some of them fit her situation. Little John seemed to appreciate them, too. He stopped his digging in the sand to sit up and smile at his mother with sparkling eyes and even made little noises himself.

"'He shall be filled with God's Spirit from his birth,'" Elizabeth repeated softly as she looked at him. "That's what the angel said. John, I believe you understand I'm singing about God, don't you?"

She started another psalm and found her voice bursting with praise as she came to the words that meant so much in her present circumstances:

> Because Your lovingkindness is better than life,
> My lips shall praise You.
> Thus I will bless You while I live;
> I will lift up my hands in Your name.
> My soul shall be satisfied as with marrow and fatness,
> And my mouth shall praise You with joyful lips. . . .
> Because You have been my help,
> Therefore in the shadow of Your wings I will rejoice.
> My soul follows close behind You;
> Your right hand upholds me.

By this time Elizabeth's voice was getting a little husky, so she decided to think back to all the synagogue services she had recently attended. She was a little surprised to find she didn't remember much of Rabbi Jannai's words. In fact, he had often irritated her as he and some of the other men argued on small points of the Law. No, the things that remained clearest in her mind were the stories her father used to tell—stories of Abraham, Joseph, and Moses. Why, of course, Moses' life had been threatened as a baby, yet God had used his mother's and sister's courage and initiative to save his life. And God had moved Pharaoh's daughter's heart to adopt him. What God had done for Moses he assuredly would do for John. A deep peace flooded Elizabeth's heart then, and she found herself singing:

> Praise Him with lute and harp! . . . .
> Praise Him with loud cymbals . . . .

How she wished she had some instrument to sound in his praise, but instead she began to clap her hands. Little John looked and then started imitating her and she felt the cave had truly become

God's sanctuary. His very presence was there upholding her, giving her extra physical and spiritual stamina.

In spite of the rain starting again in the late morning, the day seemed to pass quickly and happily. After his nap, Elizabeth sat John up and then carefully unrolled the parchment and read the words to him. Before, she had always recited them, but now she had the feeling he should see they were written words—something different from her usual talking. So she started looking up at him between each sentence.

> And you, little one, will be called the prophet of the Highest
> for you will go in advance of the Lord to prepare his way,
> to bring to his people a knowledge of salvation
> by remission of their sins . . . ."

When she looked up at him between each phrase, trying to impress it upon him, John had given her his usual bright smile, as if taking it all in.

It was raining again the next morning, and the cave was beginning to feel cold and damp. Elizabeth had to keep her cloak on all the time, and cold water and dry bread was not a very warming diet. Still, she was conscious of the glow from yesterday's time of worship, and the certainty that God would be with her.

But how could they get away if the rain continued? The thought of clambering up the steep, muddy hillside was not pleasant, especially when feeling weak from hunger and aching joints. And there was just one bread left for tomorrow. Her prayer became a double refrain: "God, please cause the rain to cease; please send help before it is too late."

The next morning she and John awoke with the sun streaming through the cave entrance. So one prayer was answered! Elizabeth thanked God as she stretched aching muscles and joints. Very slowly she reached for the last bread in the sack and broke it in two. "You who supplied manna to our fathers in the wilderness, remember our needs here," she prayed.

Slowly the morning passed, and it was time for John's nap. As soon as he was asleep, Elizabeth thought she would stand outside in the sun and try to get the dampness out of her body.

Everything looked so fresh after the rain as she basked in the sun's warmth. Then she began to feel a little drowsy and was tired with standing, so she decided to lie down with John. Perhaps a doze would help her to forget her hunger, which she felt more conscious of than usual. She went in, drank a cup of water, and lay down on the sheepskin.

The next thing she knew, a low voice was calling, "Elizabeth."

She awoke with a start, thinking she must have been dreaming.

"Aunt Elizabeth, are you all right?"

She hurriedly sat up and looked at the cave entrance. Once again she saw a young man standing there, perhaps a year or two older than Barabbas, but this time she saw with overwhelming relief that the man was someone she knew. He was Hannah's nephew by marriage, Cleopas, whom she had occasionally met at her brother's home in Jerusalem.

"Praise God you have come! Is it safe for us to leave now?"

"Yes. Uncle Hilkiah sent a message yesterday, and asked if I would come for you this morning. How are you both?"

"Remarkably well, considering how little there has been to eat."

"I have some bread and cheese here. And a little goat's milk." He pulled a small leather flask from his girdle. "Here, have this. Do you think you will be able to travel?" he asked anxiously. "I have our donkey up on the footpath. Can you manage to get up there? If we leave at once we might get home before the moon rises."

"I'll manage somehow," Elizabeth assured him. Reverently she held the fresh bread and cheese in her hands a moment, her eyes closed in thanksgiving.

Truly she had never tasted anything so enjoyable. She then took a deep draught of the milk. It seem to carry new strength to every part of her body as she finally emptied the bottle.

"Can you manage if I take the baby now, or would you rather I helped you up first and then came back for him?"

"Please take him now!" Elizabeth couldn't bear the thought of his being out of her sight even for a short time. If he woke up he could easily crawl out of the cave.

"What else is there to come back for? Just this sheepskin?"

"Yes, but if possible I'd like to keep this cup and half piece of bread to remind me of God's goodness." She put the cup in the little food bag and quickly tied it to her waist, making sure the precious parchment was also safe inside her gown.

Then she took one last look around the cave, a prayer of thanksgiving on her lips, before lifting up baby John and rolling him up tightly in his blankets.

He yawned and looked at her in surprise. As they left the semi-darkness of the cave, he screwed up his eyes tight in the bright sunshine. Elizabeth held him until they reached the barely visible track leading upward, then handed him to Cleopas.

"Is it very slippery?" she asked.

"Not as bad as it would have been yesterday. It's easier going up than down," Cleopas answered reassuringly.

He started to lead the way through the undergrowth, but by this time little John's eyes had adjusted to the light, and he let out a yell when he realized his mother was out of sight.

"Here I am, John," and Elizabeth reached up to pat him, anxious to soothe him to silence. "Can you let him see me over your shoulder, Cleopas, then perhaps he'll be satisfied."

She found that by clinging to the bushes and vines she was able to keep going up the steep slope, though each step was painful to her hips. Cleopas' youthful stride would have taken him up more quickly, but he stopped every few steps to satisfy the baby that his mother was still close by. Eventually they reached the upper path and found the donkey tied where Hilkiah had left his the night they had arrived.

"It's still too wet to sit down, I'm afraid, but I'll be as quick as I can," said Cleopas, handing over the baby. He headed down the hill again.

Elizabeth leaned against the donkey as she tried to get her breath again after the steep climb. She attempted to balance John in the saddle when he grew too heavy. What a long time it seemed since she and Hilkiah had arrived here, and how good God had been to her and John. But there was so much she wanted to know now. She waited impatiently for Cleopas to return.

"Here we are then," he said before she had a chance to speak. "If you give me the baby, can you get into the saddle yourself? Is that comfortable? We should be in Emmaus in just a short time."

"Emmaus? Is Zachariah there?" she asked eagerly.

Cleopas hurriedly turned to untie the donkey.

"No, no he isn't," and he gave the donkey a little slap that set her on her way.

"Not there? Then where is he?" persisted Elizabeth, looking back anxiously at Cleopas as he shouldered the sheepskins.

"Uncle Hilkiah wants you stay with us at Emmaus for a few days while he decides the best thing to do."

"But Zachariah? Didn't Hilkiah know where he is?"

"Yes," young Cleopas said reluctantly, his face a picture of distress. "I'm terribly sorry Aunt Elizabeth, but Zachariah is dead."

7

Murder in the Temple

Elizabeth clutched at the horns of the saddle as trees and the pathway began to swirl crazily before her eyes. She felt as if she were going to faint.

"Stop, stop!" she screamed. "Take the baby, he's falling."

Cleopas dropped the sheepskins and grabbed John and the donkey's rein.

"I'm sorry," he said awkwardly, "I didn't want to tell you. Uncle Hilkiah said to wait until we got home."

"I had to know," Elizabeth said weakly. Suddenly the new bread and goat's milk churned in her stomach. She just had time to slither from the saddle before she vomited.

First, hot with embarrassment, then suddenly chilled, she leaned weakly against the donkey for support, feeling all her strength had drained away.

"Do you think you can carry on now? The sooner we get home the better, you know."

"I—I—in a moment," Elizabeth finally managed to get out. Then John began to cry, and Cleopas looked even more worried and helpless.

With a supreme effort Elizabeth summoned new strength. From now on this gift from God would be her responsibility alone— alone except for the promised help of the One who had given him.

"I think I'll be all right now. I'll just feed him before we go. He's hungry, I'm sure."

Elizabeth sank down on the roll of sheepskins and as John fed, the tears rolled down her cheeks. *Dear Zachariah! And I will never see him again.*

A short time later, John seemed satisfied and Elizabeth felt steady enough to get on the donkey again.

After a period of travel in silence, she felt at home with the rhythm of the donkey again, and John seemed to have settled comfortably. So she ventured to ask the questions that were hammering at her brain.

"Couldn't you tell me a little more?" she pleaded. "I promise I won't stop again. Where—how—did it happen?"

"Uncle just told me it was at the temple, and that he would tell you everything when he comes this evening or tomorrow."

Elizabeth sighed with frustration, but realized her brother must have been trying to shield her from the shock and anguish that would make this journey even more difficult.

"Tell me at least what you do know. What happened after your uncle left me in the cave? Did he have any trouble on the way?"

"Not that I know of. He arrived at our place soon after we were in bed. He told us about the order from Herod and where he had taken you and the baby. He drew a very careful map of where you were and asked me to be ready to come and get you as soon as I heard from him. I was to bring more food if I heard nothing from him after ten days."

"Thank God that wasn't necessary. And then?"

"Well, word quickly got around about the slaying of all the baby boys. Hatred of Herod grows every day. They say he deserves all the agonies he's going through. It must be God's judgment."

"Without doubt." Elizabeth's heart ached for all the mothers who had lost their precious little ones, and she prayed they would soon be pregnant again.

"And when did you hear from Hilkiah again?"

"It wasn't until last night. Cousin Jason came. His father had been unable to get away, but sent the message that he thought it would be safe for you to stay with us a few days until things quiet down. He will come as soon as possible and give you all the details."

Elizabeth lapsed into silence again, her mind frantically trying to sort out bewildering thoughts and emotions. At the same time she had to remember little John and support him so he didn't slide off her lap as the donkey patiently jogged along the uneven path through the woods.

At last they emerged onto the main pack trail that would eventually lead them to the town of Emmaus.

"It should only take us a little while longer from here," Cleopas remarked, shifting the awkward sheepskin roll to the other shoulder. "Would you like to rest a bit first?"

Elizabeth shook her head. She was anxious to get there now. She remembered to be thankful for the rain that had fallen, holding down the dust that was so persistent for most of the year. She was thankful, too, that today it was not raining, and everything was fresh and cool. In some fields, people were already sowing seed for the next harvest.

The road was continuously up and down over the rolling Judean hills. The descents were always the most uncomfortable on the back of a small donkey. Elizabeth would have preferred to walk then, but knew she could not carry John far, so she hung on as best she could, her mind at least distracted during these times from the anxiety and sorrow in her heart.

At last they reached the pleasant little town of Emmaus, which Elizabeth had never visited before. Young Cleopas, whose parents had died a year or so before, had inherited a house and fields on a hillside west of the town.

Thankfully Elizabeth handed John into the waiting arms of Mary, Cleopas' wife, then painfully dismounted. It seemed as if every muscle of her body were aching.

"Come along while Cleopas sees to the donkey," Mary said hospitably. She was a pleasant-looking young woman, resembling her aunt Hannah. Elizabeth could see from her shape that she would soon have a child.

"I'm sorry to trouble you at such a time. I see God has blessed you. How soon will it be?"

"Any day now." Mary smiled. "Uncle Hilkiah thought you might like to stay here a few days to help after the baby arrives."

Elizabeth warmed to this pleasant young girl, but shrank from committing herself before she had heard all Hilkiah would have to tell her.

"Well,—if I can really be of help . . ." she began, then finished anxiously, "When will my brother be here?"

"This evening, if at all possible. Now, please lie down and rest a

67

while. I know how tired and thirsty you must be. The baby probably needs feeding, too."

Mary put him down beside his mother, hurried away to get a
drink, then excused herself as soon as she had brought it. Elizabeth had the feeling that she was avoiding her, perhaps because
she feared being questioned, as had Cleopas.

Out of Elizabeth's hearing, Mary whispered to Cleopas.

"The story of Zachariah's death has reached the village. It's
terrible, Cleopas! No wonder Uncle Hilkiah didn't want to tell
us. I hope he comes soon or we'll never be able to keep it from
her."

The simple supper was a silent meal. Though it tasted so good
to Elizabeth, she was not able to eat very much after subsisting for
days on so little. She felt the atmosphere a little strained, too,
although Mary was showing every effort to be kind.

Just after darkness fell they heard the sound each had been
listening for. Mary and her husband hurried to the door. Mary
ushered Hilkiah in and Cleopas went to take care of his donkey.

As Elizabeth stood to greet him she was shocked at the change
she saw. He looked ten years older, and his face was almost gray
with weariness.

"Oh, Hilkiah! Please tell me—"

"Yes, yes my dear. Sit down. You will need all the strength you
have to bear the news I bring."

"I know he is—dead." Elizabeth's voice faltered a little at having to put it into words for the first time. "But how?"

"Herod's orders." Hilkiah sank wearily onto a rug on the floor,
while Mary sat next to Elizabeth.

"His soldiers went to Ain Karim as I said they would. They
were angry at finding no one in your house. So they killed all the
other boys under two. Meanwhile, Ishmael had the high priest's
men detain Zachariah in the temple, thinking he might go back
to warn you."

"That evil Ishmael!" exclaimed Elizabeth in bitter exasperation. "Why would he do such a thing?"

"In order to get your nice house for his sister and Zoma, I suspect. He didn't want you to have an heir."

"That's what Zachariah thought, too. But I just can't imagine
how anyone could so hideously betray a relative."

"I'm afraid it's a very common practice in our sinful world. But they didn't escape themselves. He thought the soldiers were only to kill John in Ain Karim, but Abigail's grandson died with all the others."

"Poor little Aram!"

"When the soldiers returned, they reported there was no one in your house. Zachariah was called and they demanded to know where you and the baby were. He could only swear he did not know."

"So you hadn't told him?"

"No, I knew it was safer not to for John's sake. After a whole day of interrogating him, they had to report no success. Herod then sent soldiers back to Ain Karim again, and a message to Zachariah saying, 'Tell the truth, where is your son? Remember your life is in my hand.'"

Elizabeth shuddered, but kept her eyes fixed on Hilkiah.

"All he would answer was, 'Then you shed innocent blood, and the Lord will receive my soul.'"

"How like him!" Elizabeth's tears began to flow.

"They reported what he said back to Herod, but Herod did nothing until the soldiers returned from Ain Karim saying they had not found you. Meanwhile, Ishmael saw that Zachariah was kept in the priests' quarters under guard."

"And didn't you see him at all?"

"I knew I must not appear involved in any way or I might never get to help you. But when Jason delivered a fresh supply of incense, he got near enough to Zachariah to whisper that you and John were safe. That was a great comfort to him." Hilkiah paused.

"And then? Please tell me quickly, Hilkiah!"

"Early the next morning, the Sabbath, before the course began their duties, Zachariah asked to offer his own burnt offering. Just as he was beside the altar he was struck down—by Herod's order. It must have been one of the temple guards who did it. I suspect Ishmael had some hand in it. But take comfort, sister. Zachariah died a righteous, God-fearing man."

Hilkiah wiped the sweat and a few tears from his face, his ordeal completed, while Mary put her arm around Elizabeth's shaking shoulders.

"Why did it have to happen to him?" she whispered at last.

"Why do the wicked prosper while such a good person suffers such a death?"

"That we cannot answer. It has happened many times in our history. Yet God promises he will have the final word and reward each according to their deeds. To you, Elizabeth, he has given the care of this child who is to turn our people back to God and righteousness. You must conserve all your strength and fulfill the work allotted to you."

"Yes, I know God has spared us and will keep us safe. He was very near to us in that cave, Hilkiah." She tried to dry her eyes.

Relief showed on her brother's face at these words. "Praise his holy name! We certainly prayed that God would protect you. . . ." Again he paused, as if considering whether to continue.

"Mary says she will be very happy to have you here for a month or so. You will be a real help to her, and after a month things should have settled down. Some say Herod is so sick he is going to Jericho to try to get relief in the hot springs. Maybe then he will forget all about the star over Bethlehem."

"I'll be very glad to help here. But what about our house in Ain Karim?"

"On no account must you return there. Let them assume that you and John have perished. But I'm afraid it means Zoma and Abigail will take the house."

Elizabeth clenched her hands together in an agony of frustration. The thought of leaving her home of so many years was a tremendous shock. The thought of it being taken by those who had treated them so cruelly was even worse.

"Afterward . . ." Hilkiah was watching closely to see how she would react to what he was about to say, "we think it would be a good idea for you to go and live with Eleazer and Doris. He is so disgusted with all that goes on at the temple, he has decided to join the Essenes. There's a group of them at Bethany. He's making arrangements now to move there and go into the olive oil business."

Elizabeth stared at him wide-eyed, but no words came.

"I know this must be a shock to you. But we have all been considering and praying about it very much. The Essenes are a godly, righteous-living people, who keep very much to themselves. It seems the safest possible place for little John. Think it over carefully. We can see no other way."

Elizabeth continued staring. Yet even in her dazed condition, she recognized that the man who was now her family head had made the decision. There was nothing she could do or say but to accept it.

8

Bethany and a
Fateful Decision

Elizabeth sat under the grape arbor in the courtyard of Eleazer's house, keeping a sharp eye on John, now three and a half years old, and his cousin, Eleazer's son, Nathan, who was a year younger.

She felt inexpressibly weary and was thankful that Eleazer would be returning that evening from the big conference at Qumran. Then, at least, she wouldn't have the entire responsibility of the household and little Nathan, who seemed always up to mischief.

"No, no! You mustn't do that!" she cried in exasperation as she saw him pull one of the almost-ripened grapes and hold it out to John. "No, no!" and she slapped his hand this time.

A deep sigh escaped her. It was not so bad now, when the grapes were not yet good for the children, but when they were fully ripe, how was she to keep John from eating them when he saw Nathan doing it? She had forseen the problems there might be with the children growing up together. She had feared, too, that Doris, who doted on Nathan, would not be willing to deny him anything.

But now Doris was gone, having died with the baby in childbirth only two months ago. Elizabeth had done the best she could to run the household, but Nathan had been understandably upset at the disappearance of his mother and she was finding him very difficult to handle.

She almost wished Eleazer would take another wife, yet at the same time she feared he might marry an uncongenial woman who would object to Elizabeth and John's presence in her home. Two women under one roof was never an easy situation. Elizabeth wondered if perhaps she had found sharing another woman's home particularly difficult because she had lived so long in her own home with freedom to do as she pleased. But she had always tried to fit in with Doris' wishes. There had been no real problem until Nathan began to walk and play with John.

She thought back to her two months with Cleopas and Mary and the birth of their little James. At first, that hadn't been easy, either, since they had been complete strangers. But they had done their best to make her feel at home in the midst of her sorrow. She had been glad to help all she could during Mary's time of need. Now, she didn't seem to have the strength to cope.

She glanced at the sun again. Soon it would set, she reckoned, and so Eleazer might be home any time now. She had better draw the evening's water supply. He would be hot and thirsty, coming from that desert place by the Salt Sea. It was such a steep climb all the way back up the largely bare, rocky heights of the wilderness of Judea. She wondered why anyone would ever want to live down there when there were the pleasant hills of Judea with pretty places like Ain Karim, Emmaus, Bethlehem, and even Bethany, which wasn't quite three miles east of busy, crowded Jerusalem.

Bethany owed its importance to being the junction between the north-south road from Shechem to Hebron, which ran along the crest of the Judean hills, and the east-west road from Jericho, which passed just north of Jerusalem westward and eventually to the Great Sea or Egypt. Elizabeth had found it interesting to watch the constant caravans from distant countries passing through, with their many different wares attached to the backs of camels, mules, and pack-asses. Sometimes there would be as many as two hundred camels in a caravan from distant lands. Although much of the merchandise was destined for the needs of Jerusalem, much continued on the longer journeys. Eleazer was finding Bethany a very convenient place for his olive oil business.

Suddenly Elizabeth caught sight of Martha, the eight-year-old daughter of Eliab and Rebeccah, their neighbors. The girl was peering around the entrance gate.

"Martha, dear," she called, "Would you mind watching John

and Nathan for a moment while I draw the water? Just be sure they don't pick any of the grapes."

Martha was a very capable girl for her age, well used to taking care of her younger brother and sister. She had several times helped Elizabeth in this way since Doris had died.

Elizabeth was thankful that in Bethany they had a cistern in the courtyard. She didn't have to go to the village well except when the cistern dried up a month or two before the rains came. She always feared one of the little boys might fall in because they liked to peer down as she threw in the leather bucket.

After moving the heavy lid and the exertion of pulling up the bucket several times to fill her jars, Elizabeth was breathless and exhausted. She sat down on the bench again for a moment's rest, then carried two of the jars into the house while Martha was still with the boys. She poured a cup of water, filled a basin ready to wash Eleazer's feet, and then returned to the children.

"Thank you Martha. Perhaps you should go now. I'm sure your father and Eleazer will be home soon. Your mother may need you to watch your brother and sister."

The child obediently ran off, and Elizabeth called the boys to follow her into the house as she carried in the last water jar.

While she was preparing the evening meal, she wondered if Eleazer would tell her anything about this important convocation he had attended. A lot of it was secret, not to be revealed to outsiders, and she wasn't sure she altogether agreed with what she knew about the Essenes.

Certainly they were very righteous people and were very punctilious at keeping all the Law. This was no problem to her because she had always been part of a priestly family. But they did seem to cut themselves off from ordinary society in the village. Eliab's family next door had been in it for some years. And all the members in Bethany had been very glad to have Eleazer because they needed a number of priests for their organization. But at this big meeting Eleazer's full initiation was to have taken place and Elizabeth had the feeling things might be more complicated from now on. The Essenes had some kind of common meal together, she thought it was just bread and wine, which they considered very important. No one else could share it who was not a full member.

She would have preferred not to have any wine around at all, for John's sake, and for the hundredth time wondered why the angel had specified he was to be a Nazarite from birth, when it was such a difficult thing in a society where grapes were so abundant.

She heard Eleazer bid farewell to Eliab at the gate and she hastened to get the towel and basin ready by the bench.

He greeted her with his usual courtesy and gratefully drank the cool water she offered him. During supper he told the two boys of his journey and about the great blue Salt Sea he had been beside, where nothing could sink. But not a word did he say about the ceremonies he had witnessed, even after she had put the boys to bed. She guessed he would be tired, and she herself felt so weary she soon followed the children to bed.

The next morning she was conscious of a stabbing pain in her chest and could hardly drag herself around.

"I'm sorry," she said to Eleazer after she had placed breakfast on the table, "I feel quite ill and must lie down again. Do you mind helping the boys?"

Eleazer looked up in concern. "You certainly don't look well. I have to go into Jerusalem this morning. Perhaps my mother would come back and help for a little while. I'll see if Eliab's wife will mind the boys while I'm gone."

Elizabeth murmured her thanks, adding anxiously, "You will remind them that John mustn't eat grapes?" and then retreated to her room. She would much rather have kept John with her. She couldn't bear him out of her sight. But she just couldn't manage two of them and didn't like to suggest separating them.

In the afternoon she still felt no better, but was glad to see both Hilkiah and Hannah with Eleazer. They were really concerned and soon Eleazer went out and returned with the village physician.

"She is very weak. I doubt if she will last long," he told the others out in the courtyard, as they escorted him to the gate.

With troubled faces they sat down on the bench under the grape arbor to discuss what should be done. When Eleazer had outlined his plan, Hilkiah looked even more concerned.

"It will break Elizabeth's heart, but what else can we do? We have to consider John's safety first," he sighed, as they got up to enter the house.

Elizabeth's eyes were fixed on the open door as they approached her room.

"What did he say?" she asked anxiously.

"He thinks you are very weak." Hilkiah felt they must make the situation quite plain. "So you need complete rest. Therefore we must decide what to do with John."

Elizabeth was instantly filled with fear. "What do you mean?" she whispered.

"The doctor said you may not have long to live, and so we must plan for his future. Eleazer would like to tell you what he thinks is a wonderful provision of God."

"Yes," said Eleazer with some enthusiasm. "The Qumran community is eager to accept young boys and train them up in the ways of God."

"Oh, *no!*" Elizabeth caught her breath with a sob. "Is there no other way? Will you—will you not think of taking another wife, Eleazer?" she pleaded.

"I did at first," Eleazer acknowledged, "but at this convention I came to share the view of the leaders there. They feel all sexual relations are wrong for those who want to give themselves to God." He paused, then seeing the look on Elizabeth's face, hastily continued.

"So I am planning to give them little Nathan. Eliab next door is coming around to the same view. He says he will never arrange marriages for any of his children. Little Lazarus is not very strong, otherwise he would send him to Qumran. The others are just girls." he added, with an unconscious note of slight contempt.

"But is there *nowhere* else?" Elizabeth turned beseeching eyes to Hannah, who quickly looked away.

"I would gladly take him, Elizabeth," she cried, "but Jerusalem would be dangerous for him. King Archelaus has inherited most of his father's vices and few of his talents. He would murder any potential rival to his position, no matter how remote the possibility. Truly, there is no safer place for John than at Qumran. The Herods give that place a wide berth, I've heard."

"Yes, Qumran is the most suitable place for him in every way," added Eleazer persuasively. "These men want the very best for God. They believe they are fulfilling the prophecy of Isaiah, 'Make straight in the desert a highway for our God.' What more can you want? I feel drawn to them myself, but nearly all their time is given to studying the Scriptures and praying. I know I was not made for that. I have to live an active life. But for little John, I honestly believe it's God's solution."

Elizabeth lay back exhausted. She offered no further opposition. The thought of John being able to spend so much time studying the Scripture did begin to appeal to her. He would be safe there it seemed. And above all, God would be watching over him better than she could ever do—especially if she were to die soon.

"It is very hard for you to accept, I know," said Hilkiah, his voice full of tender concern. "You feel John is so young. But remember the prophet Samuel and his mother. It was her own idea to send Samuel to the house of the Lord at an early age."

"Yes, I remember, but she had other children," Elizabeth added wistfully. "But I know John is God's gift to us for his own great purposes," she said resolutely. "Maybe I have already fulfilled the part he wants me to play."

She gave a tired sigh, then forced herself to ask the dreaded question.

"How soon are you planning for them to go?"

Eleazer hesitated. "Well, I have an order of oil to send down there in two days. I know there will be no problem about them taking the boys. They actually appealed to us all to find suitable children for them. So perhaps it would be as well if they went with me then."

Elizabeth winced as if in physical pain, but she made no protest. She knew now that she had not the strength to care for John.

"I'll wash their clothes tomorrow and get everything ready," Hannah put in gently.

"Don't forget John's parchment!" Elizabeth exclaimed with a sudden spurt of strength. "It is in the chest over there. That is a copy of Zachariah's prophecy and it must always remain with John. Tell them, won't you?" She turned anxiously to Eleazer, then weakly sank back again. In a moment the others left the room to see to the many matters now needing attention.

Since living with her nephew and his wife, Elizabeth had not repeated the prophecy to John as often as she had intended, but he had learned to say some of the phrases after her. Following Doris' death, however, Elizabeth had been so busy caring for both children, she had often forgotten the scroll. Now, she decided that she must have one more time alone with John before he left her.

Hannah readily arranged this for her the following afternoon. With all the strength she could muster, Elizabeth held out the scroll and said slowly and clearly, "John's scroll. What is it? John's scroll," and pointed at him. He put out his hands for it, but she kept it out of his reach and began repeating the familiar words for the last time.

"You, little one, will be called Prophet of the Highest—" John could repeat these words clearly, although he understood nothing of their meaning. So she slowly went through it all, rejoicing at each phrase he seemed to have memorized. She then prayed that the prophecy might be indelibly imprinted in his mind.

Although she slept little that last night, her hand resting on the warm body of her sleeping child, the hours seemed to rush by for Elizabeth and soon it was morning. Her spirit felt weighed down with sadness at her impending loss. But she must not show it. Eleazer, she guessed, was having similar feelings about Nathan, judging by the way his eyes never left the boy.

The children were to travel in pannier baskets on either side of a hired donkey. They were excited at the idea of the journey to see the big blue Salt Sea Eleazer had told them about.

Now the time had come. Elizabeth clasped John to her in a last embrace and managed to keep the tears from spilling out until the small caravan had disappeared around a bend in the narrow street. Then, sobbing bitterly, Hannah helped her back to her bed.

Qumran was only about ten miles from Bethany, but the intensely steep slope down to the Jordan Valley Rift involved a circuitous route that most travelers took two days to complete. Throughout that day and the next, Elizabeth clung to life, praying constantly for safety along the way and a future under God's protecting hand for her beloved son.

At last the afternoon of the fourth day drew on, and Eleazer appeared looking tired and strained.

"Are they—all right?" asked Elizabeth anxiously.

"Yes, yes. They were given a very warm welcome," Eleazer answered gently. "They are to be in the care of a very pleasant woman on the farm. There are several other children there, so they will be happy."

"And you told them he is a Nazarite?"

"Yes, they understand. It will be no problem there."

"And did you hand over the scroll and explain it to them?"

"Of course. I told them all about it, and the bursar registered it with other property. It will be given him when he is of age." He did not add that the head man, known as the Guardian, had laughed a little saying, "Doesn't every mother of Israel believe that about her son?" as he tossed the scroll onto a shelf with other things to be filed away.

Toward dawn, Hannah, who was sleeping in the inner room with Elizabeth, heard a faint cry come from her lips. "Zachariah, Zachariah!" A moment later her spirit had departed.

PART TWO

JOHN

9

The Vow

Sure-footed, even in the darkness, John's tall, lean figure bounded up the steep rocks behind the Qumran community buildings. His destination was a small, level, tongue-shaped promontary, which dropped away in an almost sheer precipice on three sides. Once there, he sat on his favorite rock, facing east across the now dark-looking waters of the great Salt Sea.

He began at once to recite the set prayers and psalms he had been taught to repeat over the years. As he neared the end of the list he began to open his eyes for a second after each one, scanning the horizon. In a few moments, a first faint flush appeared over the mountains of Moab. This was what he had been waiting for, and he continued to watch expectantly.

Precisely as the sun's full disc appeared above the mountains, he closed his eyes again and lifted his face.

> I give thanks unto Thee, O Lord,
> For Thou hast illumined my face
> With the light of Thy Covenant.
> Day by day I seek Thee,
> And ever Thou shinest upon me,
> Bright as the perfect dawn . . .

John continued on with the rest of the long prayer and then relaxed. In the congregation of the Men of Perfect Holiness, as the Qumran community called itself, the sun was regarded as the symbol of the divine light that was specially granted to them, the elect of God. Set prayers at sunrise and sunset were therefore mandatory. No one must speak before sunrise every morning. Immediately afterwards, they usually all assembled to receive their orders for the day's work.

Today was to be different, however. John's heart raced at the thought of the coming events. He was thankful that the leader of his group of fellow-initiates, (Joseph Barsabbas,—usually known by his nickname of Justus)—had excused them from work that morning. This was to give them time for final preparations for the great occasion of their examination and solemn oath-taking as novitiates of the community that afternoon.

This would be followed in two days time by the great annual Feast of the Renewal of the Covenant, when if at all possible, every member of the Order throughout Judea, would come to Qumran to renew his vows.

John had arranged to wait here to meet Benjamin, his friend. Benjamin was another of this year's initiates, and John wanted to give him a little last coaching before their oral examination by Simon, who was known as the great Guardian of the community. If Simon did not pass them, there was little chance of the whole assembly voting for them. Benjamin, in fact, had been deferred from the previous year. He hadn't even been given the chance to be examined by the Guardian. His leader believed he did not yet measure up to the required standard.

Benjamin was a rather simple fellow in some ways. He found study very difficult, although he was clever with his hands. He had seemed attracted to John since their early days together. Now he had sought his help because John had such a great understanding of the sacred writings.

As John waited, his quick mind reviewed all that had led up to this great day of initiation, now that he had reached the required age of twenty. It had been a strange life since the day his cousin (whom he always addressed as "Uncle" Eleazer) had brought him and Nathan to Qumran.

Six children had been given to the community around the same time as himself, ranging in age from Nathan at two-and-a-half to others of four years. Because they were too young to study and understand the rules of the community, they had been placed with a married couple who worked at the farm and industrial area of Ain Feshkha, two miles south of Qumran. The wife, Anna, was a kindly woman who was not allowed within the community proper at Qumran, but still had accepted its teachings. The boys had had a lively time together, even going down to the Salt Sea sometimes and enjoying the strange sensation of floating in its thick, saline solution.

Benjamin had been brought to them as an orphan when he was six. By that time John was five, and the boys had begun to help weed the crops and herd the flocks. No one could sling a stone to turn back a straying goat as accurately as Benjamin and he taught John. From that time, too, they were taught to recite various psalms, prayers, and Scripture verses. At ten years they had begun serious study of the Mosaic law and to read and write Hebrew and Aramaic. To Benjamin, this had been a horribly difficult task, but to John it had been an exciting new experience.

A few years later, when they were transferred to Qumran, John periodically peered into the big writing room called the scriptorium, and longingly watched the Brothers who sat at the huge table made of plaster-covered mud bricks. The only sound was the constant dipping of their pens into the inkwells as they painstakingly made new copies of various sacred Scriptures, commentaries, and the sacred manuals of the Order.

The young boys still had to live in the buildings outside the community proper. They could not associate with the full members, except for their teachers, until after their initiation was complete. In fact, it was a tense matter being near any of the Brothers, for even to touch their garment or any of the pots, pans, plates, or food connected with their common sacred meal was to render them unclean.

Apart from that, John had not found the life particularly restrictive. Perhaps the fact he was from a priestly family had given him a favored position, but his obvious eagerness to learn had earned him the approval of most of the instructors. Not all the boys had fared so well. Benjamin had often had his food ration cut for breaking one of the many rules.

He was not really a mischief-maker, John reflected, and certainly wasn't afraid of hard manual work. In fact, Benjamin was very honest and good-natured, although there was a streak of stubbornness sometimes which often stemmed from an intense desire to be certain about something. He also enjoyed a laugh and was somewhat clumsy. His clumsiness often caused defilement, which was probably why Benjamin didn't get on so well with his group leader, Zimri, who was very different from Justus.

John realized with a start that the sun was now well above the mountain skyline. He wondered what could be keeping Benjamin. The deep waters of the Salt Sea before him had turned to their usual azure, while farther south they appeared first aqua, then bright turquoise. The shade varied with the depth of the water.

What a marvelous slash of color it was amid the arid surrounding country! John put his hand almost affectionately on the light gold-colored rock beneath him, then glanced up at the deeper tones of the tawny cliffs towering behind him. It was all beautiful to him, but especially so on this late spring day. It was Friday, the thirteenth of the third month. John was aware of a strange stirring within him—a sense of expectancy that he could only suppose was due to his having come of age and to the closeness of his initiation into the deeper secrets of the Qumran community.

He had never prayed in words other than those he had been taught to memorize. In fact, to utter the most venerable name of God, YHVH, while reading or praying was a terrible sin, punishable by expulsion from the community. Consequently, few dared pray extemporally. But now John suddenly felt he *must* express something personal.

"Oh, Holy One, here I am. Take me for your use. Help me to keep all the conditions of the covenant, and guide me in your service. Amen."

He felt almost scared as he finished and opened his eyes. There was his friend coming up the rocky pathway at last.

Mechanically they uttered the customary greeting of the community.

"The Lord bless thee and open for thee from heaven the perpetual spring of knowledge."

"The Lord keep thee from all evil and deliver thee from domination by Belial."

Benjamin was almost as tall as John, but of heavier build. He was panting a little as he sank onto the rock beside him.

"Sorry I'm late. I got involved in a chore in the kitchen. Zimri doesn't intend to let us all off this morning, like your Justus. And I dare not argue with him today of all days."

"No! Do be careful!" John's voice sounded his concern. He

couldn't help liking Benjamin, although he was so different from himself. He had known him so long and knew he always meant well. "Now, shall we go through the main points the Guardian is likely to ask?"

"Yes, we'd better." Benjamin nodded gratefully.

"First, how did our community come into being?"

"It is the true congregation of Israel, the fulfillment of Moses' promise of a future teacher of righteousness and of the sayings of other prophets. Our Guardians, each in turn, have been the source of this right teaching."

"Good! What is our aim?"

"To live a holy life within the covenant. To find the secrets of heaven in this world and to stand before God forever in the next."

"And what is our specific task?"

"To maintain the law and covenant of God in the midst of our age of apostasy and confusion. To bring men back to the Truth before the final judgment overtakes them, and to fight the last great battle against the heathen and the sons of darkness."

"Good, Benjamin! Now, why are we called 'Priests after the order of Zadok'? That's very important. You forgot it before."

"The Hasmonean rulers did away with the only true Zadok line of the priesthood established in the time of our father David. They then appointed a high priest from another branch of Aaron. Thus, our teachers of righteousness have had to retire to the desert. Here they continue the pure line of Zadok in absolute holiness, having nothing to do with the corrupt worship of Jerusalem."

"Right. And the covenant?"

"It's a renewal of the old covenant between God and the true Israel, especially those here in the desert. We promise to keep all the law of Moses in every detail."

"What else do we promise?"

"To be truthful, humble, just, upright, charitable, and modest. And to share our wisdom, strength, and property with our Brothers of the community. But John, I have no property, and I can't see anyone wanting a share of *my* wisdom," Benjamin added with a rueful chuckle. "I haven't enough for myself!"

"But it will increase, Benjamin—the more you study, the more you will become a real part of the Brotherhood. Why, the master himself—second only to the Guardian—will be teaching us all the other rules and the secret truths of the Order, once our initiation is over."

"To tell you the truth, I'm scared stiff of him! I'd much rather spend my time at the pottery wheel. John, I've never dared say this before, but I've been thinking lately—I'm not sure I go along with this idea of our bodies being evil and unclean. And being told we mustn't let our bowels move on the Sabbath! Isn't that just something *natural*, not evil? And the same with women and marriage. Didn't God create them? I'm beginning to feel I need one."

John turned an alarmed face. "But you know what we've always been taught, Benjamin! We are to be men of perfect holiness and are not to follow a sinful heart, committing all manner of evil. Women have no capacity to learn and only lead men to sin. Remember, they can't even remain faithful to one man, we are told."

"Well, how did you and I get born? Was that sinful? I remember my father and mother, and they were both God-fearing people. If only they hadn't been killed resisting robbers, I wouldn't be here," he added wistfully. "Even now I wonder if I shouldn't leave."

"Benjamin!" John fixed his piercing black eyes on his friend and brought all his will power to bear. "Remember the two spirits! What are they?"

"The spirit of truth and the spirit of perversity in which all men walk," replied Benjamin dutifully.

"Just *make up your mind* to let the spirit of truth guide you and spurn the spirit of Belial, then you can discern the sons of light . . . from the sons of darkness. Never be one of *those!*" Benjamin hung his head.

"And don't forget the master says the present cycle of time is almost completed. We're living in the last days, and many calamities will occur, as you said just now. We are preparing in the desert the way of God for his anointed one. Remember, there's the holy war to fight and the Messiah will be victorious!"

Benjamin looked in astonishment at his friend and John, too, was surprised at the force of his own words. In spite of being a year younger, he felt a strong responsibility for Benjamin.

"All right, I'll do my best. But it's really hard. I had such dreams last night, and they're so frequent these days I'm always getting defiled. At least I hope I can stay pure now until after initiation! I must get back now in case Zimri wants me. Don't tell anyone what I said, will you?" he added anxiously.

"Of course not. Just remember to answer all the questions this afternoon as you did now. Then you'll have no problem."

John stayed there until it was almost time to prepare for the midmorning first meal of the day. In his excitement about initiation he had almost forgotten the Festival of the Renewal of the Oath on the fifteenth, which according to the community's peculiar calendar always fell on the first day of the week. Thus, members from a distance must either arrive in the afternoon in time to pitch their tents before the Sabbath began, or else travel through the evening and early morning after the Sabbath sundown.

Uncle Eleazer always attended the festival, bringing him and Nathan a new robe each year and some other small gift. But he had promised that this year, when John was twenty, he would have something important to tell him. John felt a little curious as he remembered this, although he thought perhaps it would just be a fatherly talk on reaching this important stage in life.

He might know in just a few hours now. The Guardian examined the initiates in the early afternoon before the Sabbath began. Then on the evening after Sabbath sundown they all came before the assembly of the congregation, who, after discussion, would vote on whether to admit each initiate. In practice they usually followed the recommendation of the master, so his examination was the most crucial part of the procedure. John was sure Uncle Eleazer would be there for the assembly, if not this afternoon.

At last the oral examination was completed. Two out of Benjamin's group had been deferred, but somewhat to his surprise and not without a secret twinge of regret, Benjamin was passed. The master had been advised that though not a bright student, he was honest and hardworking and would make a good soldier for the coming holy war.

John was disappointed to see no sign of Uncle Eleazer, and that Sabbath passed especially slowly it seemed. Then came the most solemn moment of taking the oath in the presence of the whole congregation. Each initiate had memorized it for weeks, but it was repeated after the master for fear any should make a mistake.

I commit myself with a binding oath to return with all my heart and soul to the commandments of the law of Moses, as that law is revealed to the sons of Zadok, the priests who still keep the convenant and seek God's will; and their co-covenanters who have volunteered together to adhere to the truth of God. . . .

I pledge myself to respect God and man according to the communal rule; . . . to do what is good and upright in his sight in accordance with what he has commanded through Moses and his servants the prophets; to love all that he has chosen, and hate all he has rejected; to keep far from evil and to cling to all good works; to act truthfully and righteously and justly on earth, and to walk no more in the stubbornness of a guilty heart and of lustful eyes, doing all manner of evil; . . . . to love all the children of light, each according to his stake in the formal community of God; and to hate all the children of darkness, each according to the measure of his guilt.

I pledge myself to bring all my mind, strength and wealth into the community of God, so that their minds may be purified by the truth of his precepts, their strength controlled by his perfect ways, and their wealth disposed according to his just design.

I will not deviate by a single step from carrying out the orders of God at the time appointed. I will neither advance the statutory times, nor postpone the prescribed seasons. I will not turn aside from the ordinance of God's truth either to the right or to the left.

At last it was completed, with muted sighs of relief from some, and awed awareness in the hearts of most initiates of the finality of the step they had just taken. But soon their minds were diverted by the sound of the combined priests and Levites pronouncing the blessing.

"Blessed be God for all that he does to make known his salvation and truth."

"Amen, amen," chorused those who had just taken the oath.

The priests then recited many of God's acts of mercy and power toward faithful Israel, while the Levites followed with an account of the many iniquities and transgressions of sinful Israel. This was the cue for the new members to confess their own sins.

"We have acted perversely, we have transgressed, we have sinned, we have done wickedly ourselves and our fathers before us in that we have gone counter to the truth. God has a right to bring his judgment upon us and upon our fathers. Always from ancient times he has also bestowed his mercies upon us, and so will he do for all time to come."

The priests in a loud, united voice then proclaimed the blessing upon them.

"May he bless you with all good and preserve you from all evil. May he lighten your heart with life-giving wisdom and grant you eternal knowledge! May he raise his merciful face toward you for everlasting bliss!"

Then it was the Levites' turn to pronounce the curse for those who might later decide to cast in their lot with Satan.

"May he deliver you up to torture at the hands of avengers! May he visit you with destruction by the hands of the wreakers of revenge! Be cursed without mercy because of the darkness of your deeds!"

Now all that remained was the presentation to each novitiate of the three symbols of purity, the first being a white robe, which was always to be worn. Next was a small apron to bind around the loins for the frequent ritual immersions, including before the communal meals, and for other occasions demanding purification. The last was the spade prescribed in Deuteronomy 23:12-14, for digging a hole to bury their own excrement. For the Qumran community this had to be more of an axe to hack the rocky surrounding surface to the required depth of one foot.

Once it was all over, John realized there was still no sign of Uncle Eleazer. He managed to find Nathan in one of the outer buildings, remembering now he must be careful not to touch any of the people there lest they make him unclean.

"No," Nathan replied to his query, "I can't think why he hasn't come. Perhaps he'll be here in the morning."

Among the last of the travelers to arrive next day was a sad-looking young man from Bethany named Lazarus. Having registered, he asked if he might see the bursar personally, as he had an important message to deliver. He was ushered into the inner office.

"The Lord bless thee. . . ."

"And keep thee. . . ."

"I have bad news," he began. "Our guardian at Bethany, the priest Eleazer, died suddenly a few days ago. He murmured something about an important message for John, son of Zachariah, who is here, but he died before he could make it clear. It was something about a scroll."

The bursar thought a moment. "I believe I remember something about it." He consulted a document. "Yes, it was registered as his property to be retained until he was of age. We'll take care of that. He's not free to speak with you now because he's one of this year's initiates. But what about you?" he suddenly demanded with stern gaze, "Are you unclean from touching the corpse?"

"No, no. It was four days ago and I didn't go near in order to keep pure to come here. There is another tragedy, too," Lazarus continued with a deep sigh. "Uncle Simon, one of our elders, has contracted leprosy. He has been shut away a month. If the master has some secret cure, please beg him to make it known to us."

The bursar shook his head. "Even the master cannot do that," he said a little impatiently. "Nathan will be in the outer kitchens now. Perhaps you should go and tell him the news about his father. But don't mention the scroll to him. It is a personal matter for John. We will see to it."

Not until the following day, when the great convocation had come to an end and most of the visitors departed, did the bursar arrange an interview with the Guardian. He took along the small scroll that had been registered as belonging to John, son of Zachariah. He explained what had happened and what he knew of John's background.

"Let me see the scroll."

The Guardian took it out of the beautifully embroidered case and read it through carefully, his lips pursed.

"H'm. We don't want any strange doctrines or wiles of Satan introduced here. He is a promising young man and a priest. We can ill afford to lose him. If the Holy One has truly provided that he shall be a prophet, nothing can prevent it. But we must not be responsible for putting such ideas into his head."

He thought again for a moment, his eyes moving up and down the huge blocks of light stone forming the bare walls of his austere chamber in the two-storied tower that dominated the community building.

"Put it among the other scrolls in the scriptorium in the locked section. If the Holy One intends it for him, he will direct him to it."

The bursar pronounced the official blessing upon the master, picked up the scroll, and made his way to the scriptorium.

10

A Vision in the Night

John glanced up at the low shafts of sunlight coming through the west windows of the scriptorium and realized it would soon be time to stop writing and attend evening prayers. He was in the midst of copying the prophecy of Isaiah, a tremendous work few others wished to begin. But to John it was no hardship; indeed, it was now his favorite occupation.

Today, however he had found it hard to concentrate. Benjamin's stricken face, as it had appeared in the court of judges yesterday, kept coming back to his mind. He really must pull himself together now and finish the remaining few verses of this section before it was time to stop.

Apart from the all-important Torah, the first five books of Moses, Isaiah's prophecy was the Scripture most consulted and taught by the Qumran community, hence the need for a number of good copies. As John had carefully transcribed it, sentence by sentence, many of its words had impressed him in a new way. He was disturbed to realize his new perceptions were not always the interpretations given by the community's leaders.

He had been particularly struck with the account in the early part of the prophecy where the writer told how he had seen the Lord after the death of the king, Uzziah. Isaiah had beheld the Lord of Hosts enthroned on high. His reaction had been: "Woe is me. . . . Because I am a man of unclean lips." Then God had sent an angel with a glowing coal to cleanse his lips, after which he had issued that great call, "Whom shall I send, and who will go for us?" The prophet had answered: "Here am I! send me."

As he copied it, John had thought how remarkable it was that an individual should have such a personal encounter with God himself. It wasn't something they heard much about in the community. True, their teachers of righteousness were specially enlightened in mind by God, but for the rest, the emphasis was on obedience to the six hundred and thirteen positive and negative commands of the Torah, though with a few notable exceptions, as he was beginning to realize. In addition, there were the secret teachings of the master to listen to and all the extra rules of the community to be strictly kept. Any deviation brought severe punishment, as had been the case with poor Benjamin yesterday.

The sun's rays had disappeared from the window now and he stopped writing. After a moment he held the manuscript sideways towards the light to make quite sure the ink was dry, before he reverently rolled up the scroll for the night. Then he joined the other four Brothers who had been working there and they filed out in silence.

John went to join the group of which he was now priest leader. He pronounced the opening words and from then on the prayers seemed to follow mechanically, although the words were often of real beauty and truly worshipful.

> I give thanks unto Thee, O Lord,
> because in a dry place, Thou hast set me beside a fountain;
> in an arid land, beside a spring;
> in a desert, beside an oasis;
> like one of these evergreen trees,
> fir or pine or cyprus,
> planted together to Thy glory. . . .

"Planted together,"—that was it! That was what partly accounted for John's present feeling of dissatisfaction, he realized. There was just no opportunity to be alone in the community. He had passed his twenty-seventh birthday a short time ago and as well as being leader of his own group, he had advanced to the stage of being present at the court proceedings within the community, although he would have no vote in its decisions until he was thirty. How thankful he had been that this was so in court yesterday during Benjamin's case!

From the time he began attending the court cases he had begun to get a little restive with life in the community. Up until then he had always had something ahead to look forward to. After his oath of acceptance of the covenant, there had been the great experience of becoming a member of the holy community and joining those solemn sacrificial meals twice a day. These rites were preceded by immersion and began and ended with prayer.

In their first year new members could only partake of the food; not the drink, *tirosh*, which was fresh grape juice. (Later, John was allowed citrus juice.) The reason for this delay was that fluids were considered especially susceptible to contamination through contact with anyone who had not followed every detail of the laws of purity. After this final year of probation, having proved they were really capable of keeping these laws, the new members were fully accepted into the community, truly having everything in common with the holy Brothers.

Then had followed the very special sessions with the Guardian, who taught them the secrets of the Order, which they had sworn never to divulge to anyone outside. These included methods of interpreting the Scriptures by the use of allegories, with special emphasis on themselves as the faithful "remnant" of Israel. There was also guidance on how to predict future events and interpret dreams; learning the names of the angels; and finally details of secret cures for sickness with the use of special herbs and stones.

The majority of newer members were really excited about these things, but they had left John unmoved for the most part. He had discussed it one day with Justus, who still remained his adviser.

"How can we be sure that these allegories are really the true explanation of the Scripture passages? No hint of such is given in the holy writings themselves."

"But that is the whole purpose of joining this Order. God has granted this special enlightenment to our successive teachers of the right. It is the reward for their great piety and mortification of all bodily pleasures," Justus had answered.

John said no more at the time, but a tiny seed of doubt remained in his mind, which caused him a growing discomfort. He continued to copy the Scriptures as often as he could, though he had to take his turn with the other priests in making the sacred bread for the common meals, as well as instructing initiates. He was also being instructed himself in the rituals for maintaining perfect purity and in interpreting the Scriptures according to the views of the various teachers of righteousness throughout the history of the community.

With the long compulsory communal times of prayer at dawn

and dusk, John was beginning to feel as if there was no time to be alone and think, except when he was in the scriptorium copying the sacred writings. Perhaps that was the purpose behind the community rules. They were to be as one, the true Israel of God; and being constantly in each other's presence the Brothers could easily notice if the spirit of perversity led any member astray. In this way they could keep watch on each other and report for the annual assessment of their spiritual status.

The principle was good, perhaps, but in practice John found that some Brothers were over-critical. With priests in rather short supply, he himself was one of the privileged ones. But since attending the court of the judges, he was beginning to feel the penalties were quite out of proportion. He began to dread the day when he would have to vote.

A Brother falling asleep during the assembly of the congregation, for example, was sentenced to a cut of one quarter of his food ration and exclusion from the purity meal for thirty days. The same penalty could be given a Brother caught laughing loudly, or gesturing with his left (unclean) hand. Since they ate very simply at the best of times, and fasted on the second and fifth days, this punishment could be hard. Disrespect to a companion of higher rank, or rudeness and anger towards a priest, drew a year of this penance.

This had been the terrible sentence imposed on Benjamin yesterday for alleged disrespect to Zimri. The severity of the punishment had troubled John ever since. He decided now he must see Benjamin after the evening meal. Of course, he would be very careful not to touch him in order to avoid becoming defiled himself.

The prayers ended at last and each Brother in full purity tied on his little apron, so he would not be seen naked by his fellows (which again would incur a penalty). Then each Brother took off his white robe and immersed himself completely in one of the two big cisterns within the main community building. Robed again, they proceeded to the refectory, seating themselves according to status, first priests, then Levites, then laymen. The presiding priest of the day uttered the blessing and stretched forth his hand to take bread. The others could then follow his example.

After the meal's closing prayer it was time to study the Scriptures. John gave his group a passage to memorize and then excused himself. Nathan, his half-cousin, was now in his group gaining experience and could be left in change.

Having set them to work, John cautiously went out toward the other buildings where those under discipline and also the pre-novitiates lived. There they could not contaminate the Brotherhood. Here the elder Brothers near death were also housed for the same reason, but they were tended with loving care.

But how would he find Benjamin? Those living outside had a schedule similar to his own and John supposed his old friend would be in a study group, unless he had some other duty. How could he call him away without arousing great curiosity and comment? He had absolutely no idea, and the thought suddenly came that he must pray about it.

"O Lord, show me what to do now," he said, standing still for a moment.

He turned toward a building on his left. Walking close to the wall, he had almost reached the entrance when someone rushed out and would have bumped into him if he hadn't hastily stepped aside.

The figure was swathed in a cloak, but in the moonlight he could see it was Benjamin.

"Benjamin!" he called in an urgent whisper, "Stop! I was coming to find you. Where are you going?" He had a fearful suspicion his friend might be trying to run away. "Let's go up to our old rock and talk."

Benjamin had thrust his cloak aside and pointed to the little axe in his belt. "I'll be with you in a few minutes," he panted, and sped away.

John breathed a sigh of relief. Of course, he might have guessed, since the cloak was supposed to be worn for that purpose; but he couldn't forget Benjamin's face yesterday when he heard his sentence. John had been afraid he might do something desperate—like run away.

He climbed slowly to his favorite old perch to wait for his friend. He hadn't come there for a long time and he felt a guilty relief at being alone. With deep appreciation he watched the shimmering pathway made by the moon across the dark water of the Salt Sea, while considering what he should say to Benjamin.

At last he arrived and carefully sat the required distance from John.

"It would be terrible if I defiled you, wouldn't it?" There was a note of sarcasm in his voice that John chose to ignore.

"I'm glad you've come. You know, when I first saw you I was afraid you might be running away."

"I'm not sure I won't, even yet. I had the excuse of bowel sickness for not being at Scripture study tonight. This rule of being two thousand paces away from the buildings to relieve yourself is wicked, when you feel like I do! They gave me some left-over food, and it must have been bad!" he muttered bitterly.

"John!" Suddenly the words began to pour out with anguished intensity, "I *can't* stand this for a whole year! I've a big frame, and I'm always hungry. I just can't take it! It makes me so bad-tempered, too, and that will only get me into more trouble. I *know* I'll have to leave eventually, either run away or be thrown out!"

He put his elbows on his knees and bowed his head in his hands in despair.

"Benjamin, I know how hard it is, but after a few days your stomach will contract and the fasting will be easier. If you leave, you will certainly starve! You've sworn to live this life and no one outside the community is allowed to give you food if you've been expelled. I have heard that some have died because they had nothing but the spring grass to eat when they left."

Benjamin raised his eyes with a hopeless, yet puzzled expression.

"You mean . . . I deserve a death sentence for what I've done?"

"Well, what happened exactly?" John asked, stalling for time.

"Gideon was supposed to be molding one of the thin pots to keep scrolls in and suddenly made it look like a fat-bellied man instead. It really looked comical and I laughed. Just then Zimri happened to pass by and accused me of 'guffawing foolishly.' I got angry and told him he didn't know what a real 'guffaw' was. So he brought it to the court as a case of 'rudeness and anger towards a priest.'"

"That is a very serious offense."

"But where in the Scriptures are we told we must never laugh? Surely the Lord doesn't want us always to be grim and sober."

John was nonplused for a moment.

"I—I don't think I know him well enough to be able to answer that," he began slowly. "As you say, there's no command in the

Torah—though Sarah was rebuked for laughing, remember? But of course she was only a foolish woman." He thought hard for a moment before continuing.

"Isn't it rather that the times are so serious now? The end of the age is so near! I feel something of tremendous consequence is soon to take place in the world. We must retain our purity and be ready to do the Lord's work and fight the holy war that is coming. Just hold on a little longer. Remain a son of light and you'll not be disappointed." He stopped for breath, surprised at all the words he had spoken.

"Let us pray that you will have strength to follow the spirit of truth." He prayed then in the simple, personal way he had found himself doing recently.

"O Lord, you have cared for your people like a shepherd. Look now upon Benjamin. You know his heart, you know he desires to serve you, but his flesh is weak. Strengthen him in body and spirit to bear this present discipline and to serve you faithfully. Amen."

"Amen," added Benjamin in a firm yet awed tone of voice. "Can we really pray like that—using our own words—for something personal?" he asked incredulously.

"I don't see why not. I've found myself doing it several times lately. But I'm afraid we should go back now, or we'll arouse suspicions."

"I suppose so." There was still a trace of reluctance in his friend's voice, but once again Benjamin had been persuaded by John's forceful words. "I don't know what I'd do without you, John," he added, then with a sudden change of tone, "You go ahead. I have to dash off again . . . my stomach's still upset!"

The next day as John worked on the prophecy of Isaiah again, he found he was about to write one of the favorite verses expounded by the Guardian and other community leaders.

> Prepare the way of the Lord;
> Make straight in the desert
> A highway for our God.

This, it was claimed, was what the community was doing as it shut itself away from the world there in the rugged, arid, uninhabited wilderness of Judea.

As John looked at it carefully, he was struck with the number of references to proclamation in the passage. "Speak comfort to Jerusalem, and cry out to her, that her iniquity is pardoned." A voice was to call, "Prepare the way of the Lord." Over and over the words went through John's mind. Yet here they were spending much of their time studying secret teachings shut away from the world, when God was wanting them to speak to the people! They were to give them warning. Plus the good news of his loving concern for the cities of Judea!

He must certainly have a talk with Justus about this and perhaps even with the Guardian himself.

That night as he lay sleeping amid the usual row of Brothers, John had a very clear dream. Like the prophet Isaiah, he saw the Lord, high and lifted up. With amazement he heard again the words that Isaiah heard, but with a slight difference.

"We need a voice—a voice in the desert. Who will go for us?"

John's heart beat wildly and his limbs began to tremble. His throat was suddenly so dry he could scarcely form any words, but with a supreme effort he forced them to come.

"Lord, here am I! Send me."

The vision faded and he awoke to find himself drenched in sweat. In the faint moonlight that came through the high grating in the dormitory wall, he could discern the sleeping forms of the other Brothers on their mats, apparently completely unaware of the amazing thing that had taken place.

For John, however, there was no more sleep that night. What was the future going to hold for him? He could see no pattern, no way to go. But of one thing he was sure. God, the Almighty, had summoned him for some great purpose.

11

The Discovery of the Scroll

The next day John tried to make an appointment to see Justus, but it was not convenient for him until the following afternoon. Meanwhile, John reviewed the verses from Isaiah, to ensure that he could quote them accurately. Even a priest could not take a scroll out of the scriptorium, except when teaching a class or for community studies.

Since Justus had the responsibility of guiding the various leaders of the small groups, he could be consulted without questions being asked. He suggested at once to John that they should go out and walk toward the sea. John thankfully strode along beside him, rejoicing in the unexpected freedom and fresh air.

"I need your advice," he began. "A number of things have been happening recently and I don't know what I should do."

Justus turned to him with a concerned look. "Tell me about them. Hold nothing back."

"Well, I'm making a new copy of the prophecy of Isaiah, and as I have looked at the words and thought about them, they seem to take on new meaning."

"In what sense, specifically?"

"Two days ago I was copying those words we know so well: 'Make straight in the desert a highway for our God.' But all around those words are others which make it plain God wants us to *proclaim* his message to the cities of Judah, to warn them of judgment, to tell them of God's character. He wants a voice crying in the wilderness. We are not doing that since we are shut away here."

Justus was silent a moment.

"Our teachers of righteousness taught that the life of the whole community is a witness. The ordinary people know enough about us to understand that we live by the Levitical laws and well beyond them, mortifying the body. Our life is one united voice witnessing to him. In this way we are preparing for the end time and the holy war."

"But doesn't God use individuals, too? We read of them all through the sacred writings . . . Abraham, Moses, David, Elijah. Isaiah himself had a personal meeting with the Almighty. He heard God speak and he answered 'Here am I! Send me.'"

"Yes, he has certainly called individuals and revealed himself to them in the past. Now it seems that for four hundred years he has ceased to do so. He has chosen to speak only through our congregation—through its leaders and secret knowledge."

John drew a deep breath. "That is why I must tell you what happened two nights ago after I studied those verses. I was sleeping when suddenly I saw a great light. Like Isaiah I saw the Lord, high and lifted up. Then I heard a clear voice."

"What did it say?" For the first time there was a slight rise detectable in Justus' usual level tones.

"It said, 'We need a voice, a voice in the desert. Who will go for us?' My whole body shook, but I managed to answer, 'Lord, here am I! Send me.'"

Now his secret was out. John turned in some trepidation for his tutor's reaction. There was no mistaking now the trace of agitation on his face, but he strode on in silence for a dozen paces. His reply, when it came, was totally unexpected.

"John, all my life I have hoped to have such a vision of God. I went through the school of Hillel to become a rabbi with the desire that I would attain a fuller intimacy with him, but it eluded me. So much time was given to interpretation of the oral Law." He gave a deep sigh and remained silent a few more steps.

"Then I learned about this community, shut away in the desert and completely detached from all worldly things. Here, it was said, one could acquire an unobstructed view of the Holy One. When I saw their sacrificial living so wholly given to God, I thought that there I would surely meet with God." He paused again, a look of deep sadness shadowing his face.

"It has not proved so. Some days my heart is full of praise as we sing our great hymns. God seems so near. Yet at other times, when we are so concerned with minute details of procedure, he seems so very far away."

"How has this happened?"

"The fathers meant well. The early purpose of the Pharisees was to raise the status of each of their members to the dignity of a temple priest. Thus they formed closed communities where members tithed all their possessions and kept all the Levitical laws of purity. Yet, the truth is, the spirit of darkness is still in our midst, within our own hearts at times, even here."

There was anguish in his voice now, and he stood a moment to stare across the Salt Sea to the mountains of Moab, then northward toward Mount Nebo.

"Moses was very fortunate," he went on with a wry smile. "He met with God up there while the rest of the people had to take his word for everything. And how often they failed! If only all of them might have seen God, perhaps things would have been different."

"They saw the pillar of cloud and fire. They saw his many acts and miracles. Was that not enough?" John asked in surprise.

"It should have been, yes. But as Jeremiah says, 'The heart is deceitful above all things, and desperately wicked.' But now we must turn back." His voice had returned to its usual level tone as he continued.

"With regard to what you have told me, it *could* be merely a dream, resulting from your excitement at reading those particular verses." He raised his hand for silence as John was about to protest. "It is also possible it was a revelation from the Almighty. He has used dreams many times in the past. Perhaps in his mercy he is doing so now." Again he walked a few steps in silence.

"But we must be cautious. As your superior I order you not to mention this to anyone else. I must report it to the Guardian, of course. But as you know, he leaves in two days to take our annual dues to the temple. He will then be away nearly a month visiting our various camps throughout Judea. So I shall await his return before I speak to him. During that time you should study all the Scriptures you can. The Guardian may well forbid you to study them by yourself after his return. He may think you are getting your own ideas about their interpretation."

John's heart missed a beat. Not study the Scripture alone? That was his one real joy in life! How could he exist without it? And how was he to be available to the Almighty he had met and offered himself to two nights ago?

He dared not voice his fears now, knowing all must be reported to the Guardian, but Justus evidently guessed what was going through his mind.

"Accept whatever discipline and penance is considered necessary. Remain in obedience until everything is made clear about your future. Remember, resentment is a sin. Above all, be confident that nothing can thwart the fulfilling of God's purpose."

"Amen! And thank you," John added in a submissive tone, while inwardly he thought he could now sympathize with Benjamin a little more! He himself might soon be suffering something quite alien to his spirit.

He could see Justus considered the discussion closed. They continued in silence to the gate where each gave the other the formal blessing, then they went their separate ways.

John worked almost feverishly the next few days to complete the Isaiah manuscript, trying to memorize it as he went. Soon he came to more words that struck him with new meaning. Who was this person the prophet spoke of, "Wounded for our transgressions . . . bruised for our iniquities . . . and by His stripes we are healed"? Who was to pour out his soul unto death and be numbered with the transgressors while he bore the sin of many and made intercession for transgressors?

Surely this sounded like the actions of a particular person, not the work of their community or even their teachers of righteousness. John shook his head in despair, knowing he could not ask anyone after what Justus had said.

The day came at last when he would finish Isaiah's prophecy. He had expected a thrill of joy and pride at its completion, but the last words cast a shadow over the glow of accomplishment. True, it said first, "All flesh shall come and worship before Me." But that was followed by the sinister words: "And they shall go forth and look upon the corpses of the men who have transgressed against Me. For their worm does not die, and their fire is not quenched. They shall be an abhorrence to all flesh."

Suddenly he had a great longing to go out and warn all these rebellious ones and turn them to the Lord. He had had success twice with Benjamin. Maybe he could with others as well! With a deep sigh he remembered his orders to be silent.

The ink was now dry. With reverent hands he rolled up the scroll, wishing fervently it was his own possession. Almost reluctantly, he took it to Sapphias, the Brother in charge of the scriptorium. He took also the old scroll he had used as a copy.

"Well done," said Sapphias, after briefly scanning John's work. "It is good we have another copy of Isaiah at last, we use so many of them. Put it in this jar and return the other copy to its old one. Now, perhaps you should work on something short for a change. I've recently been sorting out some we only have one or two copies of. They are in the rack over there. Go and choose the one you would like to do next."

John felt a thrill of pleasure at this unexpected privilege. Manuscripts relating to the secret beliefs and practices of the community were kept either in the Guardian's study, or a locked chest in the scriptorium. The Scripture scrolls were in clay jars and were arranged according to their respective groups: the Torah, of which there were many copies; the former prophets and latter prophets; and the holy writings, which consisted of the historical and poetic books. These could be consulted any time with the permission of the supervisor.

Having placed the old copy of Isaiah in its jar, John moved toward the two wooden racks on the wall. One of these held the manuscripts on which priests were currently working, the other one, indicated by Sapphias, now contained a dozen small scrolls.

Slowly John approached it, wondering which one he should choose. He picked the scrolls up one at a time: Zephaniah, Malachi, a commentary on Nahum. Then came an even smaller scroll in a beautifully embroidered case. This was most unusual in the community, and John was reluctant to touch it, but then he decided he would at least identify it. Suddenly he had the strangest feeling he had seen this parchment before. Then his head began to swim as his eyes caught the title, "The prophecy of the priest Zachariah, concerning his son, John."

Somehow he stumbled to his place at the big table, hoping the other Brothers wouldn't notice his agitation. Once there, he hastily began to scan the scroll's contents.

The angel Gabriel appeared to me, Zachariah, as I was offering incense in the Holy Place. He told me he was sent to speak glad tidings to me: that our prayers had been heard, and my wife, Elizabeth, would bear a son whose name was to be John. He would afford us joy and happiness, and many would be glad at his birth; for he will be great before the Lord. He will drink no wine or liquor, and from his birth he will be filled with the Holy Spirit. Many of the sons of Israel will he turn to the Lord their God, before whom he shall go forth in the spirit and power of Elijah, to turn the hearts of the fathers to the children, and the obstinate to the wisdom of the righteous, to prepare a people who are ready for the Lord.

"He shall *go forth*—in the spirit and power of Elijah—" John read the words again slowly, "to prepare a people who are ready for the Lord." Why, *the very thing his vision had seemed to imply*! He continued reading, almost breathless with anticipation.

The following is the prophecy uttered by me through the Spirit, after the birth of the child.

Blessed be the Lord God of Israel, for he hath looked with favor upon his people, and has accomplished redemption for them. He has raised up a powerful Savior for us in the house of David his servant. . . .

This must be Messiah! John's eyes raced through the rest of that paragraph, and came to the next.

And you, little one, will be called a prophet of the Highest, for you will go in advance of the Lord to prepare his way, to bring his people a knowledge of their sins, through the tender mercies of our God, by which the light of dawn will beam on us from on high, to shine on those sitting in darkness and in the shadow of death, to direct our feet into the path of peace.

With intensified excitement, John began to read those words through again. "And you, little one, will be called the prophet of the Highest—" *Where had he heard those words before?*

He closed his eyes and repeated them, "You, little one . . . prophet of the Highest—" then he sensed a strange stirring in some deep recess of his mind. Yes, certainly he had heard those words before, long, long ago in a woman's voice! But not Mistress Anna's at Ain Feshkha.

In growing perplexity his eyes strayed down to the end of the table. Suddenly he was aware of the supervisor looking directly at him and motioning for him to come.

With some anxiety he rose to obey. Should he take the scroll, or was it about something quite different Sapphias wished to see him? But now he was pointing to the scroll, so John reluctantly picked it up, fearful he might be about to lose it. Was it his, or was it now the common property of the community?

As slowly as he dared, he approached the head of the table, the precious scroll held protectively in his hands.

"So you have found it. I came across it as I was looking for manuscripts to be copied. Attached to it was a note saying that as soon as you found it you were to report to the bursar. You had better go to him at once."

Automatically John moved obediently toward the door, though he longed to ask for more information.

The bursar was a very busy man, especially these days while the Guardian was away. He was the priest in charge of all the material and business side of things in the community, as well as assisting the Guardian in matters of discipline and purity.

His assistant asked what John wanted, then told him to wait while he enquired if it was convenient for the bursar to see him then.

John stood respectfully with head bowed and uttered a desperate prayer that he might be allowed to keep his scroll.

A few minutes later, he was standing in the bursar's presence. Being mostly concerned with copying Scriptures or baking bread, John had had little contact with the busy bursar, apart from seeing him at meals, prayer times, and at the assembly of the congregation, when either the Guardian or he presided.

The bursar was a good judge of character, as his position required, and he now eyed the young priest before him with a penetrating gaze.

"The Lord bless thee. . . ."

"The Lord keep thee. . . ."

"I understand you wished to see me when I found this scroll, Master?" John wanted to say "my" scroll, but feared that might be too presumptuous.

"Yes, now you have it, I will explain its origin. Your uncle Eleazer wanted to do this when you reached the age of twenty, but was prevented by his unexpected death."

He paused to glance at a papyrus sheet on his desk, while John's eyes never left him.

"When Eleazer delivered you to the care of the community, he told us you were the only son of the priest, Zachariah, and Elizabeth, his wife. Your birth was supposed to have been foretold to him by an angel."

"So the scroll explains."

"You have read it already? So you know the rest of the scroll is a prophecy your father uttered at your dedication in the temple. By the way, did you ever hear how your father met his death?"

John shook his head.

"He was murdered by the former king, Herod, who for some obscure reason ordered the slaughter of all infants under two years in Bethlehem and its surrounding areas. Your father refused to reveal your whereabouts. Your mother evidently escaped into hiding with you. Naturally, she thought you must be destined for some remarkable purpose—as most mothers do for their sons—and so committed you into our care."

A half-smile played on the bursar's lips for a moment.

"Because of this, the Guardian decided that when Eleazer was unable to tell you the story in your twentieth year, the scroll should not be handed to you then, in case it should give you fanciful ideas. Now, the scroll is yours, but you will not discuss it with any of the Brothers until the Guardian returns. What God wills shall come to pass, without a doubt. You are dismissed."

"The will of the Lord be done." Thankful that he could keep the scroll, John carefully pressed it into his girdle and withdrew.

Possessing the scroll helped to compensate for the shock he had experienced on hearing how his father had died. He read it through whenever he could, but as its message burned itself into his heart and mind, he began to count the days until the Guardian's return.

12

Growing Tension and
a Test of Wills

The Guardian returned only five days before the annual Feast of the Renewal of the Covenant. He then had many important details to attend to, as well as examining that year's initiates. He also was to preside over the *esah*, or assembly, when the reassessment of status of each member of the community took place.

The day after his return, Justus had managed to whisper to John as he passed him in a hallway that he would not be reporting his case to the Guardian until after the Feast. John's reaction to this news was a mixture of relief and frustration. He would now have longer with his beloved Scriptures. On the other hand, he longed to get started on whatever it was God had for him to do.

At the annual reassessment, John, as usual, had a good report from all, especially from Sapphias, supervisor of the scriptorium. His status rose from sixteenth to fourteenth, and Nathan's rose to twentieth, among the twenty-five priests then within the community. Since one of the old priests had died, Justus was also promoted to be one of the three priests, who with twelve presbyters formed the small inner judicial and advisory council to assist the Guardian. Certain decisions, however, were made by democratic vote of all full members of the Brotherhood. They could only speak in turn, however, in strict order of their rank, so it usually took two or three sessions for all the business to be completed before the annual Feast or convocation.

John now realized with a sense of gratitude that Justus had probably intentionally delayed reporting his case until after the assembly, lest it should result in postponing his advancement, or even a loss of his former status. With the assembly safely over, John's thoughts returned to something else that had been on his mind recently.

It was not until a few hours after he had left the bursar that he realized he did not know how his mother died. Members of the community had, of course, renounced family ties. Because he had no recollection of his parents, he had not thought very much about them, except to wish sometimes that they had not made him a Nazarite. Recent developments, however, gave him a growing desire to know more. He had decided, therefore, that during the convocation he would try to contact the group from the Bethany commune, to see if he could find out anything about Eleazer.

When the latter used to visit, he came into the buildings looking for John and Nathan, so they had mixed very little with people outside. In fact, the younger Brothers, especially, were not encouraged to communicate with those outside. The reason, no doubt, was that there were women members in the town camps, who were allowed to attend the convocation feast if they remained in a state of purity throughout. Since many had to stay home with small children, and every woman was unclean throughout her menstrual period and the seven following days, it meant in practice that only older women were usually present.

With unaccustomed interest, John now made his way among the thousand or more tents pitched in the surrounding area. Finally, he tracked down the overseeer of the Bethany camp. On hearing his request, he directed John to a man named Lazarus.

"He's the son of one of our former elders. He may be able to tell you more about Eleazer."

Lazarus looked several years his senior, with a pleasant face, though he had the air of one with a chronically weak constitution. On hearing who he was, he gazed at John with friendly interest.

"So you are John! Your relative, Eleazer, lived next door to us. My sister Martha used to bring you into our courtyard to play when you were very small. Yes, I can remember your mother. She died a day or so after you were brought here. She seemed quite old to me then. There are relatives of Eleazer's still alive I believe, though they are not in the community. His brother is a priest in Jerusalem, I think."

This information only increased John's curiosity and frustration. He longed to know more of his background, yet that was something he had renounced and was not supposed to think about.

Finally the great convocation ended, but it was two more weeks before John received his summons to the Guardian. An assistant told him to go up to the Guardian's private room on the second floor of the solid stone tower dominating the Qumran main building.

Climbing the steep, narrow stairs, John found himself alone in that august presence. Yet somehow he didn't feel overwhelmed. By now he was so sure God had commissioned him for some great work that he longed for the chance to explain it. Even as they exchanged the formal greeting, he raised his eyes to the man seated before him, and they seemed to take each other's measure.

Simon, the Guardian, was in his sixtieth year, yet his slight frame was very upright and imposing. With a mind honed by years of administrative and teaching responsibilities, he also had a reputation for powerful secret medications and as an interpreter of dreams. In fact, it was the fulfillment of his interpretation of a dream of Archelaus, a son of Herod the Great, that had first established his reputation.

He now regarded for a full moment the tall, ascetic-looking young man before him, with the longer hair of a Nazarite and deep-set, fearless eyes that steadily met his own. Simon shifted slightly on the hard bench at his desk, then came straight to the point.

"It has been reported you have your own interpretations of the sacred Scriptures, and they are contrary to those God has revealed to our holy community. This is a very serious matter. What have you to say?"

"I don't think I have made interpretations, Master," John replied, earnestly, yet respectfully. "I have only read the Scriptures and been struck by what the words are actually saying. I deeply desire to speak of their meaning with one who knows."

"Now is your opportunity. What are your questions?"

"First, we swear in our oath to keep every command of Torah. Many of its specific commands concern sin offerings and sacrifices, yet here we keep none of them. Can this be right?"

"We have explained this many times! The whole temple priesthood in Jerusalem is utterly corrupt. You know nothing of the outside world, but believe me, it was true when our community was formed over one-hundred and fifty years ago, and it is still true today, as I witnessed this past month. In the prophet Malachi's day the corruption was the same. Then the Lord said, 'Who is there even among you who would shut the doors, so that you would not kindle fire on My altar in vain? I have no pleasure in you. . . . Nor will I accept an offering from your hands.'" Simon paused, then continued.

"Our community has endeavored to shut that door. Our Zadokite priesthood, with its purity of life, has now become a temple of God, a true Holy of Holies. Because we diligently keep the covenant, we are a 'pleasant savor' to the Lord. We atone for sin by the practice of justice and by suffering the sorrow of affliction. We thus effect the atonement of the true Israel and ensure the requital of the wicked."

"But doesn't the law say that without the shedding of blood there is no remission of sin?"

"Early in Isaiah's prophecy he quotes the Lord as saying: 'To what purpose is the multitude of your sacrifices to Me? . . . Bring no more futile sacrifices.' Remember, too, that the prophet Samuel told King Saul that the Holy One prefers *obedience* to sacrifice of bulls. Our obedient, holy way of life will prove far more effective than any fleshly burnt offering. It will be so acceptable to God he will shrive the world of guilt, bring final judgment on the wicked, and perversity shall be no more! Have you other questions?"

"I recently copied Isaiah's prophecy. There God calls for a *proclamation* as his way is prepared in the desert. He wants all people warned of the end of the age and the wrath to come. Yet, we have shut ourselves away from people."

"Even the prophets were ignorant of the full import of their utterances. The supreme talent of our teachers of righteousness is to know their ultimate meanings. *Our* interpretations offer the true enlightenment. We are the elect of God! Our very life here is a witness. We have no need to preach to the masses. The Holy One will bring those he has elected to come to *us*! Why, in every town camp just visited many were waiting to join our congregation."

John searched desperately for the right words.

"Master, I can't help thinking the Lord wants something else today, with the end of the age so near. In fact, he gave me a vision some weeks ago, as perhaps Brother Justus has told you."

"He has. We do not know yet if it was from God, or your own imagination."

"But do you not think it was for this very reason I was made a Nazarite from birth? That this prophecy of my father is a confirmation of the vision, and the vision a confirmation of his prophecy, of which I knew nothing then?" In his earnestness John unconsciously stepped forward, holding out the scroll.

Simon put out his hand and took it from him.

"It may be. Time will prove. Remember, there has been no prophet for many generations. Instead, God raised up our holy congregation. What you suggest deviates from our teaching and could lead to serious division and sinful pride in yourself." He paused to let the seriousness of his words sink in, his eyes never leaving John's face.

"Truly there is no pride. I feel utterly unworthy! But I have this overwhelming conviction that it *is* God's will for me."

"I can believe that now, but you are young and the temptation is great." The Guardian's tone softened. "You have had an excellent record so far. I had already begun to think that one day it might be the will of the Holy One that you should be Guardian of our community. So we must do our utmost to preserve you from the wiles of Belial."

He gave a faint sigh and let his eyes drop to the desk for a moment before continuing.

"To prevent the danger of pride, we have decided to prescribe a period of penance. I believe losing your food ration would mean little. You already have good mastery of your body. Rather, you must be deprived of spiritual nourishment. For three months you will not work in the scriptorium, nor look at your scroll. Instead, you will work continuously in the bakery, making the sacred bread. Try to understand more fully the way in which *that* has become part of our great sacrifice of atonement. Remember flour was also permitted by Moses as a sin offering of the poor; and haven't we made ourselves perpetually poor for the Lord's sake?"

"That is true."

"One thing more. You renewed your oath of the covenant two weeks ago. Did you do that with a clear conscience and firm commitment?"

"Yes." There was surprise in John's eyes, but assurance in his answer.

"Good. For added precaution, however, you will come and repeat it to me privately at the close of the last Sabbath of each of the next three months. You may remain in charge of your group of ten, but may not tell them of your vision, or discuss your private views. You will teach only according to the instructions Brother Justus will give you."

With bowed head, all John could manage was a low "thank you," as the Guardian's continued silence indicated the interview was over. He put out his hand for his scroll.

"This will remain with me for the three months. The will of the Almighty shall come to pass."

"Amen!" John stepped back to withdraw, when the cool voice of the Guardian stopped him.

"And the blessing?"

How could he have forgotten! But so shaken was he by all he had just heard, John had omitted the formal blessing reserved for the Guardian.

"Your pardon, I pray." he stammered, and fought to focus his mind. He recited the blessing:

The Lord lift thee up unto the summit of the world, like a strong tower on a lofty wall.

Mayest thou smite with the vehemence of thy mouth. With thy rod mayest thou dry up the fountainheads of the earth, and with the breath of thy lips mayest thou slay the wicked.

The Lord favor thee with a spirit of sound counsel and with perpetual strength, and with a spirit of knowledge and the fear of God. May righteousness be the girding of thy loins and faithfulness that of thy thighs.

May God make thy horns of iron and thy hoofs of brass, and mayest thou gore the iniquitous like a steer.

And mayest thou share the lot of the ministering angels, and be one of the company of the Holy Beings for all time. For he hath entrusted thee with his judgments, and hath made thee a holy thing among his people, to be as a light to illumine the world with knowledge, and to enlighten the faces of men far and wide. Amen.

Simon inclined his head in acknowledgment and motioned John's dismissal.

The three months passed slowly and painfully. John whole-heartedly sought to humble himself and resolutely quenched feelings of bitterness and resentment as they arose. At the stone mill in the great kitchen, he helped grind the flour needed for two meals a day for one-hundred-twenty to one-hundred-fifty men (depending on how many were in a state of defilement or discipline). This was women's work in the outside world, but here anything connected with the sacred meals must be done by holy hands. They fasted on the second and fifth days of the week, but on the sixth had to prepare a double quantity, since no work might be done on the Sabbath.

John couldn't help feeling a bit hurt at the new attitude of his tutor, too. In curt tones Justus gave him the subjects to study with his group the following week and then dismissed him. Sometimes John even had the suspicion he was listening outside to check up on him. Only in the week before the last Sabbath of the first month did he thoughtfully remind John of repeating his oath to the Guardian.

The only enjoyable parts of the day to John now were the united prayer time, when he tried to concentrate on the beautiful words they repeated, and the study with his group, if the subject was not too circumscribed. He longed to arouse in them a consciousness of God and a real love for the Scriptures. But he could usually only convey this by his example, rather than what he could say under his present restrictions.

Only as he wrapped his cloak around him at night and thankfully lay down on his mat could his thoughts be his own. Night after night he wondered how things would end, and how he was ever to fulfill God's commission.

At last the months dragged to their completion. With pounding heart John made his way to the Guardian's room for the last taking of the oath. Both times before, Simon had listened in silence and then dismissed him. John had felt a little foolish the second time. Reciting it alone made it much more personal than with a group of fellow initiates, or the whole assembly, as no doubt the Guardian intended. Now, the third time, he was afraid the words might stick in his throat, but he managed to get through without a mistake.

"Do you repeat those words with a clear conscience?"

"I do."

"I have had excellent reports of your work, obedience, and attitude from Brother Justus and the kitchen supervisor. You may now return to the scriptorium, but this month you will copy the *Manual of Discipline* and the *Manual of the War of the Sons of Light and the Sons of Darkness.* Those will give you much to think about. And here is your scroll."

This time John said the blessing over the Guardian with a full heart, then made his way to Justus for instructions for his group.

"Welcome! There is a cool breeze blowing, so let us walk towards the sea."

Happily surprised, John eagerly followed, but at first Justus walked in silence.

"So you have passed the test!" he said finally. "Now I am convinced God caused your birth for a special purpose, and your father's prophecy will come true."

"Praise be to the Lord!" exclaimed John with shining eyes.

"In a year you will become thirty and then will be the time to act. Have you any plans as to what you will do?"

"None at all. I have sworn the oath of the covenant. I can't see *how* I am to leave here."

"There is no doubt you must get into the wilderness and meet the people. And you know nothing of life outside, do you?"

John shook his head.

"In time I will instruct you about the different types of people and their particular needs. Meanwhile, study with your group the life of the prophet Elijah."

"Why him?" John began, then comprehension dawned as he remembered the angel's words to his father, recorded in the scroll.

"In the rabbinic schools there is the tradition that a new Elijah will appear shortly before the Messiah. But our teachers have tended to merge these figures into something our community is now thought to fulfill; though some also talk of *two* 'coming ones,' the Messiah of Aaron, and the Messiah of David—meaning a duly anointed high priest, and a duly anointed king. But . . ." Justus hesitated and took a deep breath, "now I believe both views wrong."

John stood still in amazement. "What has changed your thinking?"

"I was brought up to believe in a coming Messiah. And now . . ." he turned to John with a smile, "since pondering your thoughts on the prophecy of Isaiah, perhaps I must be prepared to be your student."

"Oh, no!" John couldn't imagine such a turn of events. "But isn't that what my father's prophecy is all about?"

"It is. And we must obey God and do his will. But there will be many grave problems. We must remain silent for a time and continue in obedience until next year's assembly. Then pray that God will grant a miracle, so that you may be able to leave with the blessing of the community."

The azure waters of the Salt Sea danced before John's eyes. To have Justus' full support was far more than he had dreamed of, and he felt a great uplift of spirit.

That night the vision of the Most High appeared to him again, but this time the question was, "Where is the voice that will cry in the wilderness for us?"

"Lord, I am ready. Only show me the time and open the way," came eagerly from John's lips. He heard the words "It shall be shown you in that day," then all was dark again.

From that time John had a growing inner peace and confidence. The studies on Elijah had been exciting and encouraging and Nathan especially had seemed responsive. Benjamin had managed to complete his year of excommunication with much encouragement from John. When Nathan had moved on to take charge of his own group, Justus managed to get Benjamin placed in John's. Justus also promoted the study of Elijah in other groups, too, followed by Isaiah.

At last the second month of the new year came around. One day with a rather anxious expression on his face, Justus called John to come and walk with him.

"You have only six weeks now before you must take the fateful step. Have you thought what you are going to do about food when you leave? Are you planning to break your vow?"

"Break the vow? Never! All my conscious life I have eaten undefiled food. How could I change now?"

"You know that none of the town communes will be allowed to assist you, if you are expelled from here?"

"Yes, yes." John remembered he had given Benjamin that very same warning.

"There is no way you can live off wild things in this part of the desert, except around Ain Feshkha, but there everything belongs to our community. You must go farther north toward Jericho where there is a perpetual spring and Elijah's brook, Cherith. There are plenty of good, dry caves there and growth the whole year round. There you will find dates, wild honey and the carob bean, which is very sustaining. You can pick those with your own hands, and you will not be defiled. And there will be locusts. We have our community rules for preparing those, remember, though we don't get them here. The Jericho area has plenty of fruit, too."

"Thank you. Somehow I haven't felt concerned about food or drink—perhaps because I have never had to provide it. But as the Lord provided for Elijah, so I believe he will for me."

"Well, I doubt Elijah's ravens were in purity," Justus responded with a quizzical smile, "nor the widow of Zaraphath. She was a Gentile."

John looked shocked, but then said, "I can only trust the Almighty. I am in his hands."

"There's the matter of dress, too," persisted Justus. "You will have to leave your white robe behind, and you cannot go out naked."

Again the shocked look appeared on John's face. "What would I do without you!" he exclaimed. "I've thought of none of these things. I have thought of only how I'm to get out of here and of what message I shall give the people."

"Yes, I believe that is why God has prompted me to help you. There will be some new initiates coming from outside camps to the convocation. I'll see what I can buy from them."

Seeing the surprise on John's face he added, "You probably don't know that when we join the community as adults, we must register all our possessions with the bursar so that he knows all sources of income are pure. But if there is more than is needed, it is still in our name, though he never divulges what each possesses to the other Brothers."

"I see. But . . . just *how* am I to go about leaving here?"

"I know. I have thought it through and believe I have a plan from the Lord. After we have all been assessed for status at the assembly of the congregation this year, we each have the privilege of addressing the assembly. You are now fourteenth in order of precedence, and I don't think all those before you will want to speak. So, prepare to put your case as forcefully as you can then. Do you understand?"

John nodded.

"I will then propose that you be allowed to leave the community free from all penalty, because you are manifestly following the leading of God. Most Brothers here know nothing of your background and vision, so it will be a revelation to them. Pray that they may be so impressed that we may win the vote!"

"And if not?"

"If not, there will be bitter recrimination . . . and either seven years imprisonment or expulsion with nothing . . . or even death."

The fateful day of the final meeting of the assembly of the congregation arrived. Other sessions had been held to deal with the new status. John retained his place as fourteenth in spite of his three month disciplinary period. Now in their new white robes, a fresh one being issued each year at this time, the Brothers solemnly filed into the great assembly room.

First came the priests of Zadok, led by Simon, the Guardian. Then came the bursar, Justus, and Saphiras, and on down the list of twenty-five in order. The Guardian and his three special assistants moved to the semicircle of stone seats on a slightly raised dais facing the congregation, while the remaining priests sat in the front row there. Then came the Levites, followed by the laity, the twelve presbyters moving to the remaining seats on the dais. Near the very end of the procession came Benjamin, for he had been demoted since his year of discipline.

When a few items of business had been introduced and voted on, Simon announced that now was the opportunity for any who desired to do so to speak.

The bursar had already spoken on the business matters and motioned to Justus, who stood up.

"I have something to say to the congregation. I desire permission to speak."

"Granted."

Justus proceeded to give a brief but encouraging report of the Scripture studies, and sat down.

Saphiras next asked permission to speak. He noted the inceased number of copies of the Scriptures made during the year.

The next three passed and John hardly heard what number seven had to say. Again two passed, then Zimri stood to speak. He pointed out what he considered to be some slackening of discipline and proposed that new initiates needed to be more carefully examined.

It was John's turn at last.

"I have something to say to the congregation. I desire permission to speak." Was it his imagination, or was there a momentary delay?

"Granted."

John drew a deep breath and began. First he wished to thank the Guardian and others who had shown understanding and consideration in a problem he had encountered this year. He also thanked all the Brothers for his life in the community since it had received him as a three-year-old. He looked across at Simon and saw him looking restive and troubled. Hurriedly then he launched into the story of his birth, the finding of the scroll, and finally his vision.

"The Lord Almighty has unmistakably called me to this work, which is impossible while I remain within these walls. I must therefore beg the consent of this assembly to withdraw from the community for the present, although I shall remain true to my oath in every other respect."

There was an intense hush. All eyes were fixed on this commanding young figure with flashing eyes and persuasive voice. As he now cast an appealing glance around, he was aware of a variety of reactions. The Guardian sat with compressed lips and pale face, staring ahead. Justus smiled his encouragement; the bursar's expression was hard to read, while Saphiras' was obvious sadness. Nathan looked excited, Zimri sour, while Benjamin's eyes were wide with astonishment. Most seemed spellbound and the silence continued unbroken.

Seeing Simon was making no move, Justus now quickly asked permission to speak again.

"Granted."

"We have all been deeply moved by what we heard just now. I have observed our young Brother closely over the past ten years. I am now convinced that the Spirit of God is upon him. I believe that in his gracious lovingkindness the Lord is doing a new thing in these last days. He also honors our community by calling out one of our number for a special mission.

"I therefore propose that this assembly release our Brother in good standing immediately after the conclusion of the Feast of Renewal of the Covenant. We shall thereby be cooperating with the Almighty in the furtherance of his will." He turned to Simon. "May we take the vote now?"

"Wait a minute! I have something to say first!" It was Zimri. "Have I permission to speak?" He remembered to add the request just in time.

"Granted."

"This is *peleg,*—division! No such thing has ever been done before. The only way a man leaves this community is by expulsion or death. Let us hold fast to our tradition!"

Justus sprang to his feet again. "We believe in the holy war and are making elaborate plans for thousands to fight in the coming battle. We shall all have to leave these walls to take part. I believe God has called our Brother to go out and begin winning those who will fight with us under the coming Prince."

"When that time comes we all leave together. But this—this is heresy! Excommunicate him!" Zimri shouted.

Murmured conversation now quickly spread throughout the great room, a complete departure from the rules. Hastily Simon rose and held up his hand for silence.

"There will be no further discussion! You have heard the two points of view. As our Brother Zimri has indicated, there has never been such an occurrence in our history. We will have a moment's silence while each considers the gravity of the situation and prays for God's guidance."

John sat with closed eyes and a fast-beating heart. "Oh, God, your will be done," he repeated many times. The minutes seemed to stretch endlessly, but at last he was aware that Simon had risen again.

"The bursar and his assistant will now count the votes. Those who are against Brother Justus' proposal now stand!"

A dozen or more stood up at once with Zimri, then others joined them more slowly. At last there was no more movement. The bursar announced the number was forty-one.

"How many support the motion?"

Again some rose quickly, then others more slowly all through the room. The count was eighty-three. Neither Simon nor the bursar had voted, and it was obvious a few others must have refrained, too.

The Guardian rose to speak.

"The will of the majority has been expressed, and we must accept it. Brother Justus, your motion has been carried."

Justus immediately asked permission to speak again.

"I wish to thank all my Brothers for their support in this matter. John is now free to leave in good standing. Now there is something else I must say. Because so many of you manifestly support our Brother John, I beg for your understanding on my behalf, too, when I say that I wish to follow him as my master from now on, as he goes forth as the Lord's chosen prophet."

This time the whole assembly was truly thunderstruck, until the silence was broken by a young voice.

"So do I!" cried Nathan.

"And I!" came from Benjamin's far corner.

Three other lay members from John's group quickly followed.

"No, no! You don't understand!" John was standing again, his face filled with anxiety. The murmuring continued, but all eyes were now on the Guardian.

For the first time that they could remember, he seemed at a loss, but slowly he rose to his feet, his face filled with emotion.

"This is in many ways a tragic day for our community. The loss of three priests in one day we can ill afford. Yet, I, too, believe our Brother John has been called by God for a great work, but I hoped it could be accomplished within our Order. For the others . . . go if that is your wish, but I warn you—" and here his voice suddenly rose in a strong, prophetic tone, "you will have many difficulties. Your ministry will not last more than two years, I predict!"

"Two years of fulfilling God's will is all I ask," John answered, "Thank you, for your consent. As for these others—" his glance swept from Justus right around to Benjamin, "I am not worthy to have any followers. I have nothing to offer. I only know what *I* must do. But perhaps it is his will that together we serve him. The Lord bless and keep you all here."

In a choked voice the Guardian announced the adjournment of the assembly.

13

The Voice
in the Wilderness

With varied thoughts and emotions, seven men, no longer clad in the coarse white linen robes, filed out through the thick stone entrance to the community.

John was so consumed with the urgency to begin proclaiming God's message that this outweighed all other emotions. But he did have a twinge of fear at the thought of stepping out into what, for him, was a completely unknown world. He had no concern about what he would wear, but Justus had given him a garment of rough woven camel's hair. Light in weight, this could easily be girded into his leather belt when walking. But it would also shed the rain and be warm on cool nights. It blended well with the color of the rocks and dust of the wilderness, should hiding from danger be necessary, and it would remind listeners of the sack cloth usually worn by mourners as well.

The others wore coarse brown robes similar to those used by workers at Ain Feshkha before taking the oath of the covenant. Justus had felt it would be good to show a distinction between the new prophet and his disciples, so that attention would more quickly be drawn to John. He, too, had a keen sense of suppressed excitement and anticipation, a premonition that he soon might have what he had desired so long, a meeting with the living God.

At first John had been greatly astonished, and indeed embarrassed, when he heard Justus announce in the assembly that he planned to be his disciple. For so long, it had been Justus who was *his* master and tutor. He was over ten years his senior, and John knew how much his leaving had meant to the Guardian, who had been placing increasingly heavy responsibilities on Justus. But now, it had become a great comfort to John that he could continue to have his old friend's advice in this venture into the unknown.

When he had heard Nathan express the desire to follow him, and then the other four—especially Benjamin—John had been really alarmed, fearing the whole community might split asunder. So it had been a great relief when no one else volunteered. Afterward, he and Justus had met with the five and tried to dissuade them, thinking the followers had merely been swayed by the emotion of the moment, or else might be looking for an easy way out, as he suspected might be the case with Benjamin.

"I'm of the same family as you. I believed from the beginning God willed we should be together," asserted Nathan. "I have always sensed there was something different about you. My father once told me God had a great purpose for you and that I should always stay with you. That I intend to do!"

Of the others, Jochanan had been brought to the community at a very early age like Nathan, though three years later, so they had been companions a long time. John knew he was very dependable and a good Scripture student.

Matthias had joined the community only four years before, at the age of twenty-three. He had known great sorrow and loss. His parents and young wife had been murdered by a band of marauding Arabs while he was at Jerusalem on business.

"I joined the community because I despaired that justice might never be found in the land until Messiah should come and reign," he said. "I wanted to be ready to fight the holy war I heard they were preparing for. But if you are ordained of God to prepare the way for Messiah, then I am with you."

The third man, Shobab, had been a friend of Matthias in the outside world. He had joined the Brotherhood the year before Matthias. He had a strong spirit and was something of a mystic, but he was not very robust. This caused John and Justus some concern.

"Are you aware of how hard our living conditions are likely to be?" John asked him. "Only the strongest will be able to endure."

"God has called me to be your disciple. He will provide," Shobab insisted.

Lastly there was Benjamin. John had taken him aside and with eyes seeking to bore into his very soul asked, "Are you using this as an excuse to get out of here, and—and give way to those fleshly lusts you told me about once?"

"I promise you it is not that!" Benjamin looked really hurt. "I know I can help you in small ways. I can find suitable food and drive away wild animals in the desert, and other things like that. John, I will stay with you until death parts us. Let me go with you!"

The Guardian was obviously unhappy over the way things had turned out, but did not assert any authority to prevent it. "The will of the Almighty be done," he repeated finally, after the last mutual blessings had been said.

As John and his followers left Qumran behind, they walked along in silence for the most part, afraid to voice their varied emotions. But there was a spring in their steps as they began to savor the strange sense of freedom after all the years in the community.

They had stayed for the first meal of the day, a hallowed and nostalgic time, since it was to be the last in the company of the Brothers with whom they had had fellowship for so long. Now they walked for an hour before stopping to rest in the shade of some high rocks. Justus allowed them to drink from the leather water bottles slung at their belts, but he warned that it would be still a long time before they reached the brook Cherith, which spilled from rocks high up in a deep valley south of Jericho.

"There we will find plenty of caves where we can make our headquarters until we see how things develop," he explained— "That is, if the area is not already infested with robber bands."

This sent a chill down most spines, and Nathan and Matthias began a discussion on the best way to deal with such a situation. But John cut them short.

"It is the Lord who is bringing us here. Let's trust him to prepare the way before us. Do not let your hearts be shaken with anxiety. We will sing a hymn now and be on our way."

They were beginning to tire a little, after the unaccustomed long walk. Several of the men cut themselves a staff from the stunted trees that grew in the short wadis, or gullies, that centuries of rain water had cut through the rock. After leaving the north shore of the Dead Sea, it seemed they had lost a long-familiar and beautiful friend. Ahead lay the muddy fertile flats of the Jordan River, where the deep rift of its upper valley had broadened and flattened to form the oasis of Jericho.

They had no desire to enter that city of luxury and wickedness, however, and soon turned west into the mouth of a deep valley where the sun shone but briefly each day. After a while they were cheered by the sound of running water, the first they had heard all day. It came from a thin stream that suddenly emerged from high up the rocky face of the north bank and cascaded into the valley below.

"So that is where Elijah fled from Ahab," John said wonderingly as he gazed up the valley. "A place chosen by God himself! Truly it is hallowed ground."

They reached the stream at last and thankfully drank its sweet water before filling their leather bottles in the place where it splashed into the stone pool. They examined with interest the channel of clay pipes, built by Herod and improved by the Romans, which carried the life-giving water down the valley towards the city of Jericho.

"There will be many travelers stopping here on their way to and from Jerusalem, Jericho, and many places beyond," Justus informed them. "These nearer caves will be constantly in use, so if we are to have some privacy for prayer and study, we must move farther up the valley to one of the less accessible caves."

Matthias and Benjamin offered to go ahead and find a suitable place, while the others rested beside the water.

In a short time three different groups of travelers had arrived to refresh themselves, and John's spirit stirred within him.

Advancing with firm step he fixed his intense gaze upon them and after the usual greeting said, "I have tremendous news for you! The kingdom of heaven draws near! God has sent me to proclaim this truth, and to warn you to repent of your sin and turn to him before it is too late. His anointed Messiah is even now on his way! Repent. Repent and confess your sins."

His words and his very appearance caused quite a stir. Some of the people stopped to ask questions. Others, anxious to get themselves and their animals settled, left, but continued to talk about this strange figure far into the night.

Before long, Matthias and Benjamin returned in triumph. "We've found a very suitable, large cave, high up the cliff on the north side, near the spring," announced Benjamin. "It should get a little sun during the day, too."

"It's difficult to reach," added Matthias, "but we're all young and can manage it, I'm sure."

So they set off behind Benjamin. After they had completed the climb and crept in single file along the narrow ledge which was the only approach on the cliff face to the cave, they found themselves in what was indeed a comfortable enough cave. They had plenty of head room and a flat surface where all could lie down comfortably.

"Maybe this is the very cave where Elijah hid all those weeks from Ahab," Jochanan said with awe.

They had few enough possessions. John had brought only his scroll. Justus had obtained permission to bring some of his personal scrolls, including Isaiah, Joel, Micah and Malachi and, unknown to the rest, he had also a little money. The others had between them a couple of blankets and bread enough for one day. But even before they could unpack these few things, a blood-curdling shout rent the air.

"Hold still if you value your lives!"

They turned to see what appeared to be an unending procession of fierce-looking men, each brandishing a *cica*, grouping themselves around the cave entrance. Then they advanced, their curved daggers poised.

Their leader, a swarthy man of about fifty, was closely followed by a younger one carrying a sack he held open, while another eight pressed behind.

"Hurry! Put what you have in here!" ordered the leader.

John knew instantly what he must do.

"Friends, look at us," he said firmly to the older man. "We are holy men, sent by God from the Brotherhood in Qumran to warn our nation of Israel that the last days of this epoch are at hand! The kingdom of God draws near and with it the Anointed One."

Astonishment spread across the faces of most of the robbers, and one or two shifted uneasily.

"We have nothing of value with us," John continued. "We have lived a lifetime of poverty. See, this is all I carry with me," he added holding up his scroll.

"A very fancy cover," the robber leader said. "Perhaps that scroll contains some information I might find useful."

"I hardly think so," said John. "It's only a prophecy about me, given to my father many years ago by an angel."

"Is that right?" A strange, quizzical expression came over the leader's face. "Just how long ago did your father write this prophecy? I seem to have seen that cover before!"

"It was soon after my birth, some thirty years ago."

"Could it be?" the leader said to himself. "That was when that devil of a Herod came to his deserved end, when even the worms couldn't stomach him!"

Then, staring hard at the embroidered cover, he said to John, "What is your mother's name, and what does this prophecy say about you?"

"Her name was Elizabeth. And the prophecy says, 'You, little one, will be called prophet of the Highest—'" began John.

"The very same!" broke in the leader excitedly. "By all the blood of those we've slain, who would have believed it!"

"What are you talking about, Barabbas?" one of the robbers said. Several of the others began murmuring impatiently, "Let's get on with the job!"

"This beats anything I've ever experienced," exclaimed their leader, ignoring them. "Here, let's all sit down and find out what happened." He motioned to his own men and to John and his disciples.

"What happened to your mother?" he asked.

It was John's turn to look astonished. "My mother died when I was three. I don't remember her. I was sent to the Qumran community then and have remained there until this very day."

"I can tell you something about her. She was a great and brave lady! She escaped with you from Ain Karim when evil Herod ordered all the babies slain. She hid in a cave a few miles away."

"I knew nothing of that," John broke in.

"I was fleeing from Herod's men, too, and sought shelter in the same cave. Your mother shared her food with me, though she didn't know how long she would have to stay there. And even you helped me by finding some buried treasure that kept my companions and me going for a long time! She also showed me that scroll. She read it to you every day."

"So that's why it sounded familiar to me when I read it for the first time!" John gave a relieved smile at the solving of the mystery, then listened intently as Barabbas continued.

"I heard later that Herod killed your father—all Jerusalem was talking about it—but I heard nothing of your mother. I suppose it was wisest to keep you hidden. And so now you are a prophet?"

"God has been calling me to this work for some time, but only today could I leave Qumran. I believe he has brought you to me as confirmation of his call from my mother's womb. Also . . ." those intense eyes turned first to Barabbas, then the rest of his men, "he wants to give you an opportunity to hear and repent."

With great earnestness John then proceeded to warn of the coming wrath of God and the need to confess their sins before the Anointed of the Lord should appear.

The robbers listened attentively, and two of the youngest looked really troubled. "What shall we do?" they asked.

"Give up this dishonest way of life. Determine from now on to live in full obedience to God's law."

Barabbas stood up, and the rest of his men quickly followed him.

"For me it is too late," he said with a sigh. "It was that greatest thief of them all, Herod, who forced me into this life. I have too many crimes to atone for to ever appear in public. These two may join you if they wish. They have little to answer for yet. But one thing I will promise you, prophet, for your mother's sake. I will issue orders that no one of our brotherhood is to disturb or injure you in any way. I give you my word. Let us go, men. We still have a night's work to do."

Seven men followed him silently out of the cave. The two young ones stood still, looking irresolute and frightened until John bade them sit down again.

His own disciples were regarding him now with an awe that had increased perceptibly during this encounter. Surely here was God's prophet in truth! Yet they appeared a little uneasy at the addition of two robbers to their number.

"You are welcome to stay with us tonight and learn more," John was saying to them. "But as you see, we are holy men sworn to keep all the rules of Torah, to eat nothing impure or that hasn't been tithed, and to touch nothing that defiles." He looked at them to make sure they understood his meaning.

"We have enough bread and water for this evening's meal," he continued, "which we will gladly share with you. Tomorrow is our fast day, which you may also share, if you wish. From then on, we must depend solely on God. I suggest you go to the colony at Ain Feshkha, where there will be honest work that you can do. Or if you wish, you can be recommended to one of the town communities if you wish to become part of the Brotherhood."

The bread was carefully placed for the two young robbers a little apart from the others, but Justus included them in the blessing. When the simple meal was over they continued to ask questions. They listened attentively to all the information given them and soon the time came for the corporate prayer period. Then all lay down on the cave floor for the night.

The next morning, John announced after the sunrise prayer time together that the Spirit was leading him to go off alone to pray and that the others might spend the time as they wished.

In the evening John returned with a new eagerness in his voice.

"God has spoken to me as I prayed and revealed that we need to do something more than tell people to repent," he announced as the others gathered around. "They need to confess their sins, then take some action that will show their genuine repentance. Then they must go back to their ordinary life and demonstrate daily the change that has taken place."

"What 'action' do you have in mind?" asked Justus.

"I was thinking of all we had studied about Elijah and Elisha. Do you remember? We could do what Elisha asked the leper Naaman to do . . . something that was very hard because of his pride, but was the one thing that God ordained should cure him of his leprosy. He had to immerse himself in the Jordan!"

"The *Jordan?* But it's so dark and dirty-looking! Why not the sea, or the pools at En Gedi?" asked Matthias.

"Have you ever tried to immerse yourself in the Salt Sea?" asked Nathan with a smile. "It's impossible! And En Gedi is too far. It's nearly a day's journey away."

"Yes, it is too far from the main roads, too. I believe God caused Elisha to say the Jordan, so that it might be a pattern to guide us. And far more people will be traveling in its area," John added with a note of finality.

"But Naaman was a Gentile," Justus protested. "It was only natural God would choose water from Israel to heal him. Besides, what you suggest will remind people of the immersion of proselytes. Those of you brought up from childhood in Qumran perhaps know little about that. But any Gentile wishing to accept our Jewish faith has to be immersed, completely naked, in a ritual immersion bath in the presence of two or three rabbinic witnesses. This is to signify a complete cleansing from their former impurity and a kind of beginning again, like a newborn babe. No son of Israel will do anything that would suggest he is no better than a Gentile!"

"Isaiah had to have his mouth cleansed with a live coal," replied John. "Should we not be prepared for something similar before we are fit for God's service?"

His disciples were silent.

"This immersion will be a kind of landmark," John continued, "done only once, not like our constant purifications in the Brotherhood. It will signify that we have repented of all known sin and have received God's forgiveness. It will be a sign that we are determined henceforth to live a clean, holy life, ready for the coming of Messiah."

"Will they have to be naked?" asked Shobab.

"Of course not. As we did at Qumran, they can wear a loincloth, or their under-tunics. They'll soon dry in this sun."

"I can't imagine many people being willing to do that, though, particularly in the Jordan," persisted Matthias.

"Each of *us* will first take this step publicly, after I have explained to the people what it signifies," John said firmly. "There will be those who are willing to follow, I'm certain. What about our friends here?" he added, turning to the two young robbers.

"I am willing," replied one.

"And I."

"How long must people prepare to take this step and be tested as to their readiness—a year, like Qumran?" asked Justus.

"No! No! The matter is urgent! I feel the kingdom is coming very soon. I believe the Spirit will speak through me to bring conviction and will give all of us wisdom to discern who is sincere. I shall invite them to enter the water the same day they hear."

There was a murmur of consternation among his disciples, but John motioned for silence.

"I shall warn them, of course, that if they don't take this opportunity to repent, they will one day have to face a cleansing by fire. If they do respond, the coming One will baptize them with the Holy Spirit. Once men are convinced God is going to intervene in history, in our very day, how can they not respond? Tomorrow we must leave here and find a suitable place to begin our work beside the Jordan. Now it is time for our evening devotions."

Meanwhile, unknown to them, in different directions, word was spreading of a strange prophet in the desert who claimed to have a new message straight from God.

14

The Multitudes Come

The other Brothers had not been idle the previous day, although they had diligently kept the fast. Justus had managed to buy a cooking pot and some clay cups from traveling peddlers who stopped at the waterside. He had also given the two robbers a little money to buy whatever food they wanted. The others had foraged around for food they knew would be pure and then had meticulously tithed it.

Benjamin had also collected dried grass and sticks and ignited it with his flint in the morning. They had found wild honey, as Justus had predicted, and mixed it now with hot water in each cup to make a nourishing drink. Then the small supply of locusts they had collected was carefully prepared and thrown into the remaining water in the pot. Dried carob beans added a little more sustenance.

At John's request they ate earlier than usual. He wanted to leave in good time to find a suitable place for this new rite of baptism that he was convinced God had revealed to him. He also wanted to meet many travelers along the way.

They all stood before leaving and with full hearts thanked the Lord for the provision of the cave. Then they prayed that he would continue with them as he had with Elijah.

When they had completed the steep descent to the pool at the bottom of the narrow waterfall, John was surprised to see a familiar figure among the group of people gathered there. It was Lazarus. He was with another man from the Bethany community

133

whom he introduced to John and he indicated that the two women nearby were his sisters. He explained that he had been taken ill soon after leaving Qumran, and that the friend had stayed with him in a cave near the stream while the rest of the party had hurried home to tell his sisters, who had come to care for him. He was better, now, however, and they planned to travel at least a short distance today.

"And what are you all doing here?" Lazarus asked. No word of John's coming mission had been mentioned to visitors at Qumran.

At once John seized the opportunity to explain and raised his voice until heads began to appear from a number of the surrounding caves. Soon he had an audience of more than thirty people.

"The kingdom of heaven is at hand," he cried. "God has called me to proclaim his coming judgment on Israel and on the sins of each person. But there is a way to escape his wrath! He has appointed me to prepare the way for the coming of Messiah by calling you to repentance. Confess your individual sins, change your heart and your actions! Submit to the reign of God and be ready to receive the coming Messiah!"

All were listening spellbound, then one or two, obviously under deep conviction, began to ask questions. John continued to explain his mission.

"We are on our way to perform a new rite. Just as Gentile proselytes must humbly undergo a complete immersion before becoming one of God's people, so we who have responded to God's call and have repented of all known sin and received his forgiveness, will go beneath the waters of the river Jordan. This is a sign that we humbly submit to the reign of God in our lives, and that we are ready for the coming of Messiah."

"This is what we have been waiting for all these years!" exclaimed Lazarus to his friend and sisters. "The coming of Messiah! I, too, must go and join in this new rite."

"Impossible! You are sick, remember? How can you think of such a thing now?" It was the voice of his elder sister, Martha.

"I am well enough and the day is very warm. Say no more, I'm determined to do this."

"I will come with you. I suppose our community Guardian will not have any objection, though?" his friend suddenly added as an afterthought. "I'll just inquire how they all got away from

Qumran. It seems very strange." He moved away and went and whispered to Matthias.

"It's all right. The assembly voted to let them leave," he reported when he returned. "So there should be no difficulty. What a pity they didn't let him speak to the whole assembly at the feast."

"Yes, nearly everyone would have been glad to follow him, I'm sure," Lazarus exclaimed. "To think the Messiah is at hand! Blessed be the Holy One who has allowed me to live to this day!"

Others were whispering excitedly. Two men finally asked if they could be baptized. After questioning them carefully, John agreed.

When Lazarus and his friend told him of their desire to be baptized, he welcomed them also. But he looked askance at the two women who were members of the party and said that if they came along, they must keep well to the rear and avoid contact with the rest of the group.

Martha pouted a little beneath her veil. She was already a bit nettled that this man she had taken care of as a baby had ignored her completely. The people in her little party were all riding donkeys, and it was annoying to have to keep stopping them in order to keep behind the rest who were walking. She whispered to her sister Mary that she thought the idea of immersing in the filthy Jordan was a very foolish one, and she knew Lazarus would get sick again.

"I hope not. I think it sounds very interesting," the younger sister whispered.

It was a large group that set out for the Jordan. They passed Jericho well to their left, and continued north up to where the deep rift of the upper river had flattened into a wide valley. Here the river was much more accessible.

As they struck the main road from Jericho, which would cross the Jordan, they saw several caravans approaching from both directions. John stopped, ready to seize the opportunity to address them. Not all were native Israelites, although most were Jewish merchants. Some were traveling from Antioch, Damascus, the Greek cities of the Decapolis, or from Arabia far across the Jordan. Others were headed there from Egypt, Askelon, or Jerusalem.

After sharing his message, John invited them all to come and witness something new, and a few responded. The majority continued on their way to spread the news of a remarkable new prophet they had just seen.

At last John and his party came to the place where the river was wider and less swift, and not so far below the banks that it was impossible to step down into it. Once again John told them clearly the purpose of this new rite of baptism.

"This is not just an outward ceremonial cleansing, such as we have used since the days of Moses, and for the conversion of proselytes. Nor is it that of our holy community, which is well known," John explained.

"This is a sign that we have each confessed our sins, received God's assurance of their remission, and are resolved now to put right what was wrong. It is a sign we humbly submit to the rule of his kingdom, which will soon be established by his coming Messiah."

John's voice was full of assurance and moved the hearts of nearly all who stood on the bank. They watched fascinated as he removed his camel's hair robe and waded out until the water was waist deep. Then he stood for a moment looking up to heaven. He uttered a prayer, then slowly knelt down and disappeared from view under the murky green water of the Jordan.

A moment later he was erect again and motioned for Justus to come and stand in front of him. He asked if he was willing to be baptized.

"I am," answered Justus, with deep commitment in his voice. As John raised his arms in blessing, then Justus, too, went under the water.

The rest of the Brothers followed automatically in the order of their old status in the community. Then came the two young robbers who had been trying not to be noticed as they encountered different groups of travelers, for fear some might recognize them. Now it seemed their fear was gone and a new light shone in their eyes as they emerged from the water.

Next, Lazarus eagerly thrust his robe on the unwilling Martha, looking even more fragile in his short under tunic as he walked to the water.

"This is ridiculous!" fussed Martha to her sister.

"But I have never seen Lazarus look so happy!" observed Mary. "How I wish—"

"Wish what?" demanded Martha as her sister hesitated.

"That I could do it, too," Mary finished wistfully.

"Now you are being as foolish as he is," scolded her elder sister. "Just be thankful we now have our own cistern at home, where we can do our own ritual ablutions—in privacy."

One after another, those who had requested it went into the water for John's baptism, and several of the bystanders began to ask Justus if they might, too. If, after careful questioning, he felt they were ready, he told them to go confess their sins in the water before John.

Finally there were no more, and John strode out of the water to give a last word of warning and encouragement. In the hot, dry air their tunics were soon dry. Robed once more, Lazarus came to bid John good-bye.

"This has been the greatest day of my life. I shall certainly tell everyone in Bethany. I am sure many of the men there will soon come to find you. God bless you and keep you."

After everyone else had left, John and his disciples had to go some distance west to find a camping place. There were no suitable caves in the flatter area near the river.

"This isn't nearly as good as the last place," Benjamin remarked gloomily.

"Perhaps not, but we must stay here for a time, so that people will know where to find us. Then later we will move farther north," John replied.

Everyone was excited by the success of their mission so far. They were all ready to follow John wherever he would lead. In their period of communal prayer at sunset, John thanked God for those they had contacted that day and he prayed that each one who had gone into the Jordan would truly live a new life for God's glory.

The next day John reached several more large caravans of travelers and each time had an attentive audience, with several seeking baptism and everyone eager to spread the news. At each stopping place for the night, as travelers lay in rows on the inn floors, John was the subject of every conversation. On the roads during the day as they met, after the customary greeting, someone would ask, "Have you heard about the new prophet down by the Jordan?"

"Yes, we saw him this morning," might be the reply. "There were crowds listening to him, too."

"What is he like?"

"A bit strange looking, with long hair because he's been a Nazarite from birth. His eyes, too, are so compelling they seem to look right into you! And he's dressed in camel's hair. You can't help noticing that he looks like a prophet. He has the voice of one, too."

"What does he say?"

"Something about repenting and preparing for the kingdom of heaven, which he says is coming soon. He wants people to go under the Jordan waters as a sign of repentance. Many are actually doing it, too. I've never seen anything like it."

So it went on until in every inn and on every road people were talking. Word of John's ministry soon entered the cities. Things had been generally quiet throughout the country for several years. Up in Galilee, Herod Antipas had been ruling tolerably well for nearly thirty years, being careful to avoid antagonizing the people with the senseless slaughter and cruelty his father had ordered. In Samaria and Judea the Roman procurator, Pontius Pilate, was keeping a fairly low profile after two or three unfortunate episodes had infuriated the Jewish people.

So now people eagerly embraced the opportunity to experience a novelty. They came in crowds to view this wonderful new prophet who looked and sounded like an authentic seer.

Others, like Lazarus, who had really been looking for the expected Messiah, also came hurrying to meet the one who could tell them more. Thus, from Jerusalem and all Judea, people came flocking down the main highways and narrow mountain paths to the rocky wilderness where John could be found.

Among the throng that came one day, John recognized by their robes some members of the Pharisee and Sadducee sects. These were the very ones the community had warned them against. They were the ones who were corrupting the worship in God's holy temple, and whom the Brotherhood had vowed to hate!

Striding forward, John fearlessly pointed an accusing finger at them and called out, "You viper brood! Who warned you to flee from the wrath to come?

"Therefore bear fruits worthy of repentance, do not say to yourselves, 'We have Abraham as our father.' For I say to you that God is able to raise up children to Abraham from these stones!

"And even now the ax is laid to the root of the trees. Therefore every tree which does not bear good fruit is cut down and thrown into the fire. . . .

"But One mightier than I is coming. . . . He will baptize you with the Holy Spirit and with fire." Here John's voice rose to a new, warning note. "The winnowing fan is in his hand, and he will thoroughly purge his threshing floor, and gather the wheat into his barn; but the chaff he will burn with unquenchable fire."

Most of these religious dignitaries turned away in anger, but there were some who stayed and willingly confessed their sins. Following this, they humbly entered the waters of Jordan.

There was great rejoicing that evening as John and his disciples left the river to make their way back to their camp.

As they walked, Benjamin came up to John and asked, "Master, I have a question. What was that you said about the Coming One baptizing with the Spirit and with fire? Whatever does it mean?"

"Yes, I wondered that, too," added Matthias.

John stopped a moment so that the others might catch up and hear the conversation.

"Even I do not know what it means. I only know that those were the very words the Spirit gave me to speak this afternoon."

"When do you think Messiah will come?" Jochanan asked eagerly.

"I don't know. But it will be soon, I'm sure of it," John answered with conviction as he walked on again.

Justus was watching for an opportunity to speak to him privately. A few moments later he had his chance to speak as Benjamin and the others were discussing the strange concept of baptism with fire.

"Those were very strong words you used with the Pharisees and Sadducees. Did you feel the Spirit gave you those words to speak also?"

John gave him a puzzled glance. "I . . . think so. It just seemed the most appropriate thing to say. The words just came. Haven't we always been told to hate those who have corrupted the true worship?"

"Yes. I just want to warn you that we may begin to expect trouble from them. They will not tolerate any undermining of their authority."

"Some of them responded. It was worth it to bring a few of them to repentance."

"Indeed it was. But that will make the others even more angry. I know them well. Don't be surprised if there is bitter and even dangerous opposition."

"So be it," was all John said, and he walked on in silence.

15

Stirrings in Galilee

In a house in the busy little fishing port of Bethsaida, a suburb of the city of Capernaum on the northwest shore of Lake Gennesaret, a tall, middle-aged woman glanced out of her doorway. The position of the sun told her it was time to begin preparation of the late afternoon meal.

Salome had three hungry men to feed, but they were comfortably off now, due to the lake's rich supply of fish. Her husband, Zebedee, was a hard-working man, and now that their sons were grown they could operate two good-sized fishing boats with the help of their partners and a couple of hired men. Thus they were able to take advantage of the greatly increased market for fresh fish that had developed in the ten growing Greek cities known as the Decapolis, situated across the lake. Even nearer was the new capital of Tiberias, which the Tetrarch of Galilee, Herod Antipas, had recently built south of Bethsaida on this side of the shore. When he was in residence there, as he was just now, there was an even greater demand for fish.

Before long, Salome heard the men in the courtyard and went out to greet them.

"Well, how did things go today?"

"Very well. We had an excellent catch, and we took it straight to Tiberias," Zebedee answered. "The servants of the Tetrarch and some of his courtiers were at the dock waiting, so we didn't even have to set foot in that accursed place."

"Oh, come now, Father, it's only a very small area of the city that is built over the old graveyard," protested the older son, James. "The Pharisees have made altogether too much fuss about it. Fortunately there seem to be plenty of Gentiles who are willing to live there, and they really like to eat fish!"

They sat cross-legged on the floor and lost no time in eating their supper. When she thought their hunger had been partially satisfied, Salome ventured to ask the queston that was always uppermost in her mind.

"Did you hear any news of interest today?"

"We certainly did," answered the younger son, John, with evident relish. "One of the men who had just come up from Jericho told us of a new prophet. He looks and speaks like one, apparently! Why, he even stood up to some of the leading Pharisees and Sadducees from Jerusalem when they went to hear him. Called them a brood of vipers! Pretty courageous, wasn't it?"

"It was! But . . . what is his message? What is he trying to do?" Salome asked.

"Something about repenting and preparing for the kingdom of God that will soon be here—with the coming of the Messiah, he says."

"The Messiah? The kingdom?" Salome's eyes were alight with purpose. "We must learn more about this! If he is really coming, we must get involved as soon as possible. Don't you agree, Zebedee?"

Her husband merely nodded, knowing his wife's strong interest in the subject.

"Where is this prophet?"

"Beside the Jordan, just north of Jericho."

"Well, one of you must go and hear him. Try and persuade Simon or Andrew to go, too, or they'll think you are leaving them to do most of the work. You can spare them for a few days, can't you Zebedee?" she asked anxiously.

"Well, I have some news, too. I heard today the High Priest's palace in Jerusalem wants a contract for a regular supply of salt fish. If we're quick, we have a good chance of getting it. So John, you go and ask Andrew to accompany you. He's more dependable. You never know what Simon might say to upset things. Then while you're there you can take a look at this prophet, but don't stay long."

Excited at the prospect of a trip, John quickly left and later returned to say Andrew would go.

"Did they give the name of this new prophet?" Salome asked him.

"Yes," John answered with a grin, "the same as mine."

"John? Are you sure?" There was growing excitement in his mother's voice.

"Of course I'm sure! Why are you surprised?"

"It's brought back memories! My sister Mary told me long before you were born that our relative, Elizabeth, down in Judea, was going to have a son who would be called John. The father, Zachariah, had a vision in the temple. The angel Gabriel told him Elizabeth was to bear a son at last—they were quite old and had had no children—that his name was to be John, and that he would be a prophet."

"Well, why haven't we heard anything about them before?"

"We thought he had been killed by Herod, as his father was. I must try and see Mary to find out more," Salome added purposefully. "What a pity Nazareth is so far. I haven't seen her since her husband died. But I really must do something about it now."

She did not add that neither she nor Zebedee had cared to keep in touch with her sister after it became known she was pregnant before her marriage.

Farther down the west shore of the Lake of Gennesaret was another town of more importance than the fishing community of Bethsaida. Magdala was a fishing port, too, but was also the home of a few other industries. One was the weaving of fine woolen textiles. In addition, there were many springs and rivulets flowing into the lake. This plentiful supply of running water made it especially suitable for dying cloth, and shell fish on the beach provided a source of certain dyes.

Since doves were such an important part of many purification sacrifices at the temple, the plentiful supply of them that gave its name to the valley also provided an important source of income for the town. There were well over a hundred shops selling pairs of turtle doves. In fact, the small city's wealth was so great that its contribution to the temple in Jerusalem had to be sent on a specially guarded wagon at the times of the great festivals.

Magdala had its own synagogue, of course, and its merchants were anxious to keep the letter of the Law. But for most of the citizens, business was the most important fact of life, and wealth had brought much moral corruption with it.

One well-to-do owner of a wool-weaving business was a man named Jeremias. Not only was his cloth of the finest quality, but he also produced patterned varieties whose fame had reached as far as Greece and Rome. This was due mainly to his artistically talented Greek wife, born in one of the cities of the Decapolis.

They had been blessed with one son and a daughter, Mary, who early showed signs of becoming more beautiful and gifted than her mother. A number of his customers approached Jeremias with propositions for having Mary as a bride. An engagement was arranged on her twelfth birthday to a wealthy man from the city of Scythopolis, the ancient Bethshan, which was at the main ford across the Jordan River.

When they had been married for ten years without having a child, the husband divorced Mary, as was common practice, and returned her to her father. There she took her dying mother's place in creating new and beautiful patterns for the weavers to follow.

Soon, however, a lesser Roman official from Antioch, the Syrian capital, came looking for the famous wool for a new toga. When he caught sight of Mary, he urged Jeremias with all the persuasion and pressure he could that Mary should become his wife. When her father asked Mary about it, she raised no objection. In fact, she was quite attracted to the handsome figure of the Roman.

Mary had been happy with him for three years, although still unable to produce a child, until one day he came home with an announcement. The Emperor had ordered his immediate return to Rome, where, he now told her, he already had a wife. He therefore thought it best, since Mary had had no children, for her to stay in her own country. He would, of course, return her dowry money, plus additional compensation to her father. All Mary's tears were to no avail to make him change his mind.

Once more she returned to her father's house, but this time she could not focus her attention long on anything, so great was her grief. Impatient that she was no longer contributing to the advancement of the business, her father willingly agreed to the proposal of yet another suitor. This was the middle-aged, fat owner of the biggest dove shop in town, whose wife had recently died and whose children were all married.

Stimulated at first by his beautiful new wife, this man soon grew weary of Mary's obsession to bear a child.

A few years after this marriage, Mary one day made a request to her husband. She said her father's housekeeper, Susanna, had told her of a wonderful temple north of Dan where a certain fertility god was reported to help those who went to pray to him for a child. Would he agree to her going there with Susanna?

Although a Jew and in close business with the temple, her husband was used to the cosmopolitan society of Galilee. And since he knew his wife was part Greek, he saw no particular harm in her going, as long as no one else knew anything about it. In fact, he thought it might be a good way of satisfying her with a baby.

From the time of her return from this journey, however, Mary had acted strangely and would not tell him what had taken place there. After a few months, when it became obvious she was not getting pregnant, she grew even more depressed, doing nothing but staring vacantly or weeping, or else wandering aimlessly about outside. Tiring of this, her husband sent her back to her father, saying he was divorcing her without returning the dowry, because she was doing no work.

With her father she occasionally invented some beautiful yet strange designs. But at other times she escaped to wander all night in the Valley of the Doves, saying she must have some birds for her purification. Occasionally, as travelers saw this strange, yet beautiful woman wandering alone, they had come to the conclusion that she was a prostitute, and she had been ravished by them. Susanna had pleaded with her to stay at home, but she kept repeating, "I'm a worthless creature. God has forsaken me and closed my womb. Now I belong to the devil."

After a while, her father began to keep her locked up. Her consequent neglect of herself led to physical ills of various kinds, but she refused to see a doctor. She was also filled with envy and anguish at the sight of any mother with a baby. Such experiences seemed to unbalance her even more.

It was amid this desperate state of affairs that a traveler from Damascus, who had come to buy wool, began telling the people in Jeremias' work rooms about the new prophet who could be seen in the Judean desert. He was drawing all men to hear him and then baptizing them in the Jordan for the remission of their sins.

"Does he cure sickness?" asked Jeremias eagerly.

"I don't know, but they say he came out of the Qumran community. They are certainly noted for their secret remedies. Perhaps he does. Who knows?"

Jeremias clung to this slender thread of hope, and began to make plans to take his burdensome and highly embarrassing daughter down to the lower Jordan where this new prophet was said to be living.

South of Magdala on the shore of Lake Gennesaret, stood Herod Antipas' new capital of Tiberias. Here, one of his courtiers, a man named Manaen, was preparing to take a journey. His father had been one of Herod the Great's closest associates. His children, together with those of a few other high officials, had been invited to study under the same tutors with the king's sons. Thus, following the Greek custom, they were known as "foster-brothers." Manaen was a little younger than Antipas, but they had been good friends.

Now Manean was deep in thought, worried about a new development Herod Antipas had confided to him. Antipas was planning to marry his sister-in-law, Herodias, his brother Herod Philip's wife!

For more than thirty years Herod Antipas, with astute cunning, had managed to hide any secret failings from his subjects and had governed his Tetrarchies of Galilee and Perea with some credit. But such a thing as he was now planning would be an affront to all orthodox Jews, as Manaen well knew. If only he would take her quietly as a second wife it might soon be hushed up and forgotten. But Herod had intimated before he left for Rome that Herodias insisted on his divorcing his present wife of many years and publicly marrying her.

The Tetrarch's present wife, however, was the daughter of Aretas, king of the Nebateans whose territory was immediately south of Perea. Manaen, as captain of Herod Antipas' household cavalry, was acutely aware of the threat that might develop in the face of such an obvious insult as divorce without any justification from a royal princess.

Furthermore, she had asked permission from her husband before he left for Rome to go and stay a short time at the palace in the fortress of Machaerus. Situated high on the top ridge of the majestic mountains of Moab across the Salt Sea, Machaerus would be cooler than the summer heat in lower-lying Julias, or even Tiberias. But Manaen was beginning to fear that she might have received word from a spying slave of what was transpiring between her husband and Herodias. She had seemed very moody and secretive lately, and she had already sent an unusually large amount of baggage on ahead. Manaen himself had been given the responsibility of escorting her to Machaerus. He wondered if she was planning to flee to her father to escape the indignity of a public divorce. What in the world would he do then?

It was while he was pondering these things that Manaen heard some of his soldiers excitedly discussing something.

"What's the news?" he demanded abruptly.

"A new prophet, down near the Salt Sea! They say he eats only locusts and wild honey. He even called some leading Pharisees and Sadducees a brood of vipers!"

"He's certainly got courage, if not much sense," another soldier added.

"Everyone is going down there to get a look at him and hear his preaching about the kingdom of God," said another.

Was there no end to his problems? Manaen made a mental note that he must check up on this prophet on his way back from Machaerus. There must certainly be no riots or insurrection while the Tetrarch was away in Rome, nor would he want the religious leaders to be upset. Antipas depended too much on their support against the influence of Pontius Pilate. Yes, he must look into it.

16

A Big Decision

The first listeners to John's message had been those who happened to be traveling through the area. They could usually only spare a short time to stop and listen. As they began to spread the news of the prophet wherever they went, however, a different type of people began to swarm to the Jordan. These came with the express purpose of seeing him. These people were prepared to camp out for a few days to hear all the prophet might have to say.

Some came just out of curiosity. After all, wasn't he the first prophet in four hundred years? Most were attracted and thrilled by the very sound of the words, "the kingdom of heaven is at hand." Some of the more self-indulgent hoped for a new king who would annul the restrictive law, and create peace throughout the land. The poor hoped for wealth and justice. Many others dreamed of having power and position in the new kingdom. Some were deeply devout and longed to see a manifestation of God's holiness and power, with his anointed Messiah in open control of the land.

For whatever reason, they now thronged all the roads leading to the Jordan. John and his disciples were busy during all the daylight hours between the morning and evening meals. At first it had been mostly people from Jerusalem and Judea who came. But as the word spread people from both sides of the Jordan, and from Galilee, began to make their appearance.

As John and his disciples sat together in the evenings and discussed the events of the day, he soon came to the conclusion that he could not himself do all the interviewing of those wanting baptism. So he appointed Justus, Nathan, and Shobab to do this, while the others were to sort the people into some kind of order.

Among those who arrived first from Galilee were the two young fishing partners, Andrew and John. Nathan, who interrogated them first, felt strangely drawn to them, in spite of their northern dialect. He advised them to spend two days listening to the teaching before taking the step of baptism. This way they would really understand what it required, and then perhaps they could go back and instruct others in Galilee.

Not far behind these two, there had traveled along the same road another group. This consisted of a well-dressed older man and a younger one riding on mules, and two litters carried by four slaves. They arrived just as John began a fresh speech before inviting those ready for baptism to join him in the dark water.

The older man motioned to the carriers to move a little to one side, away from the crowd, and set down the litters. The servants stood at attention behind the litters while the two men edged their animals beside them and finally turned toward the speaker.

John was once again explaining the message God had given him and the true meaning of the baptismal rite. As those electing baptism stepped forward and followed John into the water, a weird scream came from one of the curtained litters. The older man hastily knocked on the door with his foot, and all was quiet again.

While the baptisms were taking place, Matthias moved over to this group to ask if they wished to talk with anyone. The older man in a low voice asked him to walk a few steps away from the others.

"We do indeed have a very serious problem . . . a case of severe demon possession in my daughter. If your prophet can do anything for her, pray beg him to do so. I will reward him handsomely."

"What he has to offer is not for sale," Matthias told him bluntly. "And we are from the Qumran community. We have no dealings with women. But wait here a little longer and I'll get one of our teachers to speak to you. What is your name?"

"Jeremias of Magdala."

Presently Matthias reappeared with Justus. Jeremias immediately went to meet them to explain the situation more fully.

"My daughter is childless and has been divorced by three husbands. While with the third something strange took place, but what, I have never been able to discover. She is now back with me, apparently possessed by devils. She calls herself cursed by God and unclean. Could the prophet not show her how to repent, and let her go into the water like the others? My housekeeper is here and could accompany her into the water."

"And what about yourself?" asked Justus pointedly. "Have you no need of repentance? Will you prepare for the coming of Messiah?"

"I have a large business to manage. I haven't time for much religion. But I pay my tithes and more. It is my daughter I have come about."

"I'm sorry, but we have no dealings with women. It is getting late now. We must get back to our quarters before dusk for our time of prayer. I will discuss this with John this evening, and let you know tomorrow."

On hearing that, Jeremias turned away, annoyance on his face.

After their frugal meal was finished that evening, when they would normally have studied some portion of Scripture, either from memory or from one of Justus' few scrolls, the latter announced there was an important matter they must discuss.

"What?" John asked in some surprise.

"This afternoon a man from Galilee came seeking baptism for his daughter and a woman servant."

"For *women?*" John said in shocked surprise. "Whatever put such a thought into his head?"

"Apparently the great need of his daughter. She is demon-possessed, according to him. He thought you might be able to heal her."

"God has given me no command, or power, to heal—only to proclaim the coming of the kingdom of heaven. That is certainly no place for the demon-possessed. And of what concern can it be for any woman?"

Justus felt in his precious bag of scrolls and brought out the one of the prophet Joel.

"We have not studied this for a long time. Perhaps the Almighty has something to say to us from it," he said quietly. "Benjamin, can you get me a little more light?"

Benjamin thrust a faggot into the dying embers of the fire. When it was alight he held it close to Justus.

A BIG DECISION

"At Qumran, a passage from it was used as a basis for the future war of the sons of light. Do you remember it? Listen!" He held the scroll toward the flaming torch and began to read.

Declare a holy war; arouse your warriors,
let all fighting men draw near, let them all go up!
Beat your plowshares into swords and your pruning hooks into spears.
Come and help, all you nations, from every side,
gather yourselves there;
thither bring together Thy heroes, O Lord.

"You remember that, I'm sure. But before that, after warning of the terrible coming judgment, God had spoken through his prophet Joel thus:

My people shall never again be put to shame,
and you shall know that I am in the midst of Israel,
that I am the Lord your God, and that my people shall
never again be put to shame.
It shall come to pass after this
that I will pour out my spirit upon all flesh,
Your sons and your daughters shall prophesy;
Your old men shall dream dreams,
and your young men shall see visions,
even upon the servants and the maids I will, in those days,
pour out my spirit.

Justus stopped and looked around the group.
"What struck you most in those words?"
"My people shall never again be put to shame," Nathan volunteered.
"I will pour out my spirit upon *all* flesh," said Shobab.
"So what does that 'all flesh' imply?"
"Everybody, I suppose, or at least, all the people of Israel, the sons of Abraham."
"But it says specifically 'sons and daughters' and 'servants and maids.' So women are to be included, according to this, in God's plan for his coming kingdom."
"But what can they do? We have always been taught they are fickle, unreliable, and they are so often impure," John protested.
"So I always used to think," Justus admitted. "In fact, I believed it very firmly. But in reality God has used them remarkably in our

nation's history. Just think, Israel would have been wiped out if it hadn't been for the midwives' action in Egypt. We would never have had our great law-giver, Moses, if not for the courage and ingenuity of his mother and sister. Deborah saved the land from the tyranny of her enemies. Queen Esther by her bravery prevented the extinction of our race. I always thought it a pity that that Scripture was never given a place at Qumran."

"What do you mean?"

"There is a scroll called the book of Esther that many consider one of the holy writings. The Feast of Purim, kept by many people outside the community, celebrates Esther's brave acts. Perhaps that is why our community preferred not to study it! It contains no mention of the Holy One, but is, I believe, a wonderful illustration of his loving care and protection of his people, Israel. And he chose to use a woman for that purpose."

"You really think this is an indication we should baptize women?"

"If you have received no clear leading of the Spirit not to do so, I am beginning to believe it may be right. What do others think?"

"I overheard one of Lazarus' sisters say she wished she could be baptized," Nathan said. "They've been brought up in the community since they were small, though, so they are used to immersions."

"But that would be in the privacy of their home. What do the Rabbis do with Gentile women proselytes?"

"They are naked, of course, but are attended by women. The rabbinic witnesses stand outside the door. As soon as the proselyte's head is completely submerged, the attendants call the men in so they can testify the baptism has taken place," Justus explained.

"We can't do anything like that here," said Shobab.

"But Justus just read that women are to have part in the kingdom. Surely there will be some who want baptism if you put so much stress on it," came unexpectedly from Benjamin. "I know my mother would have been worthy of it, and from what that robber said about John's mother, there's no doubt *she* would have wanted it."

The mention of his mother startled John, but he remembered her bravery and faithful teaching in his earliest years. The others remained silent now, waiting for his verdict.

"I—I cannot say that God has spoken to me against such a

thing," he began hesitantly. "I am very reluctant to consider it now. I can't see what it will accomplish. Yet we certainly need godly mothers in Israel." He paused in obvious anguish. "So, if there are those who very seriously ask for it, we will not forbid them. But do not suggest it."

There was a murmur of assent from his disciples.

"Since you are the oldest among us, Brother Justus," he continued more firmly, "we will leave the interviewing of women to you. But be sure they are in a state of purity and are well clad and veiled to enter the water. There must be no lustful temptation for those watching."

"Very well. I will see those two women tomorrow," Justus responded. "But I think you should speak to the father. He is a hard man, and apparently has no concern about himself."

John was already preaching the next morning when Jeremias and his party arrived and joined the crowd. Unnoticed by them, Justus stationed himself nearby and watched the faces of the two men. Jeremias appeared to be listening today, though his eyes often wandered. It was the younger man who attracted Justus' attention the most. There was a strained look on his face and he seemed to be drinking in the message thundering from John's lips.

At the end of his sermon, John moved straight toward Jeremias and motioned him to one side. Justus immediately stepped up to the rest of the party and asked the younger man who he was.

"My name is Daniel. I'm Jeremias' chief assistant. He asked me to accompany them on this journey because he expected there might be some trouble." He gave a meaningful glance toward the litters.

"Yes, I understand the problem and have come now to interview the two women."

"Before you do so, I must speak to you alone! What the prophet said has shaken me very much. I have something to confess that may help you understand—but I dare not let my master, Jeremias, know."

"Can we leave these women for a time to talk?"

"Yes, I'll give orders to the men to stay by the litters and keep them locked."

"Very well, let us move back to this rock where we can keep an eye on them."

Daniel hastily began his story, his voice trembling at first.

"I don't know why I'm telling you this. It is only in the hope that it may help her situation," and he motioned to the righthand litter. "I'm so ashamed of it now."

"It is well to confess it, then."

"I have a brother, Reuben, who was her late husband's chief assistant. He fell madly in love with her. She refused all his advances, although she was obviously unsatisfied with her husband.

"I had just returned from Rome where a story was circulating about a lady named Paulina, who was beautiful, wealthy, and of excellent character, as was her husband. But another man, Mundus, was wildly in love with her. She refused all his attempts at seduction, until he finally decided to starve himself to death. This grieved a freed slave woman of his father's, who offered to get him what he wanted.

"She asked him for money, then bribed the priests of the temple of Isis, suggesting they tell Paulina that the god Anubis had sent a message saying he loved her, and required her to come to the temple for a night. Paulina was a devout worshiper at this temple. She took this as a great honor. She told her husband, and he agreed she should go.

"Mundus, of course, had hidden himself in the holy place. When the priests had put out all the lamps and locked the doors, he sprang out in the darkness, pretending to be the god. He had his will with her for the night without her suspecting anything. The only trouble was that the silly fellow couldn't keep quiet about it. When he met her three days later, he boasted about it. She was horror stricken and told her husband, who in turn told the Emperor. He had the priests crucified, but let Mundus go, because his passion had been so great.

"It could so easily have turned out all right that I suggested to my brother he should do something similar. Mary was so desperate to have a son. So I suggested that we approach Susanna, the housekeeper who had known her from her childhood, and tell her that one of the temples up at Paneas near Dan, specializes in fertility rites—as indeed they do. If Mary mated with one of the gods there, she would undoubtedly bear a child.

"Susanna was very fond of Mary and was easily persuaded since she thought it would help her. She went and told Mary of the temple where a god really came and impregnated women suppliants. She agreed to go, with her husband's permission, and

Reuben bribed the priests to let him be in the temple. She seemed to be all right when he was with her, he said, but after he had hidden himself again, he suddenly heard her give a terrible scream.

"She has never been the same since. And I—I feel responsible. I cannot live with myself!" Daniel then buried his face in his hands and cried.

"I am not surprised. How could you, an Israelite, propose another child of Abraham should enter a heathen temple? Moses would have had you stoned for that! Such places have always been the undoing of our people!"

"I know, I know," he said between sobs. "I suppose I have traveled in Gentile countries so much, I've lost all sense of religion. And she was only a woman—half Gentile, too. Her mother was a Greek proselyte. But now, since hearing John speak, I long to be clean again. Is there any hope for me?"

"If you truly repent, as I believe you do, and determine to live a different life—if you are ready to serve the coming Messiah, you may be baptized. Now ask the carriers to bring the housekeeper here and leave her with me."

In a moment the litter was deposited beside him. Through the curtains Justus was vaguely aware of a middle-aged woman who was weeping.

"Daniel has just told me what he did that seems to have affected your mistress' mind," he began. "Can you tell me what happened when you reached the temple?"

Susanna tried to stifle her sobs. "I only know that I was sleeping in one of the nearby rooms for pilgrims when Reuben hurriedly came and asked me to go into the temple and get Mary. She had fainted. She has never been right since, especially when she found she was not pregnant. She would never tell me what had happened. I feel terrible that I agreed to taking her to the pagan temple. She was such a beautiful girl, and so gifted. Now—"

"It was a very wicked, evil thing to do. Have not all our nation's problems arisen from the worship of idols? Moses' punishment was stoning to death."

"I would gladly die if only Mary could recover," gasped Susanna through her tears. "And now that I have heard the prophet, I feel more convicted than ever. What can I do?"

"If you truly repent and determine to obey the whole law from now on, you may accompany her into the water and be baptized. This will be the first time we have allowed women to do this. Remember, you have a great responsibility."

"I promise with all my heart. But I cannot answer for her. I do not even know if she understands or will be willing. Her father had to drag her to the litter to get her here."

"We must see. I will talk to her now." Justus waved for the other litter to be brought over. He was shocked to see the curtain pulled aside as it was set down beside him.

"Who are you?" its occupant demanded in a strangely harsh voice.

He was so startled at being addressed first that he involuntarily looked at the speaker. It was a woman in her mid-thirties, with a most beautiful profile and luxuriant hair. But the brown eyes turned toward him had a fierce, almost inhuman look.

Quickly he turned away his own eyes and looked straight ahead.

"I am an assistant of the prophet. Have you understood what he has been preaching?"

A strangled cry came from the litter.

"I understand! What he says is not for me! I'm unclean, cursed of God! A castaway!"

"Perhaps not. Tell me what is the trouble."

"I am barren, childless. God has forsaken me. I have been ravaged by a man who is not my husband and—and by demons and I am still barren! And unclean, unclean!" She shuddered again, then rage seemed to drive away other feelings. She demanded fiercely, "What can the prophet do for me?"

Justus' gaze seemed rooted to the ground, and he remained motionless. What *could* John do in this sordid situation? In other times, as he had already said, such a woman would have been tried and then stoned. He was sure John would say there was no place for such in the kingdom of God. Probably he was right. How could women be so foolish as this! Yet he remembered they received so little teaching. And, in the case of both Paulina and Mary, the husbands had consented. But now he must make some kind of answer.

"He has been called by God to preach repentance," he said finally, "repentance and a change of life. Can you do that?"

"Change? How can I change? I'm possessed, I tell you! *Pos-*

sessed!" Her voice rose in a weird shriek that brought Daniel and the servants running back to her litter.

As many in the crowd began to stare, they retreated some distance with her. Then Daniel came back to Justus with an anxious look on his face.

"Was it no use?"

Justus shook is head. He had never felt so helpless. He was conscious of a sudden surge of anger at this man whose thoughtless scheme had wrought such tragic evil.

"You have committed a great sin. I see no remedy for that woman whom you have wronged so grievously."

"I know, I know!" Tears were rolling down Daniels cheeks, and his genuine sorrow was evident. "I truly repent and although I cannot undo the damage, I will pray for her. I also pray that now my life will be lived in obedience to God. May I please enter the water of baptism?"

Striving to control his anger, Justus could not but consent in the face of this evident penitence.

Meanwhile, John had spent some time with Jeremias. He told him he was neither a healer nor an exorcist, and he tried to stress to him some of the duties of a father. John then urged upon him the need to repent himself.

By this time, fresh crowds were impatiently waiting for John to speak. Jochanan and Benjamin approached, excitement written on their faces.

"Master, there are some tax collectors here in the crowd today! They need to repent more than anyone! Can't you preach again before the baptisms?"

Jeremias left John then, muttering he needed more time to think, and the prophet turned toward the riverside. This time Matthias strode up to him and whispered urgently in his ear.

"Some of Herod's soldiers are here, too, with a high-ranking officer! Take care!"

"I must speak what the Almighty gives me to say, no matter who is here. We must level the mountains, remember, to prepare the way of the Lord!"

When he reached the river bank, John turned to face the crowds. His disciples thought he now preached with greater eloquence than ever before. A gradual hush descended on the motley crowd, and they listened spellbound. Justus, as usual, was scanning faces for signs of the Spirit working in hearts. When Matthias came up to whisper a warning about the presence of the soldiers, his eyes had come to rest on a group of about twenty soldiers from Herod's militia, standing on the edge of the crowd. A little apart from them was an obviously high-ranking officer on a beautiful Arabian horse.

Have they come to interrogate, or even arrest the prophet? he wondered. There was no doubt they were listening with undivided attention.

John came to his final appeal for repentance and change of life that was to be signified by public immersion in the Jordan. Already some were sobbing openly, in others the struggle going on in their minds showed on their faces.

"What else can we do to change our lives?" one wealthy-looking listener asked earnestly.

"Why, he who has two coats, give one to those who have nothing. And if you have plenty of food, do the same. There are many desperately poor and unjustly treated people in our country today, while others have more than they need."

Just then one of the tallest soldiers, who looked as if he might be a platoon leader, pushed his way forward. Justus' heart sank. He moved closer to help defend John if necessary, but then he marveled at what he heard.

"And what must we do?" There seemed no trace of arrogance in the voice, only a yearning to know the truth. What would John answer?

The prophet turned his piercing gaze directly to the soldiers and looked them full in the eye.

"Don't take advantage of people or intimidate them with your weapons. Don't make false accusations in order to get bribes. Be content with your wages!"

A laugh went up from the crowd. This prophet certainly knew a thing or two. Soldiers never were content with their pay. It was assumed that they would fight harder knowing that some of the spoils would be theirs. In any case, they knew how to help themselves at the expense of the people.

Justus anxiously watched the soldiers' faces to see if they were angered by this response from the crowd. A few obviously were, but the majority, including their spokesman, seemed oblivious of others and kept their eyes still fixed on John.

A very short man then edged his way to the front. He was known to a number of the audience as one of the customs men in Jericho, Zaccheus.

"And what must we do?"

"Don't collect more than your appointed rate of tax."

Again a murmur of approval swept through the crowd. John moved into the water. Those who had already been examined and passed for baptism began to remove their outer garments and follow him.

The vast throng at first watched in fascination. Then others began throwing off their garments and streaming into the water. Justus was amazed to see several of the soldiers doing so and could hardly believe his eyes as he saw the officer dismount from his horse, throw the reins to a soldier, and remove his uniform.

Justus immediately went up to him to make certain of his sincerity.

"Do you understand what you are doing, Sir?"

"I believe so. This is not an easy thing for me to do, I can assure you. But all that the prophet says has the ring of truth. If God in his mercy is sending his Anointed One soon, then I desire a cleansed life with which to serve him."

Justus stood aside then and allowed him and the other soldiers to enter the water. As he turned, he was shocked to see a woman's veiled figure coming forward. After his distressing interview with Mary, he had forgotten about the housekeeper and had not supposed she would think of such a step as baptism on her own.

He made his way toward her to be sure it was Susanna. When she answered yes, he asked her if she was sure she wished to take this step.

"With all my heart, I long to be rid of this burden of guilt. Never will I be part of such a thing again, and I shall pray daily for Mary to be healed."

Justus watched her timidly step into the water, and there was an increased murmur from the crowd when they saw it was a woman. Then another figure hurried forward to join her. It was Daniel.

It seemed that was to be all for the day, but just then Jeremias plunged after them into the dark waters of the Jordan. Truly this was a strong evidence of the compelling message God's new prophet proclaimed.

17

Messiah Has Come!

The crowds continued to increase each week, especially after word got around that women could be baptized, and that even publicans and soldiers were moved by the prophet's preaching.

Salome saw to it that her elder son, James, went to be baptized, and their partner, Simon, went also. He in turn invited a friend and neighbor, Philip. They were all impressed with John's preaching as they listened to him for several days, and then they were baptized. When they returned home, they spread the word further among all their acquaintances.

Everywhere now there was a feeling of excitement and suspense, and the word "Messiah" was on nearly everyone's lips. When was he coming? Where was he coming from? Most of all, *who was he*? Some began to suggest it must be John himself, so powerful was his influence upon all who heard him.

At last John heard people whispering this among themselves. Indeed, even some of his close disciples were beginning to wonder the same thing. Immediately he set himself to quell the very suggestion.

"No, no! My work is just to prepare the way. I baptize you with water, but there is One coming who is much greater than I. I am not even worthy to unlatch his sandals and wash his feet! He will baptize you with the Holy Spirit and with fire!"

"There he goes again," whispered Benjamin to Matthias. "I just can't imagine what it means to baptize with fire and the Spirit. Can you?"

160

"No," Matthias confessed, "it sounds like something directly from God. We'll just have to wait and see."

Summer was drawing to a close, and the crowds were a little smaller while people were busy getting in the harvests, first of grain and then of vine and olive. After that came the early rainy season, when even fewer cared to be on the roads—when the Jordan might turn to a whirling torrent that couldn't be forded. John and his disciples moved closer to Jericho, where there was more local traffic and also drier caves for them to live in. There, many people still sought him out, but John and his disciples were able to have a little more rest, which was welcome after their very busy summer.

They spent their spare time searching the scrolls for every hint of the Coming One. John began to grow restless, saying he felt sure Messiah was already in the land. He called them all to more earnest prayer that he might fulfill everything God had called him to do. He prayed, too, that they would recognize the Messiah as soon as they saw him.

One night, after a day of fasting, John had a dream. In great excitement he called his disciples together in the morning.

"God spoke to me clearly last night," he told them. "Praise to his glorious name! He told me that the One on whom his Spirit descends in the form of a dove will be Messiah! Now we need have no doubts! All that remains for us to do is to be pure, obedient, and ready for his appearing."

His excitement and assurance spread to the others. Those of his disciples who, in secret, had occasionally begun to wish for the warmer and more regular life at Qumran, now felt that all their trials would be worth the great moment of meeting the Messiah.

At last the rains grew less frequent, and with the returning warmth a miracle suddenly took place on the barren hills of Judea. Green grass sprang up, as well as clover, lilies, golden broom, honeysuckle, and aromatic herbs.

John and his disciples felt the urge to be on the move again. He began to plan that he and two others would go farther up the Jordan Valley than before to find other suitable places for the immersions, and also search for their living quarters.

He decided to take Matthias and Benjamin, leaving Justus in charge to receive those seeking the prophet. The day before they were to set out, however, John awoke with that strange stirring of his spirit that he knew was the work of the Almighty. Quickly he called to the others, his eyes shining.

"I am sure God is going to reveal something to me today. I must go out alone, that is all I know. Perhaps we must delay our departure until tomorrow."

Their wonder was tinged with disappointment as they watched him go.

John's feet instinctively turned toward the Jordan. There he stopped. Should he turn south toward the ford leading to the road to Jerusalem, or go farther north to the ford that led across into Perea? This latter was the road usually taken by Jews coming from Galilee, if they were particular about keeping all the Pharisees' rules, for this way there was no danger of defilement by passing through the province of the half-breed Samaritans.

John was planning to spend more time on the far side of the Jordan this summer, so he decided to go north. Eventually he reached the ford, still high from the rains, and headed toward a village named Bethany, like the one near Jerusalem where Lazarus lived. Instead of turning east into the village, however, John stayed on the trail beside the river, looking for suitable places for his baptismal rite. He looked for quiet pools or backwaters where the currents weren't too strong, yet which were deep enough to immerse an adult.

He soon found what looked an ideal place, and he waded in to test the depth of the water. Satisfied, he sat in the sun to dry on a fallen tree trunk the earlier rushing flood waters had evidently uprooted. The trail was empty of travelers at the moment, so he closed his eyes and once again asked for God's will to be made clear to him.

When he opened his eyes again, he saw a solitary figure striding along the road from the north.

Instantly John's heart began a rapid beat, and every nerve in his body felt strangely vibrant. He had an odd impression that this sensation had occurred once before in his life, yet he could not remember when. He had the presentiment now that something tremendous was about to take place, almost as if the whole purpose of his life was to be fulfilled in one supreme act.

The man drew nearer, and John's eyes never left him. He was a man about thirty, a little above medium height, and dressed in the ordinary garb of an artisan. Yet there was an air of authority in the upright posture and in the easy stride with which the stranger steadily advanced.

Should John go and greet him, as was his usual practice with travelers when he wished to preach to them of the coming kingdom and the need for repentance? Something seemed to be holding him back, so he remained motionless on the tree trunk.

Soon the traveler had only another fifty yards to go before he would be level with him. John could see that the man's eyes were upon him. Still, he made no move. Steadily the man strode forward until he was level with John, then he turned toward the tree trunk.

Immediately John sprang to his feet.

"Peace be unto you," said the stranger, and John returned the greeting, his eyes never leaving that arresting face.

"I have come to receive baptism from you."

John was speechless a moment. He did not feel the need to say the usual words, "Repent of your sin, begin to lead a righteous life, for the kingdom of heaven draws near." There was a serenity, a strange sense of purity about this face that he had never before witnessed in all the previous months when thousands had stood before him wanting to be baptized.

"Who are you?" he asked finally.

"Jesus of Nazareth."

Jesus. That was a common enough name, chosen in remembrance of the nation's great leader, Joshua, who had led them victoriously into the promised land of Israel. It sounded appropriate. To his astonishment, John found words pouring out of his mouth.

"I have need to be baptized by you! Why do you come to me?"

"Let it be this way now. The origin and authority of your baptism is from heaven. To accept it means to welcome the reign of heaven which it proclaims. We need to fulfill all the righteous acts God has planned for us. You have been given the great work of preparation for my coming. You are the bridge between the old covenant and the new and have done your work well." His smile of approval sent a thrill of joy through John's whole being.

"Now, as others have been through these waters as a sign of their will to lead a new life in preparation for the kingdom, for me, too, it is as a vow of devotion to the establishment of that kingdom. It is God's will that I should identify myself with other men and that this should be the official endowment and sign of my mission."

"And what is that mission?" John's voice was barely above a whisper.

"To be the Lamb of God, which takes away the sin of the world."

This wasn't the answer John was expecting, but speechless with awe, he led the way into the water.

He looked up as the stranger went under the water, and in that instant it seemed the heavens opened, and a light brighter than the sun beamed down upon them.

As Jesus arose from the water he stood in prayer, and suddenly John saw a dove flutter down and gently rest on the wet head. Then he heard a clear voice say, "You are my beloved Son; in you I am well pleased."

In a flash John remembered his dream, and felt he would have known this was the Messiah, even without the sign, and the confirming voice from heaven. Full of the profoundest gratitude that God had honored him in this way, his instinct was to fling himself down in worship, but this was impossible in the water. Instead, he closed his eyes in a long prayer of thanksgiving that God had allowed him to see the fulfillment of his ministry.

When he finally opened his eyes, Jesus had disappeared! A wave of disappointment swept over John momentarily. He had already begun to see the establishment of the kingdom! What was he supposed to do now?

Again he sat on the tree trunk to dry, his mind in a whirl as he gazed at the spot where the miracle had taken place. Yes, it was real, there was no doubt. He could remember every word spoken between them and then that amazing voice from heaven and the sign of the dove. At last he became calm again as he realized that the God who had done all this would surely continue to lead him.

When he was dry and there was still no sign of Jesus, John departed on the return journey with quickened footsteps. What news he had for his faithful disciples!

He found them sitting together, a little disconsolate at his long absence.

As he began telling them what had happened, a thrill of intense excitement passed through them all.

"What is he like?" asked Shobab.

John was able to answer that question fairly easily, but then came the one he was dreading.

"Where is he now?" came from Nathan.

"I don't know," he confessed. "I was so full of praise at the confirmation of my dream, I closed my eyes to utter my deep thanksgiving. When I opened them, he had disappeared!"

All were deeply disappointed on hearing this, and even a little disgruntled that they had missed the first sight of Messiah.

"Well, what are we to do now?" asked Justus, with rare impatience.

"Proceed as before, I believe, until God instructs us otherwise. After all, if the Messiah desired baptism, then surely all who come into the kingdom need it, too."

"And didn't he baptize you with the Spirit and fire?" Benjamin asked.

John shook his head.

As days passed with no sign of the new Messiah, Benjamin one day whispered to Nathan, "You don't suppose that John imagined all that, do you? After all, he'd been fasting, and strange things can happen to you then. And when he knew he was *supposed* to see a dove come—"

"You mean it might be a hallucination? Oh, I don't think so. John has fasted all his life and knows its effects."

Meanwhile in his preaching, John was even more forthright, stating, "The Messiah is here, the kingdom is at hand!"

Word of this was carried up to Galilee by a young man named Thomas, who had entered the waters of the Jordan. His mother soon told her friend, Salome.

As soon as Salome's sons came home that night, she greeted them excitedly.

"John, you and Andrew must go down to the Jordan again as soon as possible! Thomas' mother told me the Baptizer is now saying the Messiah is here! Go and find out all you can!"

18

The Lamb of God

In Jerusalem, the news was on everyone's lips that John the Baptizer, as he was beginning to be called, was speaking of the Messiah. Some of the leading Jewish council members therefore decided to send a deputation to John to ask him who he was, since many people were beginning to suggest he was himself the Messiah. Remembering his stinging rebuke to the Pharisees who had previously gone to hear him, they decided this time they would send some of the lesser priests.

This group found John near Bethany, his latest preaching place across the Jordan. It was just forty days after he had baptized the Messiah.

During a short interval when John was resting, the delegation approached him and greeted him in a polite way.

"Will you please tell us who you are?" their leader asked. "Are you really the promised Messiah?"

"Certainly not!" he answered.

"Then who are you? Are you Elijah, or that prophet promised by our father, Moses?"

"No, I am neither of those."

"Then who are you? Please give us an answer for those who sent us. What have you to say about yourself and your ministry?"

"I am just a voice," he answered, "the voice of one crying in the wilderness: 'Prepare the way of the Lord,' just as Isaiah the prophet foretold."

"Well, by what right do you baptize, then, if you are neither the Christ, nor Elijah, nor the prophet?"

"I baptize with water, but there is One already in our midst whom you do not yet recognize—the One who will come after me. I am not even worthy to unloose his sandals. You must wait for him. He will baptize with the Holy Spirit and with fire."

"There it is again!" muttered Benjamin to Matthias.

John felt he had now said all he could say. As he turned away, he noticed one of the priests following him. He was an older man, and John had been aware of him staring hard throughout the interview, although he had not spoken.

A moment later, he heard a whispered voice. "Can I speak with you alone for a moment?"

"Come this way. What do you wish?"

"My name is Jason. I am the brother of Eleazer of Bethany. I am your cousin, the son of your mother's younger brother, Hilkiah. Have you heard of us?"

John stared at him in wonder. "Eleazer visited us once a year, but never spoke of the rest of the family. Lazarus of Bethany told me recently that there were relatives in Jerusalem. Did you . . . know my father and mother?"

"Of course! They always visited us when they came to Jerusalem. So did you, when you were a baby!"

"Please tell me all you know!" John could hardly believe that he was face to face with a relative at last.

So Jason began to tell him of the angel's appearance to Zachariah at the altar of incense, the prophecy about Zachariah's son, and all the rest that had happened.

"And . . . do you know who is to be the Messiah?" John asked.

"Well, there was some talk about that, too. A young cousin of your mother and my father, Mary of Nazareth, married Joseph, son of Jacob. She visited your mother when she was six months pregnant with you and told her that she, too, had been visited by the angel Gabriel. He told her she was to bear a son whom she was to name Jesus."

"*Jesus?* Are you sure?"

Jason continued with all he knew about John's background and early childhood.

"The others will be suspicious of my spending all this time with you," Jason said. "I told them I was thinking of being baptized, and I really mean it. I know what you preach is the truth we have been waiting for."

Together they entered the water, and with a full heart John

167

lifted up a prayer of thanksgiving for this encouragement and confirmation about the Messiah. And to think it was his own cousin! The other priests were watching curiously, however, and he thought it better not to tell Jason of his own meeting with Jesus.

Before leaving his side in the water, Jason whispered a final warning.

"Be careful! The chief priests in Jerusalem are very jealous and uneasy about you. They don't know who you are or that we are related. It will be wise for you to stay here in Perea, out of their immediate territory. The Roman governor isn't interested in religion, so they have free rein in Judea. You should be safe under Herod Antipas, as long as you don't start any political unrest. God be with you."

Later that evening John shared with his disciples all he had learned from his cousin. Great was their excitement when they heard about the birth of the Messiah and that he was actually a half cousin of John. He was of the lineage of David, however, and had been born in Bethlehem, just as the prophet Micah had foretold!

Justus got out the scroll and read the prophecy to them to refresh their memories.

"It is the meaning of the name that is so impressive, though," John told them. "Jason said the angel Gabriel told Joseph the child was to be called Jesus—Savior—because he will save his people from their sins. At last, perhaps, we may begin to understand a little of what the prophet Isaiah meant. But it's hard to see how that relates to the conquering Messiah we are expecting to cleanse and free our land from all evil and oppression."

The next day as John stood with the usual crowd on the river bank, he happened to glance up at the main road, which at that point ran parallel but one hundred paces or so back from, and well above, the river. Instantly he felt that mysterious vibration throughout his body. He recognized at once the unmistakable figure.

Excitedly John turned to his disciples and the crowd.

"Look! Look!" he cried, "There is the Lamb of God who takes away the sin of the world!"

Seeing their astonishment, he tried to explain more clearly.

"He is the one of whom I said, 'He who comes after me is preferred before me, for he was before me.' I did not recognize him earlier, but I have come to baptize with water so that all Israel will know him and be prepared to receive him."

The crowd eagerly asked more questions. After he had answered them, John was disappointed to see that Jesus had disappeared around a bend in the road and had not come down among them as he had hoped and expected.

Later that afternoon he was pleased to see his young disciples from Galilee, Andrew, John, and Philip. In answer to their query, he told them he had indeed seen the Messiah.

"Come back and spend the night with us," he said to them. "Perhaps he will appear again tomorrow. If not, perhaps you may be able to find him back in Galilee. That is apparently where he comes from."

"From Galilee?" Philip was plainly puzzled. "But surely the Messiah will come from Judea?"

"He was born in Bethlehem, it is true, and of the house of David. But his mother was from Nazareth. Perhaps he has been living there."

Nazareth! John, the son of Zebedee, remembered something of his mother's sister in Nazareth. Could it be the same? Neither he nor his brother had had the courage to ask the Baptizer about his own background when they had come to hear him before, since most of their time had been spent with Nathan. Now things were getting even more complicated. If this Messiah came this afternoon, though, he would certainly ask if he were Mary's son. He might even recognize him, although it was a long time since he had seen his aunt and her children.

The next morning the three young men from Galilee kept close to John so they could hear at once if he saw the Messiah.

They were down at the river all morning. Well past noon as John was just coming out of the water after a group of baptisms, he caught sight of that familiar figure.

"See, the Lamb of God!" he cried, pointing up the road.

Immediately Andrew, John, and Philip took off, while John's other disciples disappointedly continued their counseling and handling of the present crowd. Their curiosity was even further piqued when they saw no more of the three young men from Galilee.

Two days later in Galilee excitement was rising to a feverish pitch.

The usually quiet Andrew had rushed in to see his brother, Simon, exclaiming, "We have found the Messiah!"

"What? Where? Tell me!" demanded Simon.

"We spent the night with the prophet, and he told us he had really met the Messiah, and baptized him! That was nearly six weeks ago, and he hadn't seen anything of him since. But earlier on the day we arrived, he saw him walking along the upper road."

"But who *is* he?"

"Wait, I'm trying to explain. We went to the river again in the morning and waited and waited, but there was no sign of him. Then just when we were giving up hope, the Baptizer called out: 'Look! There is the Lamb of God!' Then we three rushed away up onto the road to try to find him.

"He heard us coming and turned and said 'What are you looking for?' When we got close we really saw his face. I can't describe it—so full of purity, concern, kindness, and authority all mixed up. It felt as if he was looking right through us, knowing all our thoughts! I was speechless and embarrassed, as usual, but finally John blurted out, 'Rabbi, where are you staying?' And he invited us in such a friendly voice, 'Come and see.'"

"Well, where does he live?"

"He was staying in a cave near the roadside. I think he had been down in Jerusalem, but he also mentioned being in the wilderness forty days. He looked very tired, too. We spent the night with him, then rushed back up here."

"You still haven't said who he is!"

"His name is Jesus, and his father was Joseph, a carpenter in Nazareth, dead now. But here's the really amazing thing! His mother is Salome's sister, Mary. She claimed that it was a supernatural conception, announced by an angel before she was married. But mostly only her husband believed her, according to John. However, according to the Baptizer, the heavens opened as he was baptized, and a voice said, 'This is my beloved Son, in whom I delight.' There's no doubt God has called him. You can feel there's something very different about him. He told us he's going to need followers when he begins his ministry, and he'll be here in Capernaum in a few days. Then you must come and meet him right away!" Andrew was still breathless from excitement.

Meanwhile his partner, John, had reached home where Zebedee and Salome, and his elder brother, James, had almost finished supper.

"Why, we didn't expect you back until tomorrow at the earliest," exclaimed Salome, jumping up to get him something to eat. "Wasn't there anything new to learn from the prophet?"

"There certainly was! We have seen the Messiah! We spent the night with him! And do you know who he is? He really is Mary's son, Jesus!"

"*What!* Mary' son!" Salome's heart missed a beat. So perhaps that tale she had told the family after she became pregnant had been true! Oh, why hadn't they kept in touch with them more! But it had sounded like such an unlikely story.

"Where is he?" Zebedee asked.

"He expects to be here in Capernaum in the next day or so and said he'd contact us! It was a wonderful experience to be with him. I can't describe it. You'll just have to meet him. The prophet John is quite sure he *is* the Messiah, because as he was baptizing him he heard a voice from heaven saying, 'This is my beloved Son, in whom I delight.'"

"I can't wait to meet him," exclaimed James as he finished his last mouthful of supper.

"Another strange thing is that the prophet called him 'The Lamb of God that takes away the sin of the world.' We couldn't understand, but we were afraid to ask him yet," continued John.

Salome had no comment to make, and reluctantly turned to the kitchen, afraid she might miss some other detail of this great news. But already she was planning how she would get in touch with her sister, Mary. Then a thought struck her. She hurried back with food for John.

"Did you tell me before that women are going through this rite of baptism in preparation for the kingdom?"

"Yes, many of them now."

"Why don't *we* both go, Zebedee?" she asked, turning to her husband. "The boys can take care of things here. They've had a few days off. Now it's your turn."

Zebedee shook his head. "You know I don't care for travel that much. It's more than enough being tossed about in a boat every day. Maybe on our way down to the Passover we could do it."

Salome did a rapid mental calculation. "Why, that's only just over two weeks away!" she exclaimed. "We certainly must not lose an opportunity to be ready for the kingdom!"

19

A Rival Force?

Hundreds of people continued to tramp the caravan routes to the Jordan specifically to hear John the Baptizer. In addition, all those traveling on normal business heard his preaching.

Among those who had moved down to John's region were the sisters of Lazarus of Bethany. As soon as Mary had heard that women were accepted for baptism, she pleaded with Martha to come with her. Lazarus encouraged them and escorted them down. As usual, it was Justus who interviewed them, and their sincerity and suitability impressed him.

It was not long after the coming of the deputation of priests from Jerusalem that John's other remaining relatives appeared— Cleopas and his wife, Mary. Cleopas told John that Jason had informed him of his visit. Now they were eager to meet the man who had been the baby they sheltered so long ago.

After listening to him preach, they, with their sons, James and Joses, begged for baptism. They had come prepared to camp for the night, and in the evening they told John all they knew of his early life. Finally, they invited him to come and stay with them.

John shook his head: "Thank you, but my place is here," he said simply. "I know nothing of city life, and I know what God wants of me here. But the Messiah, whose way I have prepared, has come. I advise you to meet him as soon as you can."

By this time, the week of the Passover was drawing near. One day among the crowds he saw the young fisherman, John, approaching, with an older man and woman whom he introduced as his parents. The prophet hadn't seen any of the three young men since they had left to be with Jesus, so he was very anxious to hear what had happened. John, however, said that his parents wished to be baptized.

Not until the crowds had left to have their evening meals did John and his disciples have the opportunity to talk privately with the family from Galilee, and even then they were hesitant to begin because of Salome's presence.

The young fisherman was eager to tell of their meeting with Jesus, however, and began to describe a recent experience.

"He invited five of us from Capernaum and Bethsaida to be his disciples, and what do you think was the *first* thing he wanted us to do together?"

John and his disciples looked at him eagerly.

"Attend a wedding! It was a friend of his family in the little town of Cana."

There was a stunned silence on the part of his audience. The Messiah, the Son of God, attending a village wedding? It was utterly incomprehensible to them.

"And he performed a miracle there! It wasn't nearly time for the guests to go home, but the waiters found there was no more wine! Jesus' mother heard about it and told him. He just ordered the servants to fill the big purification jars with fresh water and then draw it out and take it to the master of the house. And do you know . . ." John paused for the greatest effect, "it proved to be the best wine most of us have ever tasted!"

"Yes," added Salome, "and they haven't stopped talking about it since."

Again there was shocked silence on the part of their listeners. They had not touched fermented wine all their years at Qumran, nor since their nomadic life had begun, yet here was this strange new Messiah acting in such a questionable way!

To John's relief, Salome wanted to go farther to spend the night more comfortably in an inn nearer Jericho. After they had left, the disciples at once bombarded John with questions.

"I just don't understand it," was all he could answer.

With the exception of the Essenes, everyone who possibly could spent the Passover week in Jerusalem. So once the crowds from a distance had passed through the Jordan area, things were very quiet there. This gave John and his disciples more time to think, and grow more and more curious about this Messiah.

To counteract some of their restlessness, John decided they would move farther up the Jordan Valley than they had ever been before. If the Messiah was to begin operating mostly in Galilee, it would be good to be nearer to his work.

Zebedee and Salome happened to find them there on their return journey. This time their son John was not with them, and they said with a slightly regretful note that he had stayed behind with Jesus.

"I really don't like it," added Salome. "I'm scared, in fact! Do you know what he did there? As soon as he arrived and entered the temple courtyard—so James tells me—it made him mad to see all those traders selling sheep, cattle, and doves at exorbitant prices, and the money changers cheating visitors. So he got a rope, made it into a whip, and lashed out, driving men, cattle, and sheep right out the gates! And he tipped over the tables with all the money standing in neat piles! He couldn't let all the doves out of their cages, but ordered the dealers to take them out of the courtyard, saying, 'Do not make my Father's house a house of merchandise!'"

There was a gasp from her audience.

"Whatever did the priests do?" asked Justus, anxiously turning to Zebedee. But Salome answered for him.

"They were furious, of course. Some went up to him and demanded, 'By what miraculous sign can you prove to us your authority for doing this?'"

"And what did he answer?"

"'Destroy this temple,' he said, 'and in three days I will raise it up again.'"

"What did he mean?"

"No one knows. The chief priests protested it had taken forty-six years to build. How could he possibly rebuild it in three days? But for some reason they seemed so shaken, they didn't try to arrest him there on the spot. Once they talk it over, it'll be a different matter, I'm afraid. I hope he will establish his army soon, or it may be a dangerous business being one of his followers."

The account of the cleansing of the temple cheered John and

his disciples considerably. This was one of the very things they believed the Messiah would do. Perhaps everything was going to be all right, after all.

"Perhaps there's one other thing we should tell you, too," Salome added before they left. "People in Jerusalem are whispering that some of the priests and Pharisees say you are just possessed with a demon and are not an authentic prophet at all. So be on your guard."

"Thank you," said John, his face unmarked with anxiety, although there was an indignant murmur among his disciples. "And what is Jesus going to do now?"

"Well, they plan to leave Jerusalem soon. I'm thankful for that. He told James and John they would spend some time in the Jordan Valley."

"I hope it won't be for long." Zebedee's voice was heard for almost the first time. "That will be four of our crew gone, counting Simon and Andrew."

"But think of the kingdom! That must be our first consideration now, remember. Then perhaps you won't need to fish any more!" Salome encouraged him.

John and his disciples moved up the Jordan Valley above the boundary of the province of Judea, until they were opposite the border of Samaria at Aenon, near Salim. There were deep pools of water there, fed from springs in the area that gave them a good supply of drinking water, too. And there was the added security of being farther from the threatening rumblings in Jerusalem.

At first there were the usual crowds of listeners, many of whom now wanted to be baptized. Then numbers began to dwindle markedly. John therefore sent three disciples across the river to contact people there to persuade them to come across and listen to him. While over there, Nathan, Jochanan, and Benjamin happened to meet a certain Jew who started arguing with them about the baptism rite. He contended that the ordinary Pharisaic laws of purification were enough. Public immersion should be required only of Gentile proselytes. Nathan tried to assure him that John was a prophet ordained by God from birth. It was God who had given him the special command to baptize everyone in the Jordan.

175

"Then why is that other man, Jesus, baptizing farther down the river? I passed them yesterday. There were hundreds of people waiting to be baptized by him."

John's disciples were shocked to hear this, and hurried back across the Jordan to tell him.

"Master, one of the Pharisees told us that the Messiah is baptizing farther down the river. Everyone is flocking to *him!*"

John looked at them for a moment, then smiled.

"No one is able to lay claim to anything unless it has been given him from heaven. You can testify that I plainly said I am not the Messiah, but am only sent ahead of him. The one who has the bride is the bridegroom. But the bridegroom's friend, who stands near and listens to him, is very happy over the bridegroom's voice; so this joy of mine is complete."

John was surprised himself at the illustration that had come from his lips. Weddings were not a subject to which he had given any thought. Perhaps it was the report of the Messiah himself being present at a wedding that had lodged the thought in his mind. But he remembered, too, that it was a scriptural idea that God was the "husband" of his people. John himself was in the fullest sense the "go-between" required in an eastern wedding. Then he concluded with words that consciously came from his heart with the utmost sincerity.

"He must increase, and I must decrease."

His disciples looked at him with puzzled expressions, and several began to whisper among themselves.

"But John, what are we going to *do?*" It was Justus who voiced their feelings. "Why do we not go and join forces with the Messiah?"

John looked surprised. "He has not asked me to do so. My commission is to preach, baptize, and prepare people for his coming. I can still reach many, awaken them to his claims, and send them on to him."

"Master, none of us here, except yourself, has had the privilege of meeting this Messiah. This is what we have been looking for, and preparing ourselves for, for a long time."

"Why, of course! Anyone who wishes can certainly go and see him! Three of you go tomorrow, while the others stay here to help, and then the others go later."

It was decided that Justus, Matthias, and Shobab would go first.

In three days time they returned, their faces alight with excitement.

"We saw him! We saw him!" cried Matthias first.

"How is he baptizing?" demanded Benjamin, "is it with the Holy Spirit and with fire?"

"No, it seemed much the same as ours, except that Jesus himself didn't do the baptizing as far as we saw, but the fishermen, Simon, James, and John."

"*What?*" Nathan sounded really shocked.

"Yes, it is true," confirmed Shobab, "And we saw Jesus heal a *leper!* Can you imagine that! And he actually touched him! We couldn't believe it."

"He invited us to spend the night with him and some of his disciples," Matthias continued. "Simon was there with John. They—they just ate anything that had been given them, without knowing where it had come from!"

"So what did you do?" John cast a searching look at Justus, who, strangely, had not spoken yet.

He took a deep breath. "We ate it, too. The Messiah said it isn't what goes into our mouths that defiles us, but what comes out from our hearts: envy, jealousy, murder, lust, and so on. There's so much truth in that. I feel I shall never be the same again. And he has invited us to go back and follow him!"

"You?" John could hardly believe his ears. Somehow it had never occurred to him that his own disciples might be affected.

"Yes. Why don't we all go? You said just the other day that your joy was to stand by and listen to the bridegroom."

John sat with his head in his hands for what seemed a long time. For once he was at a loss for words, but at last he spoke with quiet finality.

"All my life I have lived according to the laws of purity. I cannot conceive of any other way for myself, as a life-long Nazarite. The very thought of breaking them makes me ill. And I remember the oath I swore three times before leaving the community. I have to continue this way. I believe there is still work for me to do for the present. The future I cannot see clearly. But for you . . ." he looked around at each in turn, "each of you is free to leave, if that is your desire."

As he said this his thoughts suddenly flashed back to Qumran, and he found himself understanding the Guardian's feelings more fully. What would they decide?

177

The strained silence continued a moment longer, then it was broken by Benjamin.

"I swore I would never leave you until your death, or mine, remember. I stay with you."

"And so do I. It was my father's wish," Nathan announced next.

"I choose to stay, too. Like you, I have known no other life than the community," said Jochanan.

A look of relief swept across Justus' face.

"In that case," he said, "I have no hesitation in leaving. I have found what I have been seeking all my life. Truly this Jesus is the Son of God, and I have much to learn from him. I can't help wondering if you should at least ask him what you should do. But he doesn't require us to be with him all the time, as yet. Peter and one or two of the others are married men, so they could hardly be. We shall visit you from time to time, and support you in any way we can. I humbly give thanks for all you have taught us, for all your courage and determination in fulfilling God's call to you."

Matthias and Shobab then each quietly announced they would be leaving, too, but John scarcely heard them. He had gladly seen the crowds turn to the Messiah he had pointed them to, even Andrew and John. But Justus! He was all John had ever experienced in the way of a father. Even when he had unexpectedly turned into his own disciple, he had been a tower of strength, meeting their needs in so many quiet ways.

But Messiah must have the best. John had said it, and had meant it with all his heart: He must increase, and I must decrease.

Yet what of the future? John wondered. He was only thirty-one. Surely there would be a place for him when Messiah set up his kingdom? And what about all the Brothers at Qumran, faithfully preparing themselves for that kingdom? But however he tried to figure things out, no pattern would emerge. He must study his scroll tomorrow, and see if he had missed anything of his father's prophecy.

That night as the others lay sleeping, he softly whispered the words again, as a reminder to himself and as an offering to the Almighty: "He must increase, and I must decrease."

20

A Royal Confrontation

Their last meal together the next morning was strained with repressed emotions for all seven men. They had been through so much together: the trauma of leaving the security of Qumran; the thrill of triumph at seeing the great crowds pressing to hear the prophet; the joy when many willingly humbled themselves in the murky Jordan water. There were times, too, when they had been short of food and adequate shelter from the fierce summer heat of the Jordan Valley and the chill of the wet months. Above all, they had had times of rich spiritual fellowship in prayer and study of the Scriptures.

As the three prepared to leave, Justus approached John with his precious scrolls in his arms.

"I will leave these with you," he said gently. "It will be easier for me to obtain copies—and I shall be near the very source of truth."

There were tears in John's eyes as he accepted them. He knew very well that this was a tremendous sacrifice for Justus, and that it was a token of his great regard.

"We will use them well," was all he managed to say.

At last they were gone, after committing each other to the care of the Almighty. John experienced an overwhelming sense of loneliness as he watched them ford the river to disappear amid the bushes lining the bank.

He turned then with gratitude to the faithful three who had elected to stay with him They had all been children together at

Ain Feshka, and perhaps each thought back to those carefree days now.

"I think we'll keep to the Perean side a little longer, and perhaps move farther north tomorrow," John said with forced cheerfulness. "Now that we are fewer, it shouldn't be so difficult to find adequate food and shelter."

Benjamin privately disagreed, but said nothing. It had often been Justus who had supplied needed money in the past. Justus had in fact left a small sum with him now for emergencies.

After a time of prayer, they approached the road to speak to travelers, but strangely, most today didn't seem in the mood to listen to John. Instead, those from the south were in a flurry of indignation at the latest news.

"Have you heard? That sly old fox, Herod Antipas, has fallen in love with Herodias, his brother Herod Philip's wife! She's divorced her husband, and Antipas would have done the same with his wife, but she had already fled home to her father, King Aretas. Now Antipas and Herodias have had a big public wedding!"

The same story, with varying details, was endlessly repeated. Everyone was shocked at this adulterous breach of the law. Some regarded it as incestuous to marry a brother's wife while he was still alive. The fact there was a child by the marriage, in this case Herod Philip's daughter Salome, made the situation even more repulsive.

For the Essenes, however, it was also sin on another count. The Mosaic law forbade a man to marry his father's sister. Because it did not specifically forbid a daughter to marry an uncle, many rabbis taught that this was lawful, and even laudable, whereas the Essenes believed and taught strongly that what applied to men applied also to women.

John and his disciples, therefore, were doubly horrified to hear this news, which they felt would bring down God's wrath on the whole land.

As he walked along the river, John thought of the story from the Scriptures of the prophet Nathan going to challenge King David about his sin with Bathsheba. And then his own forerunner, Elijah, had confronted the wicked King Ahab with his sin in the province of Samaria. Was God giving him a fresh challenge and commission?

At any rate, he decided to get as close as possible to the palace at Julias, where they said Antipas was staying, to see if there was any possibility of meeting the Tetrarch of Galilee and Perea. Julias was east of the Jordan, but farther south, so John headed there at once.

By mid-afternoon they were at the Jordan ford nearest to Julias. John and his disciples posted themselves at the fork of the road.

In a short time a small crowd gathered and John began preaching. In the midst of his address some soldiers approached. At their head was Manaen, the captain of the Tetrarch's body guard! He halted his men, listened, and afterward warmly welcomed John to the area.

"Will you be here long?" he asked.

"A few days, at least."

"Good. I have some friends. I would like for them to hear you. They were too busy with the Tetrarch's affairs to come out to hear you before."

The next day a very well-dressed, middle-aged man and a young teen-aged boy came riding down the road attended by several servants, two of whom carried an ornate litter.

Some of the bystanders whispered to John that this was Chuza, Herod Antipas' chief steward, and presumably his wife, Joanna, and their son.

John started preaching as if he were unaware of their presence. With great conviction he poured forth his message and finally appealed to those who were ready to repent and be baptized to come forward.

Several in the crowd did so at once, still others hesitated, then finally stepped forward. While Nathan was instructing them in what to do, John saw the boy whisper to the well-dressed man, then dismount and come and join the others. Assured that each was really in earnest, Nathan led them to the water in which John was already waiting.

After the baptism was over, the boy asked John if he would come and meet his father. Was this the opportunity he was hoping for, he wondered, as he followed the boy back to the road.

"That is a very impressive message you have. I should like many more to hear it," the father remarked. "We have all heard about you, and how God is blessing your work."

"God wills that you not only hear, but respond," John replied, fixing his eyes on him. "I pray you will not hinder your son from obeying the truth, and that you, too, will repent, while there is still time."

Chuza turned to lead his party away without another word, but his face was very thoughtful.

That evening several of the Tetrarch's spies reported the presence of John the Baptizer. Antipas' curiosity was immediately aroused by this novelty. He called Chuza to him and asked if he knew anything about this so-called prophet.

"Yes, I heard he was becoming known while you were in Rome, and I saw him this morning when I was passing by the river. He really looks the prophet, and what he says is honest and forthright."

"I hear that thousands have been out to hear him."

"I am not surprised, your Excellency."

"But the Pharisees think he may be dangerous. People may be willing to follow him to the point of revolution."

"I hardly think there is that danger, from what I heard him say. It is merely a personal, inner revolution that he preaches. Probably the Pharisees are jealous of his popularity."

Antipas chuckled. "You understand them well, Chuza. But what you say intrigues me. I should like to hear this fellow. Have him brought here tomorrow."

"Sire, I have heard he is from that very strict sect at Qumran. They will not enter any house that is not purified according to their rules. I would respectfully suggest that you have your throne set up in the courtyard, then perhaps he will feel free to come."

Grumbling at having to accommodate himself to a wild prophet, the Tetrarch nevertheless issued the necessary orders. Manaen was given the task of issuing the invitation and escorting the prophet to the palace.

Joy coursed through John on hearing the invitation. Surely it must be God who provided so quickly and easily the opportunity he had been seeking. His joy was tempered only slightly with dread at having to venture into a largely Gentile establishment. The Tetrarch was known for his Hellenistic tastes, although he outwardly complied with Jewish law when in devout company.

Manaen briefed John on court procedure, and finally the party strode past the numerous guards at the palace gates, through the outer courtyard and into the beautifully sculptured inner one.

182

John firmly kept his eyes from all the nude statues, and indeed, his attention was almost immediately drawn to the Tetrarch. He was seated on a portable gilded throne, inlaid with ivory, which had been placed on a raised platform at the side of the courtyard nearest the royal dwelling quarters of the palace.

Antipas was just over fifty years old. He had the square-shaped chin and rectangular face of Herod, his father, as well as the deep-set eyes. John tried to forget that it was this man's father who had had his own father murdered. Antipas himself could not be blamed for the sins of his father. But now it appeared he had plenty of his own.

For a second, John's eyes turned to the throne beside the Tetrarch, and then away in horror at the sight of a woman sitting there unveiled. There was a similarity of features, for Herodias was the granddaughter of Herod the Great. There was an air of regal beauty about her, enhanced with the aid of liberal make-up and glittering jewels.

John shuddered at the very idea of this woman twice married to her own uncles. Maybe she had been helpless the first time, for her grandfather had made the arrangement when she was very young. But according to rumor, she was as responsible for this second match as Antipas himself.

At this thought John's eyes began to blaze. He kept them resolutely turned from her as he approached the dais.

"Welcome," said Antipas in a slightly languid, patronizing tone. "We have heard much about our new prophet, and we thought fit to provide an audience for you here." He waved his hand toward the group of courtiers on his right, and the soldiers and minor officials on his left. Discreetly in the background stood a number of servants and slaves.

"Thank you, Excellency, for this opportunity," John answered gravely. "I believe it is according to the will of the Almighty." He then raised his voice so that those in the farthest corners of the courtyard might hear.

"I believe God has called me for a special purpose, to make known to all the people of our land of Israel the warning that his judgment is coming and that we should prepare for the kingdom of heaven."

He then went on to give his call to repentance and change. The Tetrarch seemed to be listening with genuine interest, but

John noticed slight movements of impatience or irritation in the hands of the one seated beside him.

Finally, John lowered his voice, and spoke directly to the Tetrarch.

"It is with great grief, Sire, that we and all your people, have heard of this wicked thing that has come to pass within your house." There was a horrified stir among the nearby courtiers, but John pressed on with flashing eyes and accusing words addressed at the two thrones.

"Not only have you entered into an adulterous relationship with your brother's wife while he is still living, but you have consorted with another brother's daughter. This is against the law of Moses, it is an abomination to the Lord God, and it will bring nothing but evil upon your house and upon the whole land. God is not mocked. What a man sows, that will he reap."

Before he could say another word, Herodias stamped her foot, her eyes flashing as much as John's, but with rage and hate.

"This is treason. Treason!" she screamed. "Antipas, have him arrested at once!"

Antipas, too, was angry and utterly flabbergasted at the audacity of this lunatic in the camel's hair robe. He broke out in a cold sweat, uncertain what was the best thing to do. Then he gestured to a nearby guard. "Throw him out," he muttered.

"There is no need," responded John with dignity. "I have accomplished what the Almighty commanded me to do. Let us go," he added, turning to his disciples.

No sooner had they turned to go than the Tetrarch hastily dismissed the assembly. As they themselves walked toward the palace doors, Herodias whispered vehemently, "Why did you let him escape? He'll be preaching about us all over the country!"

"The people think so highly of him, it could touch off a riot if we did him any harm."

"They'll soon forget. And what he said was outrageous! I never dreamed the day would come when I would be so humiliated! Send soldiers to arrest him! Please, for my sake, Antipas!"

At last, against his better judgment, Antipas called for the captain of the guard and ordered him to take ten men to arrest John immediately and keep him securely in the guardhouse.

As he made his way back to the Jordan with his disciples, John felt deep satisfaction at the opportunity he had just had to denounce sin in high places. Jochanan was just congratulating him on his great courage when they heard shouts behind them and turned to see the group of soldiers. *Were they wanting an opportunity to repent and be baptized?* John wondered.

"Herod the Tetrarch has ordered your immediate arrest," snapped the group's leader as they drew level with them.

John could hardly believe what was happening to him as two soldiers grabbed his arms and dragged him back up the road. His terrified disciples determined not to leave him, but when they all reached the guardhouse, they were rudely pushed outside and stood there helplessly, at a loss what to do next.

"Let us all pray," suggested Nathan at last.

While they were still engaged in this, Manaen appeared. He beckoned to them, his face grave.

"I am very sorry indeed this has happened. I never dreamed the prophet would attack the Tetrarch! Though all he said was true enough. It is best for you to go, or you may be imprisoned, too!"

"We cannot leave him. Sir, you don't understand," pleaded Benjamin. "The master needs us to prepare his food. He will never touch anything that may have been defiled. Will you allow us at least to bring him food while he is here?"

"I hope it will not be for long. But I'll give orders for them to allow one of you to come with food. The guards will probably be glad not to have to share any with him! Keep out of sight as much as possible, however. The Tetrarch is usually careful not to do anything to offend the people unnecessarily. Herodias is responsible for this."

So Benjamin faithfully brought honey, locusts, and carob beans twice daily. On the third day he learned that Herod had sent for John and talked with him in a private room. His whole life had been so surrounded with flatterers and self-seekers that he appeared to enjoy listening to John's refreshing, but painful, honesty.

There were a number of these occasions. Each time John hoped that he was to be set free. Herodias, however, learned of what her husband was doing and jealousy was added to the bitter animosity she felt toward this interfering prophet.

She stormed into Antipas' room after one such meeting and begged him to kill John, as his father had so readily killed all who offended or threatened him.

"Yes, including your own father, remember, Darling? I don't

185

think I want to begin such a slaughter. This prophet is only doing what his conscience tells him."

"He's totally misguided. He's mad! You've only to look at him to know that he's a dangerous troublemaker, too. He speaks of a coming kingdom and the people are easily influenced by his words. He could start a rebellion among these excitable people! The Pharisees want to see him done away with, too. You'd be popular with them if you kill him. They might even petition Caesar to have you made king of Judea as well, like your father!"

Antipas didn't know how much longer he would be able to resist Herodias' constant pressure. Finally he called in Chuza for a secret conference.

"I'm sorry to say it, but her Excellency is set on seeing this prophet, John, killed. I fear for his safety if he stays here any longer. See to it that he is quietly taken down to the fortress at Machaerus very early in the morning. He'll be safe there, and she'll forget all about him. I'm sorry to have to do this, but I see no other way out."

21

Misery at Machaerus

The fortress of Machaerus was situated at the southern limit of Perea on the high ridge of the mountains of Moab. It stood 3,800 feet above the Salt Sea and three or four miles to the east of it. Machaerus was a defense against the Nabateans and Arabs to the south and east. The original fortress had been built by one of the Maccabees, and then destroyed by the Romans. Herod the Great, however, had not only rebuilt and strengthened the fortress, but also constructed a handsome palace for himself within the circumference of its walls.

With John chained between two soldiers, they had traveled most of the night along the King's Highway, lying east of the scarp. It was not until they were about level with Machaerus that they finally turned west along the narrow road leading to it. Valleys in the north and south protected the high plateau, while its western boundary was a 1,000 foot precipice. From its center rose higher yet the cone-shaped hill that the fortress covered. It was not until they were at the top of the steep, winding path, which was the only access, that John at last caught a glimpse of his beloved Salt Sea.

Longingly, he looked northward across the expanse of water, to the Qumran community buildings now highlighted by rays of the early morning sun.

The sight was a great comfort after the shock of his arrest by Herod, the three weeks of imprisonment, and now the forced nocturnal march with the rough soldiers. He would gladly have stood a few moments to savor the scene, but the weary soldiers hustled him toward the fortress. At least Manaen had allowed his three disciples to go with him. But that was on condition they did not speak to anyone on the way or leave word of John's whereabouts.

The soldier who had been in charge of the journey thankfully handed over his sealed orders to the commanding officer of the fortress and then departed.

After the officer had read his instructions, he expressed surprise and annoyance that they were to have charge of an important prisoner. He was especially annoyed at the order that the prisoner's friends were to have access to him and provide his food. He thought that was asking for trouble. However, the garrison was changed every three months, so he was thankful he had only one month more before transferring to Tiberias. This was a desolate place, hot in summer and very cold in winter, with snow lying sometimes for weeks. So everyone was glad when their turn came to transfer to Tiberias, or even Julias.

"Put him in the dungeon," he nodded to two soldiers awaiting his orders. "And you—" looking at Benjamin, standing dejectedly in the background, "be here at the appointed times with this absurd diet for the prisoner. Otherwise you will not be admitted."

As he was hustled away from the guardhouse at the entrance into the inner courtyard, John caught sight of Herod's magnificent palace at one side of the huge enclosure. He was led, however, to the citadel at the opposite end, surmounted by watchtowers 160 feet high.

John was led into a windowless room at the base of this citadel. He shrank back in horror as another soldier brought a flaming torch and held it over a huge, yawning black hole. As his eyes grew accustomed to the darkness, he saw it was hewn out of the limestone rock, and that a few iron staples and wooden pegs had been driven into the wall down one side.

"There's your staircase! Down you go!" the soldier ordered in jeering tones.

Unable to see the bottom, John gingerly felt his way down, until at last his probing foot struck solid rock beneath him. Assured that he was at the bottom, the soldiers departed. John could hear the huge key turn in the lock as he stood in the darkness.

He leaned against the wall as if stunned, holding on to one of the pegs. Finally he gathered courage to try to feel his way around, but he could make out nothing but a rock floor beneath, with the faint stench of old urine. At least this dungeon had not been occupied recently. For that he could be thankful, but he shuddered at the thought of the impurity of his prison.

He sank to the floor, despair overwhelming him. Had God deserted him? What had he done wrong? Everything seemed to have gone so well that he had come to expect only success. Was it foolish to have spoken so plainly to Antipas of his sin?

It seemed an eternity before he heard the door open, and a shaft of light appeared in the space above.

"You can come up to eat," called a rough voice.

John felt for the staples and slowly climbed up, his eyes dazed by the light. As he pulled himself above the rim of the pit, he thankfully recognized the figure of dear faithful Benjamin, standing beside a soldier who looked vaguely familiar.

"Oh, Master," the soldier said in a low, shocked voice, "I was baptized in the Jordan some months ago. How grieved I am to see you here! I have managed to get duty here this week and will do what I can to help. I'll try and get you a blanket later. Now, here is Benjamin with your food. Sit near the door and enjoy the sunlight, while I keep guard outside."

There were tears in Benjamin's eyes now. "Master, Master!" was all he managed to say, as he gasped in horror at the dungeon.

His presence somehow helped John to regain his composure.

"Where are Nathan and Jochanan?"

"They are out looking for food supplies. It's going to be difficult here."

"The Lord will provide, as he did for Elijah."

"I suppose so. But Master, I can't bear to see you in a place like this."

"It is hard to understand. Perhaps Jochanan should go to find the Messiah. Or that officer, Manaen, may be able to arrange my release."

The soldier appeared in the doorway. "I'm afraid your time together is finished. But I'll try to get permission for you to have some exercise after the second meal."

Slowly John returned to the depths of his pit and prayed, then he planned how he could pass the time. It was agonizing that in the darkness he couldn't read. Even if he could, he only had his

189

own special scroll with him, having decided it might be safer for the others to have the Scripture scrolls. He must ask Benjamin to read to him while he ate. Then he remembered, with a little grimace, his disciple's rather halting reading ability. Perhaps Nathan could come sometimes, instead.

Once his disciples had found a suitable cave to live in and places where adequate food supplies might be found, Nathan and Jochanan decided Benjamin could now be left while they crossed the Jordan to find Jesus. John was thankful to see them go and eagerly awaited their return.

It took Nathan and Jochanan much longer than they expected to find Jesus, as they learned that after hearing of John's imprisonment He had moved back into Galilee. Knowing how eagerly John was awaiting them, they hurried back as soon as their mission was accomplished. But they dreaded having to tell him what they had discovered.

"Well, what did you find?" he asked, their greetings completed.

"We had to go right up into Galilee to find them," Nathan began. "What beautiful country that is! It took us a day or two to find Jesus, even there. He seems to be trying to keep his presence secret. He has done many remarkable healings there, but then instructs the people not to tell about them."

John looked puzzled. "Why does he do that?"

"Some suggest it is because of what happened to you."

A chill crept over John. Was this the conquering king who was to establish the expected kingdom?

"The chief priests and others are still furious with him for what he did in the temple at the Passover. And even the leaders in his old synagogue at Nazareth have turned against him," added Jochanan.

John was even more puzzled. "But didn't you speak to him? And what about Justus and the others?" There was an eager, wistful note in his voice.

"We saw Matthias. That was in Capernaum. But he said Justus and Shobab had gone to Magdala on some business for the Messiah. As we had already taken much longer than expected, we thought we had better return without waiting to see them this time." ·

"But . . . what about the Messiah? Surely you saw him?"

"Yes, we saw him." Nathan spoke reluctantly, and then decided there was nothing to gain by withholding information.

"You'll never be able to believe this. The day before we arrived Jesus had walked into the customs office in Capernaum and called the manager there, Matthew Levi, to follow him! Actually he's one who came to hear you several times and was finally baptized, Matthias told us. He has become more honest since, and everyone has noticed it. But the next day he put on a big feast and invited all the publicans he knew, and other ungodly people—at least they were people who never kept the purification laws. The idea was for them all to meet the Messiah and his disciples at the meal!"

"So what happened?"

"They all went! And it was the *fast* day! We just couldn't believe it!" Jochanan burst out.

John's startled eyes seemed to bore into the two returned disciples as if desperately hoping to prove they were mistaken.

"Are you *sure?*"

"Absolutely," Nathan answered earnestly. "We saw him in there with Matthias, Simon, Andrew, James, and John."

"Some of the Pharisees found out about it and came to see for themselves," Jochanan said. "They were as shocked as we were. They beckoned for Matthias to come outside. They asked him why his master ate with publicans and sinners. Jesus must have overheard, for he walked over and said in a loud, clear voice, 'Those who are well do not need a physician, but those who are sick.' And he said, 'I have not come to call the righteous, but sinners, to repentance.'"

"Yes, and since he was outside the entrance, we quickly went up beside the Pharisees," said Nathan, "and we asked, 'Why do we, John the Baptizer's disciples, fast and your disciples do not?'"

"What did he say?" John's voice was sharp with anxiety.

"It was a strange answer. It went something like this: Can the wedding guests mourn while the bridegroom is with them? But the days are coming when the bridegroom will be taken from them, and then they will fast. No one sews a new patch of unshrunk cloth on an old coat, for the patch would tear away from the coat, and the tear become worse."

"Whatever did he mean?"

"We have no idea."

191

"Why didn't you ask him?"

"Just then a ruler of the synagogue came along and actually knelt on the ground before him, saying his daughter had just died, but he believed that if Jesus would just come and put his hand on her she would come to life again. Imagine! He actually suggested the Messiah should touch a corpse! But he agreed to go! No sooner was he out on the street than a crowd followed him at once. We tried to keep fairly close, without getting defiled ourselves, when suddenly Jesus stopped and said, 'Who touched me?'"

Jochanan took up the tale as Nathan appeared to be getting breathless.

"Simon said it was useless to ask such a question with the crowd pressing on them all around, but Jesus insisted he had felt healing pass from him. So then a woman confessed she had done it. She'd had a bloody issue twelve years—just think—and was wicked enough to come into a crowd she could so easily defile, and deliberately *planned* to touch him!"

"Was he very angry?" asked Benjamin.

"Angry? Instead, he turned to her and said, 'Be of good cheer, daughter, your faith has healed you.' We had seen enough, then, and decided to leave right away before we were made unclean."

John's face appeared paler than usual and he put his hand against the wall to steady himself. Just then a soldier came to lock him up for the night, forcing his disciples to leave.

Again and again John tried to go over everything Nathan and Jochanan had told him, but he couldn't be sure he completely understood. The things Jesus said just didn't seem to make sense. Eating in the very house of a publican was the last thing a Pharisee or Essene would ever do. Surely God's Anointed One would never do such a thing. And yet, he had called himself the bridegroom, the very thing John himself had called him once to his disciples. But he had said the bridegroom would be taken from his friends. How could that be? What about the kingdom? He said he had come to call sinners to repentance, and that was understandable—that was what he had done himself. But the part about a new patch on an old garment—it was true literally, he supposed—but somehow he felt Jesus hadn't been talking merely about clothing. What did it all mean? John's head ached with these constantly nagging questions.

MISERY AT MACHAERUS

The more John thought about these things, the more puzzled and anxious he became, until at last depression gripped him and he became quite ill. Another month had passed, and still there had been no word from any of his former disciples. This hurt most of all.

There was only his rough camel's hair cloak between him and the uneven rock floor. His thin frame tossed and turned on it, in spite of all his years of disciplined living at Qumran.

He found his thoughts turning with longing to Qumran. Perhaps Herod Antipas might allow him to return there if he promised not to preach again. Could he do such a thing though, and renounce God's call to be his prophet and voice in the wilderness? But he was not, and *could* not do any preaching shut away in this prison! Surely it would be better to be silent at Qumran? After all, this Jesus was apparently preaching the same message as *he* had given, and everyone was flocking to hear him now. It seemed there was no need for him anymore. But why was God treating him in this terrible way?

Then an even worse thought occurred to John. *Is this Jesus really the Messiah?* The memory of his baptism had faded somewhat. Had John really heard that voice? Although there was the dove, too, and God had previously told him about that. But why, *why* did God not speak to him now?

Tormented by these thoughts, an anguished groan escaped John's dry lips one night. He feared his reason might leave him. Then the words of the psalmist also in trouble flashed through his mind and seemed to meet his own need. "My soul clings to the dust; Revive me according to Your word." He knew now there was only one thing to do. He would tell his disciples in the morning. With that resolution, he finally fell asleep.

"How would you like to go with Nathan to see Jesus of Nazareth?" he asked Benjamin when he appeared with his morning food.

"No. I'm staying with you," Benjamin answered firmly. "Don't you remember my promise? Besides, you're sick now, and certainly shouldn't be left. I don't think Jochanan could manage alone."

"Well, thank you," John answered with secret relief. Benjamin by now seemed to have a real genius for finding honey and locusts. And though John had little appetite, he was very grateful for all his care.

193

"Where are Nathan and Jochanan today?"

"They went out onto the King's Highway. Nathan's doing a bit of preaching himself now. They also want to hear any news from travelers. It seems many people have heard of Jesus recently, though most here haven't seen him."

"Ask them both to come and see me as soon as they can."

The two disciples arrived the next morning and appeared quite excited, although they first enquired anxiously about John's health.

"What news did you hear yesterday?"

"There were some travelers from as far away as Ephesus. They said many people there are talking about you, Master," Nathan answered. "Then there was a couple from Galilee. They said they had heard that Jesus had actually raised two people from the dead! One was the daughter of that synagogue ruler we told you about; the other the son of a widow woman from the village of Nain. We didn't know whether to believe them or not. But everyone certainly regards him as a new prophet."

Again John's thoughts were in turmoil. The various healings he had heard about had not impressed him. He had had little experience with illness, and like most people, he thought sickness was probably a punishment for sin. But raising people from the dead certainly sounded miraculous, if it were true. Yet, was that what the expected Messiah was supposed to do? What about establishing the kingdom? And if he could raise the dead, surely he could bring about his forerunner's release from prison!

"And what about Herod Antipas? Is he taking any notice of Jesus?"

"He's off on a trip to some Greek islands with Herodias. He probably thought it best to be out of the way in case there were any angry demonstrations about your imprisonment. But most people are so taken up with this Jesus, they don't notice you are not around. Herod tried to keep it as quiet as possible, of course. Many don't even know about it yet."

"I want you both to go and find Jesus, and don't leave until you have personally asked him this question and received his answer. Do you understand?"

"Yes, Master. What is the question?"

"It is this. Are you truly the Coming One, or should we look for someone else?"

"Do you really mean that?" Nathan asked in surprise.

"I do."

"Very well. But do you think it is wise for two of us to leave you just now?"

"It is more important that I get a reply. God keep you in his care and grant you a favorable journey."

More than ten days had passed, but still there was no sign of Nathan and Jochanan. Of course, it was an eighty mile journey, even if they found Jesus at once, but growing anxiety for their safety was added to John's already troubled mind. The guards had told him they had received a report of a strong band of robbers not far north along the King's Highway. John feared his disciples might have fallen into their hands.

The last detachment of soldiers to arrive had also confirmed that Herod Antipas was indeed out of the country, so there could be no word of John's release for some time. Manaen had seen to it, however, that when the garrison changed there were two men who had been baptized by John, so he continued to receive sympathetic treatment at their hands. He was now kept in the room above the dungeon and was allowed outside earlier in the hot, midsummer afternoons.

There was often a cool breeze blowing from the far Mediterranean Sea, and John's favorite occupation then was to pace the west side of the fortress and stop to view the landscape. Always he looked at Qumran, if there was no thick mist rising from the Salt Sea, and he prayed for the Brothers there. Then farther north his eyes would rest toward Jerusalem and the Mount of Olives. He was a little surprised that he had had no desire to go there, but after all, he had heard little good about it over the years.

Then his gaze would skip over toward Samaria—the half-Gentile province that no orthodox Jew would willingly set foot in, preferring the longer route through Perea to and from Jerusalem. Finally he strained his eyes toward Galilee. There he tried to imagine all that might be taking place between Jesus and his own disciples. Surely they would not follow Justus and the other two, and decide to stay with him?

At last Benjamin arrived one morning with the news that the others were back, but had had a difficult time because of the robbers blocking the main road. They had scrambled down a steep precipice to avoid them, and Jochanan had fallen and hurt his ankle. But after they had had a bit of rest, they would be up to see him that afternoon.

John tried to curb his impatience as the hours seemed to stretch interminably, but at last it was time for the exercise period. This had been extended to an hour since the garrison commander had noticed the prisoner's health was deteriorating.

As his disciples approached, John could see Jochanan limping. "Welcome back! I'm very sorry to hear of your fall, Jochanan!"

"The Lord watched over us. We are thankful to be back, though," said Jochanan with feeling.

"Well, did you . . . receive an answer?"

"We did," Nathan answered, with just the slightest hesitation, John thought. "It took us quite a while to find him. He still seems to be trying to keep things quiet and moves constantly. He has now chosen twelve disciples to be with him as a kind of inner circle."

"Are Justus and Matthias among them?" John interrupted abruptly.

"No, there are the four fishermen, and Philip and Nathanael. Maybe you don't remember them, but they are friends of the others. And who do you think is one? That chief publican, Matthew Levi!"

"He can't be!"

"Yes, he is. The others you may not know, but they all came to you for baptism. I remember talking to Thomas, and hearing his confession. Two of them are called Judas, one from Judea I think. And there's another James. I forget the other."

"Simon, the Zealot," put in Jochanan.

"That's right. He's sent them off in twos to do some preaching and healing in various towns and villages. This way no one is sure where they will find anyone, but somehow the sick and their friends always find Jesus."

"So you found him?" John was obviously getting impatient.

"Yes, after quite a search. But the crowd! We couldn't get near him. In the end we just had to push our way in, clean or unclean, and said straight out, 'John the Baptizer has sent us to you with this question: Are you the Coming One, or should we look for another?'"

"What did he say?" The words rushed from John lips.

"Well, at first he went right on healing the great multitude of sick people. There were blind, lepers, demon-possessed, everything you can think of."

John leaned forward, his face lined with anxiety.

"Then he stopped a moment, as if exhausted, and turned to us. 'Go and report to John what you are seeing and hearing,' he said. 'The blind see, the lame walk, lepers are cleansed, the deaf hear, the dead are raised, and the needy are evangelized.'"

"And while this was happening Justus arrived," Jochanan broke in excitedly, "and those people from Magdala, do you remember? There was a woman with them who was the first to be baptized."

"Yes," answered John. "I wonder now if it wasn't a mistake. I don't believe we can ever trust women. If it hadn't been for that wicked Herodias, Antipas wouldn't have committed adultery and incest and I should not now be imprisoned and useless like this."

"But there was another woman, remember, who was mad or demon-possessed, and Justus couldn't pass her for baptism—"

"Of course."

"But Justus told us he'd been haunted with the feeling of his own helplessness in the face of her great need. So as soon as he saw Jesus drive out demons he went to Magdala, and begged the father to bring his daughter to Jesus. They say she was possessed with seven demons. They really tormented her and even made her tear her veil off in front of everyone! But Jesus calmly ordered the devils to come out of her. You should have seen the change! It was . . . unbelievable! She was a different person at once! Her proud father just broke down and wept."

John found it hard to share their excitement over this mad woman. He recognized Jesus' answer was a quotation from the prophet Isaiah, and so perhaps was of special significance. But was there nothing more personal than those first few words, 'Go and report to John'?

"Did Jesus say no more in response to my question?" There was quiet desperation in John's tone.

"Oh, yes, there was one other thing," Nathan said hastily. "It was this. 'And blessed is he who is not offended because of me.'"

John felt a sharp stab of physical pain. He put out his hand to the wall for support, as he dimly heard Benjamin ask a question.

"And is he baptizing with the Spirit and fire?"

"Not that we heard of. But we have no doubt, now, that he *is* the Messiah." Nathan sounded faintly apologetic as he glanced at John.

"So, you will also go away?" John asked in a weak voice.

"Certainly not—not until you go," declared Nathan emphatically. "What's the matter, are you sick?"

"I—I—don't—" Before John could finish, he had slipped to the ground, unconscious.

22

A Visit from Chuza

Even after John regained consciousness, his mind was not clear. Benjamin, stubbornly refusing the strong drink offered by the soldiers to try to revive him, managed to get some hot honey water down his throat.

At last faint sounds began coming from his lips. Nathan bent closer to listen.

"Blessed is he—blessed is he—," there was a pause, then as if struggling to find the ending, the same words were repeated, "Blessed is he—"

"Who is not offended because of me," Nathan finished with a flash of intuition.

"That is it!"

John took a longer drink then and seemed to sink into a normal sleep a few moments later.

With the commander's permission, Nathan spent the night with John, while Jochanan rested his ankle and Benjamin carried on his essential work of maintaining the food supply.

The next morning John's mind was clear, though his pulse was still weak, and he indicated pain in his chest. He begged for the prophecy of Isaiah to be brought, and when it came, he had long passages read. He ordered many pauses while he thought over the implications of the words. He was trying to relate them to what he had been told about Jesus of Nazareth.

"What a long time it seems since I copied all these words in the scriptorium," he murmured once.

After a few days, though there seemed little physical change, it was obvious to his disciples that John had regained his peace of mind. No doubt the constant study of the Scriptures, and being moved to a room with a window, contributed to his improvement. Above all, however, he believed now that Jesus had sent him a special message of gentle rebuke. He was determined to respond to it. He would no longer consider the possibility that this was not the One he had been preparing for. Even though he couldn't understand all of the Messiah's actions, surely one who could raise people from the dead must be of divine origin.

As for himself, he had no vision for the future. He had been at Machaerus nearly four months, and he felt so tired and weak that he had little desire to go on living. Could God have brought him to this mountain top, just as he had Moses, so that he might take him to himself?

Now, however, the whole garrison, and particularly the skeleton staff in the palace, were abuzz with excitement. A messenger had arrived with the news that Herod Antipas' chief steward, Lord Chuza, was on his way from Tiberias. He was coming to oversee arrangements for a big celebration to mark the anniversary of Antipas' accession to the Tetrarchy. That was thirty-two years ago now, but this would be the first celebration with his new consort, the Lady Herodias.

At the mention of her name, John's spirit quailed. Manaen had told him he was being sent to Machaerus to be kept safe from her. Now preparations were soon to begin for her very presence here! It must be back to the pit for him, but he knew he could never climb those staples and pegs in his present condition. Furthermore, the garrison commander, fearing he might have gone too far in leniency to his prisoner, ordered Nathan and Jochanan to keep away, until he found out if Chuza had any fresh instructions concerning him.

Chuza, with an entourage of over fifty assistants and slaves, arrived two days later. Within an hour, to the commander's great surprise, he asked to see John.

"He's ill. I doubt if he could make the walk from the citadel to the palace."

"Then I will go to see him."

The commander had only interviewed John in the guard house, or as he had seen him walking around. He himself would never go

200

to the dungeon unless he had no choice. "My Lord," he said, "you know how such quarters are likely to be! No place to sit,—the stench—"

"Nevertheless, I am going."

"I'll send a man with a stool, then, and you can sit outside."

Between John's self-control as a former Essene and Benjamin's faithful attendance, however, the dungeon smelled no worse than when John had first entered it. Chuza immediately ordered the stool to be placed in the room where John lay.

"Master," he exclaimed in a reverent tone, "peace be to you. The news of your illness has just reached me. I am indeed sorry. How are you feeling now?"

"Very weak, Sir." John was surprised at the respect and solicitude with which this great man addressed him. What could be the reason? Of course, he had come to hear him preach once, and John remembered how his son had come forward for baptism. One would think they would want to forget that, now. He would see.

"But your son, Sir, how is he these days?"

"That is why I have come to see you. We certainly saw a change for the better in him after he listened to your preaching and entered the water of purification." John relaxed a little, and the old glow began to return to his eyes.

"But about six weeks ago, he suddenly became very sick," Chuza continued. "The doctors, in fact, had given him up. We were staying for a short time at our own place in Capernaum while his highness, the Tetrarch, was away. I was coming out of the synagogue, when I ran into your old companion, Justus, who remembered my son and asked about him. When I told him how sick he was, he urged me to go with him at once to see Jesus of Nazareth."

"Did you go?"

"Unfortunately he was at Cana just then, a day's journey, so I hesitated to leave my son so long. But finally Justus persuaded me with stories of others who had been healed. It seemed too good to be true, but we had no other hope. My wife, too, urged me to go. When we arrived I told him at once that my son was on the point of death, and begged him to come to Capernaum and heal him." Chuza paused.

"So did he come?" John asked eagerly.

"At first he didn't seem to believe my sincerity, or perhaps was testing my faith. All he said was, 'Unless you people see signs and wonders, you won't believe.' I felt a bit affronted but was so anxious by then that I just went down on my knees and pleaded with him to come before my child died. I looked into his eyes then and have never seen such a face, so full of compassion and yet seeing right into one's heart!"

"So he did come with you?"

"No, he just said, 'Go home. Your son will live.' And I knew I could trust him. Next day, half way home, I met some of my servants coming to tell me my son was now well. I asked what time he had begun to recover. From what they told me I knew it was the very time Jesus had said 'Your son will live.' Now, my wife and I, and indeed most of our household, believe in him. With my responsibilities for the Tetrarch, it is not possible to spend much time in his company, but we are ready to believe anything he claims for himself, and we wish we could learn more of his teaching."

"Many are coming to that conclusion," said John, "and he is, indeed, the Coming One the prophet Isaiah foretold."

"I'm very concerned to see you so ill. Is there anything we can get for you? Just give the word, and you shall have it."

"Thank you, but my needs are met. It is my liberty I desire. What have I done to deserve this imprisonment?"

"How I wish I could grant that, but it is not in my power to do so. If I let you escape, Herodias would have my head—and those of all the guards here!"

John sighed and remained silent. Chuza left rather hastily, saying he would come again the next day.

Housing and catering for so large a group of guests as Antipas had planned, in such a remote area so difficult to reach, was no small logistic task. Chuza, as the Tetrarch's head steward, had oversight of every palace and residence he used. These included not only Julias and the palace in his new capital of Tiberias, but the old Hasmonean palace in Jerusalem, one at the former capital of Sepphoris, and also one that his father, Herod, had built at the former capital of Samaria. That city had originally been named Samaria, too, but had now been Romanized to Sebaste. But the palace at Machaerus had always proved the most difficult to supply.

Many people in the royal court wondered why Antipas usually

chose to celebrate there, in such a barren, isolated region. But Chuza knew the hunting was very good in the area, and guests usually came for several days to enjoy this. Also, there were wonderful hot springs to bathe in, close by at Chirrhoe. This was a Roman custom that many others in their vast empire were quick to adopt, once they had experienced its sensual pleasure and healing effects. Another reason, Chuza suspected, was that there were no conservative Jewish citizens around to fuss and frown about any Hellenistic customs and excesses in his celebrations.

One last, and very obvious reason for the choice of Machaerus, until now, was that Antipas' wife of many years was from the neighboring country of Nabatea. Her father, King Aretas, and his top dignitaries had always been invited. This year, of course, they had to be omitted.

Chuza worked hard all the next day, checking existing supplies with the permanent steward at the Machaerus palace, then issuing menus and a long list of over a hundred guests to be lodged there. But at the back of his mind was the constant nagging problem of the prophet. Should he allow him to escape, after all? He knew Herodias was determined to murder John, but Antipas would never agree. He had reigned for over thirty years without shedding the blood of his own people, trying to erase the memory of his father. He would be especially fearful of public reaction to the death of John. Yet Herodias was a new force to be reckoned with, as he was beginning to find out. Antipas' first wife had kept in the background; Herodias had much of her grandfather's character. So when they came for this big celebration, Chuza was sure she would do her utmost to have the prophet destroyed.

Compassion was urging him to release John, while his duty to his lord and fear for his own skin tugged him in the opposite direction. He almost wished he had not said he would go and see John again, he was beginning to feel so uncomfortable about the situation. He also remembered that when Herodias arrived, the prophet would have to be returned to the dungeon, as much for his own safety as for Herodias' satisfaction. Well, he must at least keep his word now and go to see John. Slowly he walked from the palace over to the citadel.

He was relieved to find John looking better, and he greeted him as cheerfully as he could.

"Perhaps one of you would be good enough to read to me from

the Scriptures some of the prophecies about the coming of the Messiah?" he asked, looking at John's disciples, who were also with him.

"Nathan, read from the Isaiah scroll," John said eagerly. "We will explain as we go along."

Chuza listened intently and had managed to forget all the cares of his work when they heard approaching footsteps. In a moment one of the servants appeared in the doorway.

"Sir, one of the Tetrarch's secret agents is here and says he must see you at once."

Chuza suppressed a sigh of regret.

"Very well. Show him into a private room in the guardhouse. I'll come right away." The guard turned and left.

"I'm very sorry for this interruption. What you have been sharing with me rejoices my heart. I hope we can meet again tomorrow."

Chuza strode off to the guardhouse and into the room indicated to him. Herod employed many spies, some from his ancestral Idumea. Here was one who worked in the area of Machaerus.

"Sir," he said hastily after producing his identification, "the other day in the market in the little town here, I overheard some travelers saying they had heard King Aretas is planning to attack Antipas to avenge his daughter's disgrace. I have been moving about on the King's Highway since then and have heard a similar rumor from another source. Aretas could be planning an attack when the Tetrarch is here for the celebration. He knows that Antipas might be most vulnerable then. Do you think he should be advised to celebrate somewhere else, either Julias or Tiberias?"

"That may be best. He will be returning in a few days. I will alert him immediately. Thank you for the information."

Chuza walked back to the palace even more perturbed than before. He doubted that Aretas could seriously challenge Antipas. The Emperor in Rome would have something to say about that, for Aretas would be guilty of breaking the famous *pax Romana.* But he might contrive some kind of hunting "accident" or raid by outlaws. He doubted, too, if Antipas would consent to change his plans, but he must certainly be warned immediately on his return.

Then Chuza had a sudden inspiration. This threatened danger gave him a good reason for removing the prophet from Machaerus, in the absence of the Tetrarch! But where to put him? In his mind he reviewed the various places under his responsibility and finally settled on the one he was convinced would be ideal, Sebaste. The beautiful palace there had been constructed by Herod the Great at the time he rebuilt the old, ruined city, and he had relocated a largely Gentile population there. It had been one of the old king's favorite residences before his jealousy ran wild. He had had his favorite wife, Mariamne I, and her sons, executed there.

Now that Samaria and Judea had been placed under direct Roman rule following his father's death and the short, misguided reign of his brother, Archelaus, Herod Antipas had mostly kept to his provinces of Galilee and Perea. The palace at Sebaste was still regarded as the family's property, however. Pontius Pilate, the Prefect, made his headquarters in Caesarea, with frequent visits to Jerusalem, and had shown no interest in Sebaste, beyond getting some good mercenary soldiers from there.

Furthermore, Chuza reasoned, the climate there would be much better for John. It was more temperate, and the breezes from the Mediterranean were good for anybody's health. Yes, that was certainly the place!

Greatly relieved at this solution, and pleased with yet another proof of his own administrative skill, Chuza slept well. In the morning he immediately went about carrying out his plans of the night before. Herod Antipas was due back at Tiberias within eight to ten days, so the utmost speed was essential. He must get John safely to Sebaste and be back at Tiberias before the Tetrarch's arrival. He wanted to tell him personally the news of the threat to Machaerus.

Chuza had not been appointed chief steward without reason, or from favoritism or nepotism. Antipas was too astute for that and had quickly recognized Chuza's great organizational ability. Though there were always others trying to pry him out of the job, Chuza had managed to retain it because of his ability and quick thinking.

His first task now was to alert the prophet to the change of plans, so that he could be ready to leave later that morning.

He found John alone. Benjamin had not yet arrived with his first meal.

"I'm sorry to disturb you so early, though I see you are already

awake. I have important news I must share with you at once."
Chuza sat down on the stool, hoping in this way to break it more
gently to the prophet and to be able to watch his reaction more
closely.

"When will your companions be here?"

"I expect Benjamin very soon."

"The problem is this. I learned yesterday that King Aretas is
planning to attack this fortress. I feel I should therefore remove
you to a place of safety."

"Could I return to the Qumran community, then?" John asked
eagerly.

"I'm afraid not. That is outside the Tetrarch's jurisdiction. We
must stay within his domain. However, I have thought of a com-
promise. He still owns a beautiful palace of his father's in Sebaste,
which he rarely visits now. So I will convey you there at once,
since I must be back at Tiberias before Antipas returns."

He saw a look of horror on John's face and was surprised at his
agitation.

"But that is a *Gentile* place! I could never live there!" John
exclaimed.

"It depends what you mean by Gentile," Chuza countered
calmly. "After all, it is the only city in the land that was built by
an Israelite, King Omri. All the others were taken from former
Gentile occupants by conquest. So what is the difference? You
can have your own disciples there to care for you, just as here.
Ah, here comes Benjamin!"

Chuza quickly repeated to the latter what he had told John,
then added, "It's a beautiful part of our country, not far from the
sea, so it has a temperate climate that will soon make you
stronger. And you will be much nearer Galilee and Jesus," he
added, thinking this would be the greatest incentive.

"But—I cannot walk," pleaded John.

"Of course not. You must go in a curtained litter. There are a
number here at the palace. We don't want anyone to recognize
you on the way. As for your disciples, perhaps they can temporarily enlist as my bodyguard, or even help carry the litter. We
must leave as soon as possible, though, after the morning meal.
Go and find your friends, Benjamin. Get them here at once."

23

A Memorable Journey

Chuza instructed the palace steward to delay ordering supplies for the feast until further word from him, but to proceed with the necessary decorating and repairs. He then went to the stables to order horses for himself and a few chief aids, donkeys for their baggage, and a litter for the sick prisoner.

Meanwhile, Benjamin hurried back to their cave, relieved to find Nathan and Jochanan still there. They hastily collected their few possessions, grumbling at the suddenness of this news. At the same time they felt a little excitement at the prospect of a change of scenery. Surely anywhere must be better for their master than this place.

At last everyone was ready. John was carefully lifted into the litter. Chuza himself was even present to see that he was made as comfortable as possible.

"I suppose you couldn't cut that beard and hair?" he asked. "You would be much less recognizable then."

"I have been a Nazarite from birth," John replied with dignity. "Not a hair of mine has ever been cut, nor will be."

"I understand. Well, at least drape this cloth across the lower half of your face, if you see anyone coming close," suggested Chuza.

John suddenly asked for one more look at his beloved Salt Sea and the distant Qumran. He had an agonizing suspicion that this might be the last time he would see them.

Fortunately it was a fine clear day, although the early rains were

207

approaching. The eight miles to the King's Highway seemed much longer to John now, being carried between two men, than when he had walked to Machaerus. Some of the grades were so steep, he had to cling to the sides of the litter to prevent himself slipping down on top of the man bearing the front poles as they were descending.

It took over two hours to reach the highway where the going was easier, and they still had several hours of daylight left. The litter carriers were replaced every half hour or so, and thus the whole party could keep going without prolonged rest periods.

There were three possible routes to Sebaste, and Chuza was still debating which to take as they turned north up the King's Highway. Two of the roads passed through Jericho, and although they were quicker, Chuza feared that since they were the most traveled, many people might recognize John or his disciples. They would also pass uncomfortably close to Julias, which the steward preferred to avoid. But would there be time for him to reach Tiberias before the Tetrarch's arrival if they went the longer way?

This last route continued farther north on the King's Highway, which had a good surface, and it would be much cooler. Later they would have to descend the Jabbok gorge, and follow it to the Jordan, where a slight turn south would bring them to the ford and the road to Shechem. From there it was an easy route to Sebaste.

While Chuza weighed these possibilities, John and the others looked around with mixed feelings. On their west rose the high scarp of the Moab mountain range, cutting them off from any further view of Judea and the Salt Sea. East of the highway, the land sloped gradually down until, over twenty miles away, it would be engulfed in the perpetual dry rocks and sand of the Arabian desert. But here beside them, wheat and barley were sprouting in cultivated fields. Farther yet were great stretches of moorland with sheep and cattle grazing, and black tents of nomadic Arab shepherds dotted the landscape.

There were occasional dips into deep gullies washed out by the rains. To forget the painful slant of his litter, John began to recall great events of his nation's history that had occurred in this area.

"Mt. Nebo must be somewhere to our west now," he said, gesturing.

"Moses must have been remarkably strong to climb up there at his great age!" Benjamin exclaimed.

With only brief stops, they traveled for five hours until they had almost reached the junction of the road that led west to Julias, the Jordan, and Jericho. Chuza ordered them to stop for the night, to the great relief of his weary servants. Jochanan, whose ankle was still not completely healed, was also thankful for the stop. Since they were in Antipas' territory, Chuza knew of a lodging place used by the Tetrarch on hunting trips where they could have privacy.

Chuza made up his mind to cross higher up the Jordan and avoid Jericho. John was deeply disappointed to hear this. He had been thinking especially of Elijah in the last hour, with Elisha accompanying him on that last journey to Bethel, Jericho, and across the Jordan. Then had come that great moment on the return journey when, as the two prophets reached the Jordan, the fiery chariot had descended, and Elijah had been caught up to heaven. His mantle had fallen on Elisha's shoulders, the latter having asked for a double portion of Elijah's spirit. A sudden, intense longing that God would take him, too, seized John. Wasn't he the Elijah who had prepared the way for Another? The Coming One had arrived, preaching, healing, and raising the dead, as had Elisha on one occasion. Clearly, his own work was done, and if he departed now he could remain undefiled! Who knew what he might encounter in a Gentile city? He couldn't bear the thought of such an existence. Oh, for the chariot of Elijah!

Morning came, and after an early start they soon arrived at the junction of the road that led to Jericho on their left. John cast a last, longing look in that direction, and even up into the sky. But there was no chariot.

For a time, the way was more mountainous, then the road wound through pleasant stretches of oak forest. Eventually the King's Highway veered northeast, leaving Perea to enter the region of the Decapolis. At this point a smaller road branched down to the Jordan Valley in a steep three thousand foot descent, but Chuza decided for John's sake not to take this short cut, but go on to the Jabbok gorge. At the top of the gorge, they spent the night.

The next morning, as they made the tortuous descent into the fairly wide, well-cultivated valley of the Jabbok, John recalled that it was here that Jacob had wrestled with an angel until break of day, then went limping on his way with the new name of Israel, full of fear at the approaching meeting with his brother Esau. Gideon, too, had come as far as this, chasing back the Midianites, and other enemies from the east.

It struck John as strange that for so long he had studied the Scriptures only thinking about the future, and the fulfilling of prophecy, yet now his thoughts were mostly in the past. It was good to be reminded of what God had done for his chosen people in this land that he had promised to Abraham and his descendants. Reuben and Gad had inherited this area, so pleasant and fertile, yet they failed to keep it because of their disobedience.

They reached the upper level of the Jordan Valley in the late afternoon. Having taken longer than expected, Chuza regretfully decided they must spend the night there and wait to ford the river in the morning. He knew of a shelter not far away, used by the Tetrarch's couriers and spies. Though this would not be big enough to house them all, he thought this better than mixing with other travelers at the regular stopping places. They had been fortunate thus far. Anyone they met concluded by his retinue that Chuza was an important official, and that the litter contained his wife or concubine. They therefore wisely refrained from trying to peer inside.

The hut was some way back from the riverside in the middle of a small clearing surrounded by the usual thicket of tamarisk, orleander, and bamboo. There was only room for ten to sleep inside, but the others could just roll up in their cloaks on the ground.

The prophet and his disciples were allowed to eat together inside, while Chuza joined his men around the campfire they had made. John therefore felt he should now share with his disciples his hope that God would take him soon, perhaps like Elijah, as they prepared to cross the Jordan.

"Nonsense," said Benjamin stubbornly. "You're just feeling weak and depressed from being sick. Now eat something. Remember tomorrow is fast day."

John was not used to having his opinions contradicted by his disciples, and this was something of a shock. However, he hadn't the energy to make an issue of it.

"We shall see," was all he said, in a slightly injured tone.

Later Chuza came in, after checking all his men and the tethering of the animals. He told John that one of the men was sick.

Because there was really no need for them all to go to Sebaste, he was sending the sick man and three others back in the morning, but with strict instructions not to mention John's whereabouts until he had been able to tell the Tetrarch himself.

Benjamin was permitted to sleep inside with John, and as the other seven men of highest rank came in with Chuza to settle for the night, John suggested they might have prayer together. A hush came over all as they listened to him raise his voice in thanksgiving to God, and then recite a psalm.

"Thank you," said Chuza, "I believe that has done us all good. Do you feel strong enough to give us some teaching as well?"

A new wave of strength swept through John at this unexpected opportunity to preach again. His voice was full of conviction as he told them of the One who had come, the Son of God, and urged them to go hear him at their first opportunity.

Chuza then added his testimony to the power of Jesus in healing his own son, and the other men asked many questions before they all finally settled down to sleep. John silently gave thanks for what he believed would be his last message to the people of God. He had been commissioned to preach in the desert, and now he was being forced to leave it against his will. Surely God would take him to himself at the Jordan!

John did not know how long he had been sleeping when he was suddenly awakened by shouts outside. Hastily Chuza and the others sprang up, with swords and daggers drawn, and felt their way outside in the darkness.

"What's the matter?" Chuza shouted.

"Lions!" came back a chorus from the men nearest the door.

There was no moon, but Chuza was gradually able to make out the figures of his men, huddled together against the hut wall.

"Someone make a light!" he ordered. "Here's a flint." It was several moments before they had enough sparks to ignite a bunch of dry grass and to light torches made from bits of pine branch.

"Is the fire out? Get it going again. We must keep it burning all night. Now tell me what happened."

It seemed that the smell of either their animals, or some leftover food, must have attracted two of the very rare lions still roaming the Jordan Valley. One of the men sleeping in the outside row had been awakened by a deep growl, and then made out the shape of the two great beasts. In terror he had yelled and

211

awakened the others, who joined in shouting to scare the lions away. This in turn had aroused their horses and donkeys, which were now making agitated noises, too.

Soon they had a roaring fire going. Chuza then ordered two men to keep watch and replenish it through the night, changing duty with others every half hour. But it was a long time before most of them got to sleep again.

"I believe it was your prayer that protected us," Chuza said to John as he entered the hut again. "We could easily have lost one of the animals, or even a man."

Everyone was tired in the morning from their disturbed night. It was cloudy, too, and although not so hot as usual, the scenery looked even less attractive. The low, ash-grey marl cliffs on the opposite side had, through the centuries, been gouged into weird shapes by the swirling winter flood waters as the river swung from one side to the other of its serpentine course.

To most of the group it was an unpleasant area. John saw it with growing nostalgia as he thought back to the triumphs he had witnessed as thousands waded out into those dark waters in response to his preaching. He especially remembered that greatest moment of all, when the Messiah himself had come for baptism.

His heart beat faster as they drew near the ford. Surely God would send his fiery chariot here and spare him the horror of going into Gentile country. His birth had been through very unusual circumstances. Surely his death might well be the same.

He watched Chuza lead the way, urging his reluctant horse to test the depth of the water. He thought the horse would not have to swim. The litter would be a more difficult problem, however, and once again John longingly scanned the sky. All was gray.

Some of Chuza's servants were busy bargaining with the ferrymen who were waiting at the ford with wooden frames of different sizes, fixed over two or four inflated goatskins. These they used to float baggage, or even the carriages of the rich, across the river, towing them with ropes over their shoulders. John's litter was placed on one, and the donkey loads on a couple of others. In half an hour the whole party was across. Those who had had to wade looked in vain for the sun to dry out their tunics.

John's spirit sank in a depth of depression as the litter was lifted off on the other side. He found himself still in it, and now in the hated Samaritan country. Slowly the party wended its way west, up the valley leading to Shechem in the steps of Abraham, and many conquerors of the land since then. But probably there had never been a more reluctant intruder than John.

At first he kept his eyes resolutely closed to avoid the sight of any abominable things and to make a desperate prayer to God, who seemed to have failed him. At last the thought came that this was indeed part of that wonderful inheritance promised to Abraham and his descendants. How divided now was the whole Promised Land, and all because of the disobedience of God's chosen people themselves! How could the Messiah ever unite the people and drive out the Romans?

He opened his eyes finally and listlessly let them wander over the lush green around him. The party was now approaching the junction with the road running south from Galilee. Suddenly, John's gaze focused on two figures walking down that road about 100 paces away. Surely there was something familiar about that walk, although the travelers were dressed in ordinary robes, not the old brown ones.

"Benjamin!" he called sharply to his friend walking beside him, "Look! Isn't that Justus?"

"It is! And Matthias! Would you believe it, here in Samaria!" And he raced off to meet them.

Chuza was up ahead of the procession, so John could not ask him to stop, especially as he knew how anxious he was to get back to Tiberias before the Tetrarch's arrival. It was a great relief, therefore, when he saw the two hurrying with Benjamin, and turning up the road to join them.

In a few minutes they had caught up and were able to walk alongside John's litter.

"How did you come to be here?" John asked after the first joyful greetings.

"The Master sent us—" Justus began, when John excitedly interrupted.

"Is he preparing to fight the holy war here? I was just thinking what a tremendous task it is going to be!"

"No, it's not that at all," said Justus with a rueful smile. "In fact, our mission is a kind of discipline for Matthias and me! I must confess I'd felt a little nagging, hurt pride that I was not one of the twelve inner circle of disciples. I thought I knew much more than those young fishermen! Then the Master decided to send seventy more disciples to towns and villages all over. When we two were assigned to come all this way to encourage the many new believers in Sychar, I thought it must be for the deliberate purpose of overcoming our background and its prejudices."

"Yes," put in Matthias, "it's so hard to think that these Samaritans could be acceptable followers of the Messiah."

"But *now,*" continued Justus, "I can see that his plan was that we should meet you! What a wonderful Lord and Master we have!"

John barely heard the last few words. "But how could there be Samaritan believers?" he asked.

"The Master came through this way once from Jerusalem. Many believed in him because of the testimony of a woman there."

"A *woman?*" John echoed blankly.

"Yes, and one who had had a very sad and sinful past, according to James. But Jesus offered her living water, springing up into everlasting life, that would satisfy her completely. She very soon recognized him as the Messiah, and went back and told the men of the town. As a result, many of them believed.

John shook his head in utter bewilderment. Matthias watched him thoughtfully.

"Did Nathan and Jochanan bring you back the Master's answer to your question?"

"They did. They told me of the healings they had seen and his final word, 'Happy is he who is not offended or turns from Me.' I fully accept now that he is the Messiah."

"Master," continued Matthias, hoping to encourage John, "that was not his final word *about* you. When your disciples had left, he turned to the crowd and asked what they went out to see in the desert. Was it a reed shaken with every wind? A man elegantly dressed and living in luxury? No, it was a prophet, and *far more than a prophet,* he said. Then he plainly told them that when Isaiah wrote 'Behold, I send my messenger ahead of you, who will prepare the road before you,' he was definitely referring to you!"

"Yes, John." It was Justus speaking now, in a deeply earnest, yet tender voice. "Then he said there was no one, born of woman, greater than John! Think of that, the very highest praise, surely!

But . . ." Justus paused, to be sure he had John's full attention, "He also added, 'yet the least important in the kingdom of God is greater than he.' Do you understand what he meant, John?"

No word would come, and John shook his head. His heart, which had swelled with joy at the first words, now had a sickening sense of bewilderment and horror. Was *he*, who had preached about it so much, to have no place in the kingdom?

"Well, it seems we've all been mistaken in our ideas of his kingdom. The Master says it is *within* us. He must rule in our hearts and control our actions. He hasn't come to make himself ruler of Israel."

"*What?*" came from a shocked Benjamin.

"Yes. Even his closest disciples cannot grasp this. I certainly don't understand it all yet, but he says he has come as a ransom for sin. This seems to fit what you said earlier, John, about his being the Lamb of God who takes away the sin of the world. Now he's beginning to tell us he will be killed soon, but no one can believe it."

"You mean he is the one Isaiah wrote of, 'He was wounded for our transgressions, bruised for our iniquities'?" John half whispered.

"It seems so, though as I said, I can't put it all together yet. James told me that early in his ministry—in fact after turning those traders out of the temple—one of the ruling Pharisees, Nicodemus, came to see him. I used to know him in the old days when I was a scribe. He's a real scholar, a meticulous keeper of the Law, and a good, honest man. Yet Jesus told him that he, and everyone, needed to be 'born again of the Spirit,' that was the only way into the kingdom of God."

"But . . . that is so different from all we've been taught."

"He also told Nicodemus that as Moses lifted up the bronze serpent to bring healing to those who looked at it, so *he* must be lifted up. Then whoever believes in him will not perish, but have eternal life."

"Yes," added Matthias, "He said God so *loved* the world, he sent his son not to condemn the world, but to save it. And another thing! Do you know, when we asked him to teach us to pray, he told us to call God 'Abba'—Father! Can you imagine anything more different from the rabbis' teaching that we mustn't even speak the name of God!"

John leaned back in his litter, all strength gone from him. His lips appeared to be forming the word "Abba," as if trying it out, but no sound came. The others continued walking beside him in silence, then Justus spoke again.

"There is another thing you should know, John. All our old ideas about ceremonial defilement are wrong."

There was a gasp of protest now from John.

"It's what is in our hearts that defiles, the Master says. In Qumran we were actually trying to earn salvation, or a place in the kingdom, with all those rules and regulations regarding outward defilements. But they never really affected our hearts. The more time I spend with the Master, the more conscious I am of sin within, which it seems *I* can never remove. But he freely offers forgiveness for our sins, I suppose because of his function as the Lamb of God. *He* provides the atonement."

"But the oath!" said John in anguished tones. "We have *sworn* to keep all those rules!"

"It was taken in honest ignorance, John. God's word is of greater weight than our words, however solemnly uttered."

"I cannot believe that an oath should ever be broken!" John covered his face with his hands in desperation. "This is all so new and strange. I must have time to consider it. How long can you stay with us?"

"As far as Shechem. Sychar is a little east of there."

"Shall we reach Shechem before the Sabbath begins?"

"I think so. But that is something else the Master is changing. All the strict rules that have been *added* to God's law can come between man and God! He has even healed on the Sabbath . . . right in the Synagogue! The leaders were furious, but Jesus pointed out they would go rescue their ass if it fell in a pit on the Sabbath, so why not heal a daughter of Abraham who had been crippled and in pain for many years?"

"A daughter of Abraham . . . you mean a *woman?*" John was again aghast.

"It seems they are just as much a part of the new kingdom, or convenant, as men," Justus replied with a smile. "Don't you remember those verses we read in the prophecy of Joel?"

John muttered an assent.

"And when one comes to think of it, God has used women in the past. Why, Deborah was a judge and leader in Israel not far from this very place. And then there was Huldah the prophetess. She brought about a great revival in Judah."

"I feel I shall always dread women and avoid them." John answered slowly. "If it hadn't been for that woman Herodias, I should not be in this bondage now. They have been the cause of all kinds of evil since the time of Eve."

"True, but many men have, too. And it is what the Master has done in the lives of women that is one of the most remarkable things about him. You remember that poor demon-possessed one, Mary of Magdala. She has been utterly transformed. She—" Justus paused, as if at a loss for words, "she . . . is beautiful now in character, in every way, and so helpful to everyone. But perhaps I should go back and talk to Nathan for a while. We must not tire you."

Chuza had told Nathan and Jochanan to keep to the back of the procession most of the time in case they were recognized as John's disciples. Though now in Samaria this was unlikely, they had not dared stay up beside John after the first hasty greetings with their friends. They were longing to hear what they had been doing and where they were going.

So the day seemed to pass very quickly as Justus and Matthias moved back and forth between John and Benjamin, and Nathan and Jochanan, sharing the things they were learning from their new Master.

John's mind remained in turmoil, but as they reached the gently sloping hills of Samaria, with their refreshing greenery of varied crops and woodland, he couldn't help noticing the great contrast with the stark Judean desert where he had spent his life. But he decided it must have been the ease of life here that had led the people to laxity, idolatry, and eventual defeat and captivity at the hands of the Assyrians.

There were so many things he wished Justus could explain more fully, and one question above all he longed to ask, yet had not dared.

Finally, Justus came alongside his litter for what John guessed was to be the last time. There was a poignant silence between them. It was Justus who broke it.

"How good it was of the Master to plan this meeting. He knows our hearts so well."

"Give him my grateful thanks. But if he knows. . . . Oh!

217

Justus, if only he had said how long I am to be a prisoner! Surely, if he can raise the dead, he could release me from Herod's power?"

At last it was out, and John felt a sense of relief, even as he waited anxiously for Justus' answer. His friend's eyes were on the road ahead as he walked a moment in silence.

"Maybe he will. Don't give up hope, John. And yet . . ." he paused, trying to find the right words, "it could be that he is entrusting you with the privilege of fellowship in the sufferings it seems certain will soon come to him."

He turned to face John as Matthias came up beside him.

"Our ways separate now, my brother. Remember the kingdom is *within*. The Lord bless you and keep us faithful in serving him."

John's face registered his anguish, and Benjamin tried desperately to think of something to encourage him. But his main emotion was anger that this Jesus, who had not yet filled John's prophecy, had apparently deserted the one who had so bravely prepared the way for him.

24

Herodias Hears Some Good News

John's thoughts were still in a state of utter confusion as Chuza's party neared the end of their journey up the beautiful valley known as Barley Vale, which stretched from Shechem to Sebaste, then on to the Great Sea.

They had traveled the eighteen miles from the Jordan to Shechem in very good time, so Chuza had decided, with great relief, that they could now do the remaining few miles to Sebaste before the beginning of the Sabbath at sunset.

They had spent no time admiring the twin mountains, Ebal and Gerizim, on either side of Shechem, where Joshua had built an altar and copied the law of Moses on stone. He had placed half the people before Ebal, and half before Gerizim and read to them the blessings and cursings of the Law. It reminded John of the Feast of the Renewal of the Covenant at Qumran, where these were read by the priests and the Levites. No doubt this was where the idea had come from!

How far away those days seemed now. And how unfamiliar were all these cultivated fields, olive groves on the hills, and sparkling streams running in the valleys! Farther west was the beautiful, long, green slope of Mt. Carmel. Again John's heart warmed at the thought of Elijah watching there for the first sign of cloud, and later offering his sacrifice and slaying the priests of Baal at its eastern end.

"Look!" exclaimed Benjamin, who was again walking beside his litter, "Carob trees! I've never seen so many! That's a good sign, I'd say."

John made no reply. They were rounding a bend in the valley, and word passed along the line that they were approaching Sebaste—his new home, or rather prison. Another glen opened into the Barley Vale now, forming a wide basin above which rose a circular, isolated hill, about three hundred feet high. It was overlooked on three sides by mountains, but commanded a wide view to the west from which any enemies approaching from the coastal plain could easily be observed. It was for this reason King Omri had built the original city here, naming it Shomeron, meaning watchtower.

The weary travelers braced themselves for the last short climb through the lower streets of the town spread below the palace area, which occupied the whole summit of the hill just as at Machaerus. Those who had not been there before were amazed at the tree-lined main street ornate with Greek columns.

A few prosperous-looking shopkeepers were beginning to bring in their wares from stands on the street and put up their shutters in preparation for the Sabbath. Most of the population of the town was a mixture of Greeks and Samaritans, to whom Herod the Great had earlier offered strong inducements to come and colonize his new city.

The palace was indeed a marvel of architecture and drew a gasp from some in Chuza's party. As they climbed the magnificent flight of steps to the outer court, they could see beyond the palace to the temple of Augustus, and farther on, the Roman forum, theater, and stadium, places of pagan worship and entertainment that made John turn away in revulsion.

A quick word from Chuza to the resident steward there soon produced two soldiers who led John's carriers, and his companions, to a small chamber in the guardhouse built in one corner of the huge courtyard. It was one of two rooms on the second floor. John was carried up on the crossed arms of the soldiers. The guards lived and slept in the room below, and could lock the door to the small staircase as required.

It was certainly an improvement on Machaerus, and from the narrow window of his room John had a wonderful panoramic view westward, with a soft breeze blowing in from the sea. As he looked out, the sun was just sinking, a glorious ball of fire between sky and sea, and he remembered it would be prayer time at Qumran. Then, with a jolt, he remembered this was where

Jezebel had lived and worshiped that sun, and built a temple for its worship in this very place.

He was brought back to the present by Jochanan, who was looking concerned.

"How are we going to live and eat here?" he asked. "Everywhere around seems to be built up, or else cultivated farmland. There are no caves I can see, except perhaps in the mountains, which are too far for us to get to you quickly. And nearly everyone is a Gentile in this city."

"Perhaps that is why Justus and Matthias were sent to meet us," said Nathan. "They told me the Messiah said it was all right to eat anything."

"There are plenty of carob trees," John said with tight lips. "They will be enough for me. I am feeling stronger now."

Benjamin and Nathan exchanged glances.

"Well, I'll go see what I can find," said Benjamin. "I think I saw some trees near the theater as we came in. Perhaps Lord Chuza will let us stay here if no one important ever comes. But what a waste! All this labor and money spent on a place that's never used."

"King Herod used it all right. It was one of his favorite places until he had Queen Mariamne executed. Later her two sons were strangled here, one of the men told me." Jochanan gave a slight shiver.

"What!" exclaimed Benjamin, still in the doorway. "Here? Maybe it was in this very building! It seems the most obvious place for it."

"Yes, and they say Mariamne can still be heard crying out for justice at night," Jochanan continued. "Then Herod used to order his servants to bring her to him."

"Oh, it was just Herod who heard her. The imagination of a guilty conscience, I suppose," Nathan added hurriedly. "But they say it's true he ordered the servants to find her. He was really mad toward the end."

"He had loved her passionately, but his sister, Salome, was very jealous. She plotted to turn the king against Mariamne by getting a steward to say she had arranged for him to be poisoned," Jochanan continued.

"We've had enough of this subject," John said firmly. "Thank God there's no sign of any woman here now." He was surprised at

221

his disciples repeating this gossip. Was this wicked place already beginning to influence even them?

Soon they heard Chuza enter the room below and talk with the guards. Then he came upstairs to check that John was all right.

"I must leave at daybreak—yes, even though it is still the Sabbath," he added, seeing their shocked faces. "It is essential that I get back before the Tetrarch arrives.

"I have left instructions for you to have proper exercise and medical attention as you need it. Also, your friends will be given employment on the premises. The other room up here is never used now, so you can stay there," he added, turning to the disciples.

"I will leave some money with you in case of any emergency," Chuza continued, handing a small leather bag to Nathan, "but the steward and guards have orders to get anything you need. If there is any serious problem come and see me at Tiberias. Pontius Pilate has allowed Antipas the use of this house of his father's, although it is no longer in his territory, since Pilate himself prefers Caesarea, but it would only be for purely private visits. But since Antipas has been away for some time, there'll be plenty to occupy him in Galilee and Perea, not to mention the threat from Aretas."

Chuza gave a satisfied smile that was largely self-congratulatory. "I'm sure we have made the best possible plan in the circumstances. So have no fear, and we trust your release will come before long. God bless and keep you."

Twenty-five miles north of the hills around Sebaste a handsome carriage, drawn by four horses, was rolling along at fine speed across the Plain of Esdraelon, on its way from the port of Caesarea to the Galilean capital of Tiberias.

Herod Antipas and his new wife, Herodias, had had a very pleasant delayed honeymoon on some Greek islands, and they were hoping all the critical talk at home would have died down. Their marriage was a fact, and mercifully people's memories were short. Besides, they had heard in Caesarea that Pontius Pilate had caused an uproar recently, having ordered his soldiers to kill some rioting Galileans right in the temple court. No love was lost between Antipas and Pilate, but he couldn't help feeling a shade of ironic gratitude toward Pilate now for transferring the people's displeasure toward himself, even if it was at the price of the blood of a few of Antipas' subjects. These Galileans were a hot-headed bunch—a little blood-letting would probably do no harm.

The only thing marring Herodias' happiness was the memory of that ugly, interfering prophet. If only she could get him permanently silenced, she would be content. He was the kind of fellow who would never change his mind, and could be neither bought nor flattered. There were few such men around. That he should attack her was an irony of fate she didn't intend to leave unchallenged. Her grandfather, Herod, had had a way of *making* things happen and changing fate. She was thankful she had inherited some of his abilities.

Their ship had made unusually good time with a favorable wind all the way, and instead of spending several days in Caesarea, as originally planned, they had decided it would be wisest to avoid meeting Pilate, or Herodias' former husband, Herod Philip, who resided there. Accordingly, they were in Tiberias two days earlier than expected.

Their arrival caused some consternation on the part of the palace staff, but Antipas chose to ignore the lack of the usual preparations. Sometimes it was good to take people by surprise.

He was irritated, however, to find Chuza, his chief steward, was not around.

"He knew I was returning here. What is he doing? Where is his wife?" he asked the steward.

"He went to Machaerus, to make preparations for your Excellency's anniversary celebrations, but has been gone longer than usual. His wife is at their home near Capernaum. Shall we send a message there?"

"Tomorrow, if he hasn't shown up."

Herodias was relaxing in the hot spring baths after the long journey, when her bathmaid came to announce that Naomi, a woman from the village, had come with a message for her from Julias.

This woman was one of Herodias' network of secret spies, and since she couldn't think of anything she was expecting to hear from Julias, Herodias' curiosity was immediately aroused. Accordingly, she ordered her wraps to be brought and was soon ready to receive her visitor.

"One of the men who went with Lord Chuza to Machaerus to begin preparations for the Tetrarch's anniversary celebrations just got back to Julias," the spy told her. "He reports there are rumors

King Aretas may be making preparations to attack Machaerus, and that Chuza is taking the prisoner, John the Baptizer, to the citadel at Sebaste."

"Where is Chuza now?"

"Probably on his way from Sebaste. He was in a great hurry, wanting to be back here before the Tetrarch's arrival. He asked that no one should mention his journey in Julias. I thought perhaps you should know as soon as possible."

"Quite right. Thank you. There will be an extra bonus for you in the morning."

Herodias dressed in one of her most becoming gowns, her tiredness from the journey forgotten. She was very particular about the way her maid put on her make-up and perfume. She must make their first dinner together at home as enjoyable as possible for Antipas.

She decided to try out the new fashion, current in Rome, of many gold "teardrops" dangling from her hair, which produced a fascinating shimmery effect as the head moved.

At dinner, after Antipas had drunk his third glass of wine, she decided to broach the subject that had filled her thoughts since she first heard her agent's message.

"You know, Dearest," she began, "I've been thinking about your big anniversary celebration. One of my maids heard a rumor that Aretas is making preparations to revenge his daughter's displacement."

"What's that?" asked Antipas, suddenly alert.

"It's just a rumor my maid heard. There may be nothing to it. Aretas wouldn't stand a chance against your forces, of course. It's more likely to be some trick while you are distracted by the celebration at Machaerus. I was just thinking, this celebration will be the first I attend as your wife . . . and Machaerus is such a stark, drab sort of place, so difficult to get to by carriage. It also has so many associations of . . . that woman." Herodias had always refused to refer to Aretas' daughter as Antipas' wife.

"So I was wondering," she continued, turning her most dazzling smile on her husband, and causing the gold teardrops to shimmer, "Why couldn't we have the celebration at the Sebaste palace this year?"

"Sebaste? But that isn't even in my jurisdiction now. Pontius Pilate wouldn't be very happy to hear of me celebrating the anniversary of my succession in his teritory! He'd think I had designs on it."

"Well, it certainly *should* be yours, as it was your father's," Herodias said petulantly. "And considering how good your relations are with the emperor, he might yet return it to you, if we act wisely. Your record for governing is much better than Pilate's! You have done a wonderful job at preserving peace all these years, while he is constantly upsetting the Jews."

Antipas was obviously mellowing under what he felt was well-deserved praise.

"But I have another suggestion." Herodias' quick mind had rallied and her voice resumed its silky tone. "Suppose instead of celebrating your accession, we say it is to celebrate your birthday. That is nearly the same time and few would know the difference. It would be a private affair, and Pilate could hardly object, especially as your mother is still in the area."

"That's true," conceded Antipas. His mother, Maltrace, was a Samaritan, and he had actually been born in Sebaste. But he preferred not to mention his Samaritan ancestry. He was a little surprised that Herodias should want to go to Sebaste, too, considering her own father and uncle had been strangled there, and her former husband lived not far away.

"Sebaste will be far better for getting supplies," Herodias was continuing. "We can get all kinds of foreign products from Caesarea, so much better than Machaerus. And I have another idea!" she said, her face lighting up. "Why not let me do all the planning for this celebration as a special first birthday present to you! I picked up some wonderful new ideas for entertaining in Greece. What do you say to that, my dearest?"

Antipas was duly flattered and put out his arm across their dining couch to draw her to him for a passionate kiss.

"If you wish it, so it shall be. I leave all the arrangements to you, my dear. But I must give you the list of essential guests. And use Chuza for anything you wish. I'll tell him he must cancel the arrangements at Machaerus. I can't think why the man isn't here. But of course, we did get back two days early."

At midmorning next day, Chuza rode his sweating horse through the gates of Tiberias. In a few moments he saw with horror that the Tetrarch's standard was flying from the palace, indicating he was in residence. What could have happened?

He hurried to his quarters, changed into fresh clothing, then immediately sought an audience with the Tetrarch.

"Well, where have you been?" Antipas greeted him testily. "We have a lot of business to see to after such a long absence."

"Your Excellency, I am very sorry, but let me explain what happened. I went to Machaerus to make the necessary arrangements for your anniversary celebration, as you ordered. When the business was almost completed, one of your spies came in with news that Aretas is preparing to attack. Machaerus and your celebration seemed the obvious target, so I thought perhaps it would be better to have the banquet here, or at Julias."

"I have already heard about the rumor and decided to change the place. I had thought of Julias, too, being in Jewish territory, and not far from our friends in Jerusalem. But Lady Herodias has asked if it might be at my father's former palace in Sebaste."

"Sebaste!" Antipas was a little surprised at the shock registered in Chuza's voice.

"Yes, I know it might not exactly please Pontius Pilate, but she's calling it my birthday party, a more private-sounding affair. And she wants to do all the planning herself, as a special present to me. She's a smart woman, Chuza. Put yourself at her service in any way she may require."

Chuza's face was so ashen now that even Antipas noticed it.

"What's the matter? Are you sick?"

"No, Sire, the truth is when I heard of the danger of Aretas attacking Machaerus, I thought it was unsafe to leave the prisoner, John the Baptizer, there. So I moved him to Sebaste, thinking he would be safely out of the way!"

Antiplas let out a groan. "You should have discussed it with me first. That prophet! He's always causing me problems! I wish I could release him and make him promise to be silent. But you can't bribe or threaten his type. The only thing is to keep him locked up for the present. Herodias can't know he is there, so we'll just have to keep quiet about it. She still seems determined to have him silenced for good." The Tetrarch added with a half-mocking smile. "You've got us into this difficulty, Chuza. You'll have to find the solution."

226

25

Strange Happenings at Sebaste

Chuza's organizing skill seemed to have deserted him. He went back to his quarters, his head spinning and a sickening sensation in the pit of his stomach.

Why had his plan miscarried? But who could have foreseen this strange turn of events? The more he thought about it, the more he began to wonder if Herodias could possibly have heard that John was at Sebaste. Yet he could not guess how she would have learned of it. He knew he could not trust all the men who had been with him at Machaerus, but he had carefully inquired at the palace gate whether there had been any messengers from Julias in the last few days, and the answer had been negative.

He must protect John. But how? Finally, by noon his ingenuity had reasserted itself. Who better to outwit a woman than another woman! He must talk to his wife, Joanna, about this. She would normally return to their apartment here after hearing he was back, but he had the feeling sometimes that the walls of the palace had ears. With the Tetrarch's permission, he would go home to Capernaum tonight. After all, he had been away from his wife for nearly three weeks. Antipas was a man who would appreciate that, although he might jokingly suggest a few substitutes nearer at hand. Chuza at one time would have fully appreciated the humor, but since he had heard John the Baptizer and later met this Jesus of Nazareth, such remarks had become distasteful.

He pulled himself together and worked hard the rest of the day checking over things with the steward at Tiberias and had another session with Antipas on the needs of Machaerus. Finally he made his request, which the Tetrarch granted, but added he should be back in time to begin work on the invitations for his birthday party without delay.

It would be late by the time he got to Capernaum, but it was a pleasant ride along the shore of the Lake of Gennesaret. He could see a number of fishing boats moving off to spend the night on the water and occasionally he heard the fishermen calling across to one another.

Before long he was passing through the beautiful village of Magdala. From there it was only another four miles to his small estate.

His wife was surprised, but delighted to see him. Their life together had improved immeasurably since their encounter with Jesus of Nazareth. She was finding she had more understanding and sympathy for her husband's difficult and highly responsible job in Herod Antipas' service. She also felt that for the first time love was beginning to develop in her heart for him.

Their's had been an arranged marriage, of course. Her husband was ambitious and Antipas was a demanding master, so she really had seen very little of Chuza. She had been thankful for the birth of a son and had idolized him as a child, but once the time for his serious education began he was removed from her care. He had just been home on a visit when they had gone, merely as a matter of curiosity, to hear John the Baptizer. It had been quite a shock when the boy said he wished to enter the water. Soon after, he had suddenly become very sick, and she had been inclined to blame it on something he had picked up in the dirty Jordan waters. But when Chuza had gone to Jesus and the boy had been miraculously healed, she had wholeheartedly put her faith in this One whom she now believed was the Messiah. During these weeks while her husband was away, she had been several times to hear him speak when he came to Capernaum.

Joanna was slightly on the plump side, but carried herself with quiet dignity. She had a pleasant smile, which she now beamed on Chuza as she greeted him. Then, to his amazement, instead of awakening one of the servants, as she would normally have done, she herself got water and a towel to wash his feet.

"Joanna!" he exclaimed, "What are you doing?"

"I have become a real disciple of the Master, now," she said with another smile. "Somehow you begin to view everything differently after knowing him."

"I understand," he said with sudden tenderness. "I've been spending some time with John the Baptizer and his disciples. They are different, all right. But I have so much to learn. And so much will be impossible to practice while I'm with Antipas. But we must try to be on our own a little more from now on. How is the boy?"

"Fine. He went back three days after you left. The father of one of his friends was going to Jerusalem, and he went with them. He was perfectly fit again, thanks to this wonderful Messiah."

As Joanna gently dried Chuza's feet, he felt a warm sense of relaxation that was not confined to his feet. He suddenly realized how tired he was after all the travel and activity of the last week, as well as the mental strain. He longed to lie down at once and leave his problem until the morning, but prudently decided it was better to share it with Joanna tonight.

"Joanna," he said at last, "I really came home because I have a big problem to solve, and I think you may be able to help me."

Joanna stared at him in surprise. This was the first time Chuza had ever asked for her help. What sort of problem could it be?

"As you know, John the Baptizer was a prisoner at Machaerus, but I was afraid that when Herodias went there for the anniversary celebration she might again try to persuade her husband to kill him. I dared not let him escape, but I heard a rumor that King Aretas is planning to attack Machaerus. So I thought that was a good excuse to remove John to the citadel at Sebaste. Antipas hasn't been there for several years, so I thought that was absolutely safe."

"Of course," murmured Joanna in assent.

"I planned to be the first to tell the Tetrarch, but when I got back to Tiberias I found them already there. They had heard the rumor about Aretas and Herodias had already persuaded Antipas to have the celebration at Sebaste, calling it a 'birthday party.' And Herodias has asked to do all the planning for it. Can you imagine that! Antipas says she had seen a lot of ideas for entertaining in Rome and Greece. But I am wondering if Herodias could have heard about John being at Sebaste. It would have seemed so much more reasonable to have the celebration at Tiberias or Julias. What do you think?"

Joanna was silent a moment. "Yes," she said slowly, "I think she probably did. That's where her father was strangled, remember. I know she never forgets that. She would never *choose* to go there."

"So, we've got to warn John of their coming, so that he and his disciples will at least keep out of sight. He was sick, too, by the way. They seemed to think there's nothing he'll eat except carob beans."

"That's just riduculous," said Joanna firmly. "Where did he get such a notion?"

"I'm not sure. He's been a Nazarite from birth, but that would only keep him from drinking wine. He used to be in that Qumran community though, and they do some odd things."

"But Jesus doesn't teach anything like that," Joanna persisted. "Anyway, we must pray about it, sleep on it, and trust God to guide us in the morning. I'm so glad you are home, Chuza." She gave his arm a little squeeze as they walked through the hall and prepared to retire.

In the morning Joanna had thought of a plan.

"You know our serving girl, Ruth, and her young deaf-mute brother we bought a few years ago when their uncle couldn't support them? She's turning out to be an excellent worker. She's been helping in the kitchen recently and he in our fields. He does good work, but the others ridicule him because he cannot speak. It makes him so frustrated and angry."

Chuza stared at her, wondering how this had anything to do with the problem of John.

"Ruth has also accompanied me to listen to the Master," Joanna continued, "and she has become a real believer. Now she is asking if she could take her brother to him to be healed."

Chuza still looked puzzled, and was also beginning to get impatient. "But what has that—"

"Jesus is now in the Nazareth or Nain area," Joanna hastened on, "so let us send them there to see if Gad can be healed. It's not far to Sebaste from there. They could take a letter from you without Herodias knowing anything about it. Her spy network will keep a close watch on anything going to Sebaste from now on, but they wouldn't suspect slaves. Why don't we have Ruth and Gad stay in Sebaste to help John and his disciples? She'll make them some good, nourishing food. I suppose you will have to go a few days before the banquet to see everything is in order?"

"I don't know. Antipas was most emphatic that Herodias wanted to be in charge of everything. But who knows if she really understands all that is involved!"

"She's been around in Rome and Greece. And she inherited some of her grandfather's traits. But she may not realize how much staff it requires."

"We'll just have to wait and see. But you find out all you can from the other women at the palace. I'll write the letter to John while you explain everything to Ruth. We must return to Tiberias as soon as possible."

Jochanan and Benjamin climbed the stairs to John's room with a load of carob beans they had just gathered, but without the honey they had hoped to find. They sat down wearily on the stone floor.

"This is a strange place," muttered Jochanan. "It's so beautiful in one way, the scenery, the architecture, and yet there's this feeling of haunting evil. One of the men showed us the place where Ahab's blood was washed from his chariot. It was all just as Elijah prophesied. And Jezebel slew all the prophets of the Lord here, too."

"With all that, and Herod's murders here, no wonder we feel their blood crying out for revenge," said Benjamin. "I shall be glad to get away from here. Even the bees don't seem to care for it. Food is a real problem."

There was a moment's silence, then Nathan cleared his throat. "Don't you remember what Justus told us? Jesus said any food was clean and we shouldn't fast while the Bridegroom is here?"

There was a stunned silence, so Nathan continued. "I remember them telling us at Qumran that it was to mortify our bodies, turn away God's wrath, and lessen his punishments. In a way we were trying to *earn* our salvation. But Justus said God in mercy is providing the propitiation for sin in his Son. If so, then I think it is wrong for us to continue like this."

Again there was silence, and everyone looked at John.

"You are all free to do as you wish," he answered coldly.

"But how are we to get anything else? The food shops are owned by filthy Samaritans, and most of the staff here are Gentiles. And in any case we have nowhere to cook," protested Benjamin, who was really feeling discouraged and still thought in terms of Jewish purity.

"Remember God provided for Elijah, and he will for us," John said with a touch of his old authority.

"Well, I haven't seen any ravens around, and certainly no widow here," Benjamin retorted. It was all very well for those who didn't do the searching to talk so airily.

Just then they heard footsteps on the stairs and a strange sound that sent a sudden wave of apprehension through each of them. It was unmistakably the voice of a woman!

In a moment there was a knock at the door. Each man looked for a place to hide, but there was none in that bare little room.

The knock came again, and their eyes were fixed on the latch, which slowly began to lift. Benjamin scrambled to his feet and rushed to the door, ready to bar the entrance of whoever the intruder might be.

He opened it a few inches, then stepped back a pace in surprise and confusion. A young man stood there in the garb of a peasant farmer, holding a large water pitcher. Beside him was a female figure wearing a short veil, carrying a tray with four steaming bowls and a basket of bread rolls.

"Peace to you," they both said, and the woman continued, "I bring you a letter from my Lord Chuza. But you are not to open it until you have eaten this."

"But—but we don't eat that kind of food," protested Benjamin bluntly. "Go away! This is no place for women."

"We are Lord Chuza's slaves. You have nothing to fear from us, Sirs." Was there a hint of a smile as she said it. Benjamin wondered afterward. "But Lord Chuza was most emphatic that you eat well before reading this letter. This is just lamb stew, made from a lamb without blemish, and the bread is from his own kitchen. Please eat now, and I will return later for the tray. My name is Ruth, and this is Gad. He has water here to purify your hands."

She held out the tray, and Benjamin found himself taking it. Then she turned and quietly closed the door behind her.

Nathan began laughing. "Well, God has indeed provided, as you said yourself, John. Praise his name!"

"And she doesn't look to be a widow," muttered Benjamin under his breath.

Again they all looked at John, awaiting his response. His eyes were closed, his face almost contorted, and his breath coming in deep gasps as if his whole body was convulsed. The others were alarmed, wondering what to do.

At last he opened his eyes, and a growing calmness came over him.

"I have never fought so great a battle, I believe, but I cannot doubt now that this is the Lord's doing. Let us give thanks for his mercy."

He then poured out his heart in a way they had not heard since the busy days beside the Jordan, and for the first time he used the term *Abba*.

His disciples each prayed from a full heart, too, then self-consciously took up their bowls and bread rolls. John nearly choked on his first mouthful, but persevered. Finally the bowls were empty. It was the most satisfying sensation, and they looked at each other with sheepish grins.

"The Lord is my shepherd . . . . You prepare a table before me in the presence of my enemies," quoted Nathan.

So great had been their trauma over the food, they had forgotten about the letter, until Benjamin collected the bowls and saw it on the tray.

John broke the seal, and began to read.

Chuza, to our friend and master, John, Greetings.
On my return to Tiberias I was shocked to find the Tetrarch already back. He and Lady Herodias had already heard the rumor about Aretas and plan to hold the banquet at Sebaste, rather than Machaerus. I never imagined such a thing happening and am deeply sorry for the renewed danger in which you are placed. All I can advise is for you to keep out of sight entirely when they arrive. The rooms you occupy are those in which Herodias' father was murdered, so I do not think she will venture there.
I am greatly concerned about your health. I am sending two of my personal servants to care for you, so that none of you need be seen in the courtyards when the Tetrarch and his wife arrive. I do not think she is aware of your presence and Antipas will not mention it to her.
Take good care of yourselves for the Lord's sake. His grace be with you all. Chuza.

"So she is following us here after all. I wonder if she really does know," said Jochanan, to break the painful silence that followed the reading of the letter.

"We must assume not, at least, and act accordingly," said Nathan. "Lord Chuza has been amazingly kind."

"It is because he has met with the Messiah and has entered the

kingdom . . . or the kingdom has entered him, as Justus told us."
There was a new exaltation in John's voice. "We are in God's
hands. Nothing can touch us that he does not allow."

Again there came a knock at the door, and Benjamin jumped
guiltily. He had meant to place the tray outside the door in order
to avoid a second encounter. He hastily picked it up now and
thrust it in the opening as he unlatched the door. But Ruth called
through, "Was it satisfactory, Gentlemen?"

"Thank you, it was very good," answered Nathan, as no one
else seemed ready to speak.

"I will be here in the morning with breakfast. Sleep well, Sirs."

"Well, I'll be. . . ." Benjamin stopped for loss of the right
word. He did not know what to do, whether to offer to fetch the
food, to relieve the others of the embarrassment of a female presence, or whether it would look as if he was wanting to see more of
her. He decided it would be wiser to keep quiet.

By that time it was too dark to read a scroll, but they each
thought of a verse of encouragement or praise to share with the
others. Then, for the first time in that place, they sang some
psalms before settling down to sleep. The guards below wondered
what was going on and were just about to shout to them to stop
when the singing ceased.

True to her word, Ruth appeared at midmorning with her tray
loaded with citrus fruit, dried figs, and bread and cheese, while
Gad had the water pitcher and one of milk. The other three men
could hardly believe their eyes as Benjamin turned around with
the tray and set it down.

"Our raven can carry quite a load," remarked Nathan with a
quizzical smile. "I think we are doing better than Elijah!"

From then on, without any discusson of the matter, it became
customary for them to refer to Ruth among themselves as "the
Raven." It seemed to come easier to them than uttering a femi-
nine name.

No sooner had they finished their meal than she appeared
again to collect the tray. They then took some exercise while they
could, before the coming of the Tetrarch's party. Even John was
feeling strong enough that, with help, he managed to get down-
stairs and outside.

When they returned, the two rooms had obviously been swept.
Even the night jar, which stood in the little hallway between the

two rooms, had been emptied. In the two-foot-wide window sill in each room stood a small clay vessel filled with flowers.

"Well!" was all Benjamin could think of saying on sight of them.

"This is beginning to seem more like a palace than a prison," laughed Nathan.

Jochanan watched to see if their leader would regard the flowers as frivolous.

John said nothing, but did manage a smile.

When Ruth came to collect their tray after the evening meal, she was alone. She stood for a moment, twisting her fingers, quite unlike the assured way she usually went about her duties.

"Master," she said hesitantly, looking in John's direction through her veil, "I have a request. Gad and I went to the Messiah on our way here from Capernaum, and he healed Gad, who had been deaf and dumb since an illness when he was a little boy. We could not stay long, and Gad has never been able to hear the good news of the Messiah before, nor learn to read and memorize Scripture. If—if you have time in the afternoons, when he has little work to do, would you be so kind as to teach him?"

John's heart was deeply moved at this request. "Very willingly," he said. "Tell him to come whenever he can."

"And perhaps we could gather some of the others. Would you preach to them?"

"Well, why not?" John's eyes were glowing.

"I will invite them for after the evening meal tomorrow," said Ruth joyfully. Then she picked up the tray and departed.

26

Light in the Darkness

Herodias lost no time in sending for the only child of her previous marriage, her sixteen-year-old daughter, Salome. She had been to stay with relatives in Damascus while her mother and Antipas were away, partly to learn some of the social graces in high society there.

Herodias shrewdly guessed that one of the main reasons Antipas had finally agreed to divorce his first wife before marrying her, was that the former was childless. Herodias herself was obviously not barren, and probably Antipas still hoped he might have an heir. By now, however, she suspected Antipas was the sterile one, as were so many of Herod the Great's descendants. Herodias was therefore beginning to entertain hopes of the Tetrarch officially adopting Salome as his daughter and heir.

To this end, she decided that the banquet would be an excellent opportunity for Salome to honor him as her father on his birthday. She would really touch his heart, which had never known the joy of children of his own.

She was pleased with what she saw when Salome finally arrived. She was now definitely a young lady, yet the handsome features of the Herodians were still not too firmly molded on her sweet, girlish face, and her grace of movement was a delight to any eye.

"Show me the dances you have learned," her mother invited in the privacy of her boudoir the day after Salome's return.

After a moment's modest reluctance, Salome complied.

236

"Beautiful! Beautiful!" her mother commented enthusiastically when the performance was over. "I hope you have brought the appropriate costumes to wear?"

"I think so. They have such lovely things in Damascus, it was hard to choose. But when will I ever have the opportunity to use them all?" she added with a sigh.

"Sooner than you think." Her mother gave her a smile that kindled her curiosity at once.

"What do you mean?"

"In just over two weeks time your stepfather is to celebrate his birthday. I believe there is nothing he would appreciate more than for you to honor him on his birthday in a special way. I know it isn't customary for someone in our position to do any of the entertaining at such a banquet, but because you are still young, and because it is such a special occasion in the *family*, I think it will make all the more impact."

"Oh! I'd be much too nervous!" squealed Salome with girlish embarrassment.

"Nonsense! There's no need to be, when you dance so divinely! Besides, my brother Philip is coming, and it will be just as well to attract him. He has already expressed an interest in you, and it would be a most advantageous alliance. You or your son might well end up with the whole kingdom, like your great grandfather, if we plan our strategy well."

Special messengers had gone throughout Galilee and Perea, as well as to Paneas, Trachonitis, Batania, Gaulitis, Caesarea, Jericho, and Jerusalem, carrying the ornate invitations, almost all of which had been accepted. Herodias was busy with her lists of menus, decoration schemes, and the various groups of entertainers who were an essential part of such a banquet.

As her chief assistant she had called in the steward of the Tiberias palace, saying Chuza's time would be fully occupied between Antipas' business there and at Julias. So he was largely in the dark about all the arrangements.

In spite of the tiring journey, and all the extra work involved, excitement over the forthcoming festivities mounted daily, and the servants who were to be left behind in Tiberias were openly envious of those who were to go and help at Sebaste. Daily now they waited eagerly to hear the date the advance party was to leave.

The week before the invasion of Herod's retinue from Tiberias was one that most of the servants at Sebaste would never forget. There was a strange spirit of peace and wholesomeness such as had never before been experienced in that place which had witnessed sin and tragedy of every description.

The whole staff, including Ruth and Gad, were very busy during most of the daylight hours cleaning up the palace and grounds. But once the late afternoon meal was over, Ruth went around inviting everyone to come to the main courtyard and listen to the prophet. As an added inducement, she told them of Gad's miraculous healing. A few said they were too tired, but most came at first out of curiosity, then continued because of the magnetic power of the prophet.

Among the guards, too, all who were not on duty felt they might as well while away an hour or two of darkness before retiring. Ruth and Gad prepared flaming torches for John's disciples to hold, and various others brought some along.

"What a picture of good triumphing over evil, light over darkness," Nathan whispered to Jochanan.

"Yes, I wonder why we never thought of doing this at Machaerus," he answered.

Gad came for his private lessons, too. After the first three days of utter bewilderment, he began to grasp a few ideas and to practice forming the written letters. Then one day his eyes opened wide with excitement as all the latent possibilities in his new knowledge burst upon him.

John and his disciples were thankful to have this new outlet for their energies, and they made the most of it, and also the opportunities for exercise. With their new diet came new strength, once they became used to it.

The almost idyllic week continued on through the Sabbath, which at John's insistence was kept as a real rest day. Then came the news that the Lady Herodias and her helpers would be there in three days. To most of the staff this was a cause of great excitement, for they had never seen her; but to John and his disciples the news cast a dark shadow over their pleasant new routine.

The last day before Herodias' arrival came and John delivered a final message to the gathering in the courtyard.

He presented Jesus of Nazareth to them as the Lamb of God who takes away sin, and he besought them all to repent while they still had time. He suggested, too, that they should go and hear the Messiah whenever they had the opportunity, or even go and visit the other believers he had heard were in Sychar.

"This may be my last opportunity to address you. I must decrease but He will increase. He is God's Son, worthy of all your devotion and service. He will baptize with the Holy Spirit and fire."

But when is he going to start, Benjamin thought impatiently, *and why does John keep mentioning it, when there is no sign of it ever happening?*

With great reluctance, it seemed, the group began to disperse, and as the last torch was extinguished, all was dark again. But a new, eternal light had begun to illuminate the hearts of a number of the listeners.

Late the next afternoon, just as they had finished their meal, which Ruth had brought earlier than usual, guards reported the approach of a carriage, several litters, and a long line of attendants, slowly advancing along the valley.

John and his disciples went down and cautiously peered over the eastern parapet. They then drew a few deep breaths of fresh air and reluctantly mounted to their little tower again. There they had a long time of prayer and encouraged one another with the Scriptures. Finally, when the noise had at last died down at the other end of the courtyard and no one had approached them, they lay down to sleep.

The next morning, there was a worried look on Gad's face as he and Ruth arrived with their breakfast.

"Lady Herodias knows you are here, Master. That was one of the first things she inquired about," Ruth said in an anxious voice. "She has also asked the steward for a complete list of all the rooms in the place. She says they will all be needed when the Tetrarch comes with his attendants."

"Then—where do we go?" blurted out Benjamin.

"The master must go to the—the dungeon." Tears began to flow down Ruth's cheeks, and unthinkingly she flung aside her short veil to wipe them away with her hand. Any other time the men would have been shocked and embarrassed, but today their minds were taken up with the news they had just heard. Only Benjamin noted the round, healthy-looking face and the big, dark eyes, now wet with tears.

"If you wish, you may remain in the dungeon, too," she said,

looking at Benjamin, "but it's very small. I think I can still prepare your food. The others will have to go into the town. Gad has
found a lodging not far away and will take you there. But stay
another night. Eat all you can, and keep up your strength." With
that they left.

The news had completely taken away their appetites, but after
the prayer they mechanically began to eat. No one thought to
question what their Raven had said. They had never had any
conversation with her, except on practical matters. They had
never asked her background, or how she had become a believer.
They had just assumed she was Gad's wife and accepted her as a
fact of life that God had ordered in their path.

The day dragged by, their tension mounting with inactivity
and the thought of the unknown future. Gad did not appear for
his lesson. It was now almost dark, and still they had received no
supper.

"Do you think our Raven has flown away?" Nathan finally
asked disconsolately.

"Had its wings clipped, more likely," answered Benjamin with
a touch of anxiety.

At last came the familiar knock at the door.

"We thought it safer to wait until darkness," Ruth began by
way of explanation. Then she pushed Gad ahead of her into the
room and shut the door.

"We have a plan," she said in almost a whisper. "I can't bear
the thought of the Master in that dungeon. So we are going to
help you to escape. Gad has a rope here, tied under his gown.
This window is wide enough for you to get through and lower
yourself outside the wall. Gad has been out to check. There is no
window under it in the guards' room, so they will not see you, or
hear you, if you wait until they are asleep. I will bring up your
breakfast as usual in the morning, so the guards will not suspect
anything until some time later. By then you can be miles away."

The four men were looking at her in amazement.

"But don't you realize what this will mean?" asked Nathan.
"You will both be tortured cruelly when it is discovered. You are
the first they will suspect, under the circumstances."

"I know," she answered quietly. "But you are the Lord's special
servants. No harm must come to you."

For the first time John was really looking at her, as if he had
never seen her before.

240

"Thank you," he said. "We thank you with all our hearts, but we cannot bring all this trouble on you. Lord Chuza would also suffer if we escaped. We are in the hands of the Almighty. Perhaps he is giving me another opportunity to speak to Antipas and warn him of his wickedness. I will stay here."

As Ruth saw the steadfast look in those deep-set eyes she knew it was useless to say more. Her tears began to flow again. As Gad stood awkwardly by, Benjamin found himself thinking fiercely that if he were her husband, he would be putting his arm round to comfort her. But almost instantly she pulled herself together, brushed the tears away and said, "The Lord's will be done. May he bless you and keep you."

As the door closed behind them the four men stared at one another.

"It's—it's unbelievable!" muttered John.

"Isn't this like what Justus told us?" Nathan said.

"I always suspected we might be mistaken about women," grunted Benjamin. "We'd better at least show our appreciation and eat what she brought."

The next morning after their meal, Gad came to escort Nathan and Jochanan to their new living quarters. After a last prayer together, they all went down the stairs, and the others watched as John, followed by Benjamin, was escorted away to the dungeon by two guards.

"We'll see you again soon," called Jochanan, trying to appear cheerful.

John merely turned with a smile on his face and waved farewell.

The dungeon was another deep, dark, and foul-smelling pit reached by a long, narrow stairway. As they descended, Benjamin said, "What a stench! How dare they treat you, the messenger of God, like this! And why isn't this Messiah doing something to win your release?"

"Hush, Benjamin," John replied. "Remember the message he sent. 'Blessed is he who is not offended in me'—whatever happens. *I am determined never to harbor any doubts about him again.*"

27

The Banquet

"This banquet hall has never looked so beautiful!" the steward's assistant exclaimed as he went in to check that the huge fireplace was burning to perfection to take the chill off the late evening air.

"Yes," the steward agreed. He signaled to the slaves to light the remaining lamps in the glittering chandeliers and numerous sconces around the walls. "The Lady Herodias certainly has a flair for decorating. Where her grandfather built great temples, palaces, and cities, she has to be content with smaller projects. But there's no doubt she has inherited his ability."

Over one hundred guests were expected. The new style of formal dining introduced in Rome was now common practice among the upper classes throughout the empire. For this, a triclinium, a special couch to hold three reclining persons, was placed on three sides of a square table, leaving one side free for serving. Fifteen of these tables were required for tonight's banquet, and the steward had had to order three extra tables, and nine triclinia from Caesarea.

He cast an eye over each table to make sure a knife, spoon, napkin, and toothpicks were set in each place; then gave word for the kitchen staff to be ready to serve the appetizers.

The usher now appeared at the great, ornate doors to the banquet hall, and the host and hostess entered. Antipas looked regal and almost handsome, while Herodias was magnificent in a blue velvet robe that offset her sparkling jewels to perfection. The usher announced each guest to them, and then had them escorted to their places, carefully assigned according to rank.

THE BANQUET

All the principal officers of Galilee and Perea were there, both military and civil. Others were leaders in the cities of the Decapolis. Those guests who were Jewish had learned to overlook some of their orthodox scruples when on official business. Many were Gentiles, a few Roman, but the majority Greek or Phoenician. Only about half had brought their wives.

All were seated at last, and while the first libation was drunk, spotlessly-clad kitchen staff hurried in with the delicious-looking appetizers. There were small, hot sausages on silver trays, sliced eggs, thrushes rolled in honey and poppy seeds, snails on lettuce leaves, goose liver cut in artistic shapes, oysters, olives, beets, and grilled damsons.

A honey wine was served next, while music was played on flutes, zithers, tambourines, and a harp. Then the main courses appeared: succulent lobster garnished with asparagus, mullet, chicken, duckling, as well as beef and lamb. Guests ate with their fingers, from a napkin spread on the couch, while servants hovered around with pitchers of perfumed water to pour over their hands when required, afterward drying them with a towel carried over their arm. Other servants were constantly filling the wine cups. The last meat dish was a whole roast boar, which was greeted with applause. By this time, in spite of the musical interludes, and even riddles being asked between the servings, many guests had to avail themselves of the small room always adjacent to a banquet hall, where, according to custom, they could empty their stomachs in order to continue eating.

Chuza and Joanna sat not far from the door and were finding themselves more and more disgusted at this ostentatious display, which was far greater than anything put on in former days. Perhaps it was partly that their tastes had changed, too.

Before the dessert, Herodias motioned to a servant, then whispered to her husband. He pulled the mysterious-looking cord the steward placed in his hand, and to the astonishment of all, an enormous hoop came down from the ceiling, filled with flowery chaplets and small bottles of perfume. There was one special wreath in honor of Antipas, and Herodias herself placed this on him with a loving look, while slaves delivered the other gifts among the most important guests. This had been one of the many ideas Herodias had picked up on her travels and she was greatly elated at its success.

Last came the dessert, heaping plates of varied fruits, some brought from Africa. Apples were considered a great delicacy, and in addition there were pears, melons, citrus fruits, grapes, figs, and dates.

Now Herodias rose majestically from her place to signal the ladies to follow her to her private suite. Some of the more scrupulous and conservative Jewish men withdrew, also.

The rest could now begin the rite of *commisatio,* a kind of ceremonial drinking match that formed the popular conclusion to banquets in many countries. The rules according to Roman custom were very precise. One man was chosen master of ceremony, and he prescribed the proportion of water to wine for each round, and the amount in each glass varied according to the number of letters in the name of the one to be toasted. Each cup must be emptied at one draught. Manaen's name was one put forward as MC, and he was most thankful the dice he threw showed an unsuccessful number.

Entertainers such as dancers, mimers, jesters, singers, performing animals or whatever was available, were supposed to intersperse the rounds of drink. Herodias herself had hired these and had carefully arranged the order of their appearance so that Salome's act would shine by comparison, and come before the spectators were too befuddled to appreciate anything.

First came a group of local peasant girl dancers of not very high standard, but with plenty of giggles and bounce. Next were some performing apes from Caesarea with amusing antics and then some human acrobats. These each withdrew after some desultory applause. Another round of drinking followed.

Suddenly, from a curtained section at the rear of the room some new music sounded, though the players were not visible. Then through the doorway ran a radiant Salome in a pale yellow, Grecian style gown. Many of the guests had no idea who she was as she tripped up to Antipas' table, where she made a deep curtsy.

"Dear Father," she said, in a clear, girlish voice, "I would like to honor you in a special way on your birthday. May I show you some of the dances I have been learning in your absence? I would like to dedicate them to you."

Deeply touched, Antipas readily agreed.

Salome gracefully backed away, and signaled toward the curtain. First she gave a rendering of some classical Greek dances, exquisitely performed, and Antipas loudly applauded, followed by the other guests. The Herods had always appreciated Hellenistic art in all its forms and Antipas was delighted.

The girl then danced her way through the door to appear a few moments later in an extravagant replica of a peasant girl's dress. She now did an attractive peasant dance during which she enticed the guests to clap along.

Again she whirled out of sight. The music changed and she reappeared in a beautiful peach-colored flowing garment, meant to represent the mysterious orient. It was studded with brilliants and silver and gold thread, which glittered in the lights of the chandeliers as she gracefully danced between the tables. Many of the guests who had been reclining now sat up, following her with their eyes around the room. She ended her performance with a dramatic, twirling finale at Antipas' feet. The applause was thunderous.

In his half-inebriated state, the Tetrarch's emotions were easily aroused and overwhelmed. What a delightful gift Herodias had presented him with in such a lovely daughter as this! He proclaimed his pleasure in extravagant terms. It was sometimes customary to offer tips or small presents to the professional dancing girls, or even request their company later in the night, but nothing like that was possible to one of royal descent like Salome. What could he do to show his great appreciation?

"Tell me, my love, what you would like. Ask whatever you want, and I will give it to you!"

Salome demurred sweetly, saying she had only hoped to give him pleasure. "If you are pleased, Father, then that is reward enough for me."

This only increased Antipas' determination. "Nay, but I *must* give you something! Whatever you ask, by heaven, I will give it to you—up to half my kingdom!"

"Please, if you insist, may I just consult Mother a moment?"

"Why, of course, go right ahead," he assured her with an indulgent smile.

With a few more girations and a kiss from her hand, Salome disappeared from view while the guests congratulated Antipas on his good fortune in having so beautiful a daughter.

Herodias, meanwhile, had been waiting in the small dressing room where Salome had changed costumes. Though putting on a smiling, gracious face to her guests and daughter, she was inwardly fuming. She had come to Sebaste with the hope of persuading Antipas to kill the prophet, but just that afternoon she had learned from one of the eunuchs in her service that her husband had sent for John and had talked at length with him! Fear and rage combined to make her even more determined to destroy John, before he should influence Antipas too far. She knew her husband was weak and that this righteous prophet held a strange fascination for him.

"Well?" she asked eagerly, as Salome came running in with flushed cheeks.

"He swore to give me anything I wanted—even up to half his kingdom! I could hardly believe it!"

"You are sure he swore?"

"Positive! It was 'by heaven.'"

"Good! The kingdom will follow, never fear, but now there is something more urgent! There is a prisoner here who is plotting to harm us. Tell your father you want, *immediately*, the head of John the Baptizer on a dish!"

"*What?*"

"Our whole future depends on it! Hurry! Hurry! Before they all forget what he promised."

The eyes of all the guests turned to follow Salome as she tripped daintily down the beautiful mosaic floor of the hall to Antipas' table. He beamed a tipsy smile at her.

"Well, my dear child, what is it to be?"

"Please give me, immediately, the head of John the Baptizer on a dish."

The Tetrarch, his face ashen and contorted with anguish, tried desperately to believe he had not heard correctly.

"You are joking, my love. What is it you really wish?"

"The head of John the Baptizer! Father, please give it to me at once on a dish. You swore, remember!"

Antipas' mouth had gone painfully dry. He licked his lips and clutched his wine cup convulsively. The voice was the voice of Salome, but he knew the request was from Herodias. The persistence of the woman! And what ingenuity, he thought with grudging admiration. His interview with John that morning flashed before him. Truly, he was a good and righteous man in no way deserving of death. What was more, he feared his many followers might stage a revolt if he killed him. But fear tore him in two directions.

A deathly stillness reigned in the hall now, every ear strained to catch his response. As the Tetrarch's eyes traveled desperately around his guests and saw the half-taunting glances, he knew that to retain the respect of his Gentile officers he must keep his oath. The legacy of the Medes and Persians was still prevalent in the east; a man must fulfill his oath once given.

Antipas was hopelessly trapped in a dilemma from which his weak, yet canny character saw only one possible exit. It would mean a life-time of guilt, regret, and possible grave political consequences.

He snapped his fingers and a slave came to his side.

Antipas' frantic gaze landed on Manaen, whose eyes were directed firmly on the table before him. The Tetrarch remembered he was one who had followed John. Better not ask him, it might lead to a scene.

"Call the guard."

A small squad was always on duty outside any room the Tetrarch was occupying. On receiving the message from the slave, they marched inside and lined the back wall. Their incongruous and sinister presence immediately removed the last semblance of festivity from the gathering. The leader advanced a few paces toward the Tetrarch's table.

"Go to the citadel immediately and bring me the head of the prisoner, John the Baptizer, on a dish," Antipas said firmly.

For an instant the man hesitated, then saluted and withdrew with his squad. Though his words were greeted with applause by some, Antipas noted that the majority were aghast.

Desperately he signaled to the master of ceremonies for a further round of drinking, but it seemed the zest had gone from his guests. It would be a while before the guards could reach the citadel, kill John, and return. With counterfeit gaiety contorting his ashen face, he called for the next entertainers.

As the eyes of the other guests followed these up to Antipas' table, Chuza turned a stricken face to his wife, his mind in as great a turmoil as the Tetrarch's.

"I am responsible for this ghastly tragedy, since I insisted he should move here!"

"Can't you stop them?"

"I don't know how, but I can try. I must hurry."

Chuza silently slipped out the door as the new entertainers, three clowns, began to tell ribald jokes that, for the most part, fell on inattentive ears. All were listening instead for the sound of the guards.

Salome, certain of her request, was perched on Antipas' couch, beaming smiles to the assembled company.

The Tetrarch's frenzied gaze kept returning to the banquet hall doors. Finally the guard appeared, his eyes fixed fifteen paces ahead as if to avoid the sight of what was in his hands.

"Your order has been carried out, my Lord."

He was about to place the dish on the table when Antipas roughly stopped him, revolted and terrified at the calm countenance facing him from the platter, the long hair and beard draped to one side amid a pool of blood.

"There you are, take it!" he muttered in strangled tones to Salome. "I have kept my oath. Take it out of my sight!"

Salome seized the dish from the guard and was surprised at its weight. She staggered a moment, then held herself proudly as she walked the length of the hall and out the door.

She just managed to hand the platter to her mother in the dressing room before vomiting violently down her beautiful costume.

In the banquet hall many guests were hastily rising to take their leave when another guard hurried up to Antipas' table.

"My lord," he whispered, "the chief steward, Lord Chuza, is dead."

Part
Three

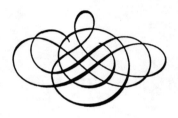

THE
FULFILLMENT

28

A Painful Separation

Once outside, Chuza had half-run, half-stumbled across the great courtyard in the darkness and hurried to the room in which the steep stone stair led down to the dungeon.

Guards now crowded around the doorway there. As Chuza reached them, two of the permanent staff who had known John longest pushed their way out with shocked, angry faces. Chuza impatiently thrust them all aside, then stopped dead, an anguished groan escaping his lips.

By the light of two flaming torches, a guard was gingerly picking up by the hair a severed head. He dropped it in the dish one of the others held ready. The body lay on the ground, with faithful Benjamin kneeling beside it, weeping uncontrollably.

Chuza then impulsively rushed forward, intending to kneel on the other side and beg forgiveness from the lifeless body. Suddenly his foot slipped in the pool of blood already seeping across the floor. Chuza plunged headlong down the steep stairs into the cell.

A horrified gasp went up from those in the room, and they cautiously approached the edge. As a soldier was about to push John's body from the top of the stairs with his foot, Benjamin angrily struck his leg aside, then tenderly lifted the thin frame of his master and laid it back along the wall.

Two soldiers now held the torches over the dungeon and could just make out the form of Chuza at the bottom.

"There's no sign of movement," muttered one. "We'd better go down and investigate."

In the midst of his own grief, Benjamin was now greatly concerned for Chuza. "Sir," he said to a guard he knew, "call Gad so that he can inform his mistress of her husband's injury."

The soldier holding the platter still stood there, waiting to see what had happened to Chuza, but a superior angrily ordered him off to Antipas, then approached the edge of the dungeon.

"How is he?" he called down.

"Unconscious, but there seems to be some faint breathing."

"Get him up."

Clumsily the two men dragged Chuza up the steep stairs and laid him on the floor near John.

"Looks like his neck is broken," muttered the officer, "and there's no sign of breathing now. The Tetrarch is going to be upset about this. He knew a good steward when he saw one. Not a very happy birthday, if you ask me."

The next hours passed like a blurred, yet horrifying nightmare for Benjamin. Gad had fetched Nathan and Jochanan, and Nathan had automatically taken control, planning what should be done with John's body. There had been just one ray of light for Benjamin in the whole horrible business. This was when Joanna, attended by Ruth, came to view the two bodies lying in the prison. They shed many tears over both, and yet there was a restraint, even a peace, so different from the professional wailings that had soon arisen outside when the news of Chuza's death reached the palace.

Antipas ordered no expense to be spared in hiring mourners for his chief steward, so relays of both wailers and flute players were soon in constant attendance. He also assured Joanna all funeral expenses would be met and Chuza would be buried wherever she wished. He seemed anxious to ease in any way he could the oppressive guilt he experienced since ordering John's execution.

Joanna decided Chuza should be buried in the family grave near Capernaum. Then she had another idea and asked Gad to summon John's disciples to her apartment.

"I wondered if you would like the prophet to be buried with my husband?" she said. "It would be an honor to have him laid with our family. I'm sure Chuza would have agreed."

Their astonishment at this generous offer of burial among the nobility was obvious.

"He surely deserves the best!" blurted Benjamin, wiping away fresh tears. "Jesus of Nazareth even said no one greater than he had been born of woman, didn't he?"

The mention of that name caused Nathan to shake his head.

"Thank you most sincerely for your generous offer, but I doubt if the Tetrarch would agree. Our Lord Chuza's funeral will be such a public affair. Antipas will want our master's death to be kept as quiet as possible for fear of a riot. Also, a lot of public display about John's death may make it more dangerous for Jesus. Many religious leaders would be glad to get rid of him."

"I understand. What are you planning to do with John then?"

"I've been offered a cave tomb in the hillside north of here, so we'll use that temporarily, at least. Perhaps some relatives may wish to remove him to Judea later."

"Well, please allow me to provide the burial perfumes and spices. Ruth and I will come very soon to—to complete this last service to those we love and revere." Tears came to Joanna's eyes again as she turned to Ruth, who had just brought in some refreshment for the guests. "Let me know as soon as your brother has returned with the spices," she said.

Benjamin was surprised at this last remark. He hadn't known Ruth had a brother. He wondered if he would be like his sister.

As the disciples left Joanna's quarters, they met Gad returning from town loaded with burial spices. Again Benjamin was puzzled. Here was Ruth's husband, but no sign of a brother.

Soon the women appeared at the citadel again, Gad following with the spices, and the women began their preparation of the bodies with loving care. When he had a chance Benjamin whispered to her, "Where is your brother?"

Ruth stared at him, wondering if grief had deranged his mind. "Why, he's over there, helping my mistress."

"You mean—Gad?" Benjamin suddenly experienced a wild heartbeat.

"Of course!"

"Why did you say he was your husband, then?"

"I never said so!" Then comprehension dawned. "Oh, when we came here we thought it safer to let it be assumed we were husband and wife. In all the excitement and anxiety I forgot no one knew differently."

Benjamin kept his eyes down to hide the excitement this news

253

generated in him, even in the midst of this sorrowful task. How thankful he was he had not known before, when John was alive. He felt guilty that anything could ease his sorrow, but now he must try to get a private interview with the Lady Joanna as soon as decently possible.

Nathan made cautious inquiries to try to locate John's head, so the whole body could be buried together. But no one in the men servants' quarters seemed to know. When he told the group busy with the spices, Ruth offered to go see what she could find out.

She soon returned, obviously upset.

"I asked one of Herodias' maids," she said hesitantly, then shuddered. "She says her mistress has it in her apartment and has stuck a bodkin in his tongue, because it had publicly accused her of adultery."

The news stunned and sickened them all for a moment. Then Nathan said, "We must bury the body this afternoon. It is not wise to leave it any longer. Who knows what other evil she may devise? Perhaps two of the more friendly guards will help carry him. Would you allow Gad to come, too?" he asked Joanna.

"Of course. We will all three come." Joanna was surprised to find she was beginning to feel more at home with these fellow-believers than with any of her court acquaintances. "What are your plans for after the burial?" she continued.

"We haven't even discussed them yet," confessed Nathan, "but I have no doubt what I must do. I'm sure John would have me go join Jesus, as our former disciples did."

"I agree," Jochanan declared unhesitatingly.

"Well, I'm not so sure," Benjamin said, and the frown on his face deepened. "Why didn't he release our master from prison? Why didn't he prevent his death? If he's really the Son of God, he could do that. Besides, John said he was to baptize with the Spirit and fire. Until he does that, I will not believe."

"Do you remember what the Guardian predicted in our last assembly of the congregation: that John's work would not last more than two years? And John himself said 'He must increase, and I must decrease.' We must accept it now as God's plan that his work is done," Nathan said gently, knowing it was better not to argue with Benjamin in his present bitter mood. After a minute of awkward silence, he asked, "What do you want to do, then?"

254

"I haven't had time to think yet. But I'm a skilled potter, remember. I can find work somewhere. But how strange it will feel! I—I just can't think of life without him!" With that, Benjamin ran and flung himself down beside John's lifeless body.

A small procession wound its way up to the hill tomb. Joanna insisted on walking and explained to John's disciples on the way that it was a test to see if she could do it, because a new plan had come to her.

"Mary of Magdala, who was miraculously released from seven devils by Jesus, feels a group of women could help him and his disciples on their busy journeys. She said her housekeeper, Susanna, and also Salome were anxious to go, too. So I thought while my son is away for his education, perhaps I would join them for a time, if I can stand the hard travel."

By now it no longer seemed strange to the disciples to be talking to a woman, and they nodded sympathetically.

"That sounds good—if the Messiah will allow it," which seemed unlikely to Nathan.

"Mary didn't think there would be any problem. Salome is his aunt, and—well, he's just so different from any other person in the world. One feels so safe, and pure, and full of kindness and goodwill in his presence."

Benjamin wondered how this might affect what he was now hoping for, but he put it from his mind as they approached the tomb.

After a brief service of committal, they each bade a tearful farewell to the body of the one they had revered and served for the two years of his great ministry.

"To think a hundred thousand people have listened to him and he ends like this," Benjamin sighed bitterly, and the others had difficulty dragging him away.

Now came yet another moment of great emotion when Nathan and Jochanan had to say good-bye as they continued north to Galilee to find Jesus and inform him of his forerunner's execution. Not only the physical separation after almost a lifetime together, but the difference in their response to the Messiah compounded the strain and sorrow.

Nathan drew Benjamin aside and handed him their common purse with most of what remained of Chuza's generous provision.

"This will help until you find work," he said sadly. "Where do you expect to settle?"

"I don't know yet." Benjamin dared not mention the new hope stirring in his heart, even amid his agonizing sorrow for the loss of John. "I shall wait and see Lady Joanna off tomorrow," he added gruffly.

A sad and silent little group returned to Sebaste, but on their arrival at the palace, Benjamin whispered to Joanna that he would like a word with her in private.

"I don't know how to say this," he began. "It's something I would never have thought possible once, but now that I'm planning to return to ordinary life, would you consent to my betrothal to your maid, Ruth? That is, if you have no plans for her already?"

"No, I haven't. She was the only one able to communicate with her brother before Messiah healed him. Now that is no longer necessary of course."

She saw Benjamin's eyes brighten and she felt deep regret at what she must now say, for she had learned to appreciate his many good qualities.

"I know Ruth thinks well of you, having told me of your wonderful care of John. But don't you understand she is a believer in Jesus? She cannot marry someone who doesn't share her faith."

"But we both loved and served John and accepted his teaching! Isn't that enough?" An agonized expression spread over his face.

"He taught that Jesus is Messiah. Why won't you accept that?"

"John doubted it for a time! And Jesus has not done what he was supposed to. He shows no sign of setting up the kingdom! He was to be the Lamb to take away sin, yet he eats with publicans and sinners! He was to baptize with the Holy Spirit and fire but never has. Most of all, he abandoned John, his most faithful servant, and left him to die! How can I follow such a man?"

"Some of these things will yet be fulfilled. Have patience. If only you would come and meet the Master, Benjamin, you would be convinced he *is* the Truth. In spite of my husband's death, I still can trust him and I thank him for the new happiness he brought into our family since knowing him. This you could never share with Ruth, if you are not his follower."

There was a finality in her tone that sent a numbness through Benjamin, quelling the throb of excitement that had coursed in him earlier. So this was the end of his hopes! And it was all because of Jesus.

A PAINFUL SEPARATION

That night his depression and despair allowed Benjamin little sleep. With a very haggard face he went to watch Joanna's party set out at dawn. Antipas had provided a chariot for Chuza's bier and a litter for Joanna. Before she left she motioned to Benjamin to come closer.

"Thank you again for all your help. Where will you go now?" she asked.

"To Jerusalem," he answered with a stubborn expression.

"The Master will go there for the Passover. Perhaps we may see you then. We shall keep praying for you, Benjamin. The Lord bless and keep you."

29

The Lamb is Sacrificed

Driven by his misery, Benjamin marched with long strides toward Jerusalem. When he arrived he inquired at the temple to learn where John's elderly cousin, the priest Jason lived. At Jason's house he gave the tragic news of John's execution.

Jason and his wife invited Benjamin to stay a few days. On the second day he told them of his desire to go into the pottery business.

"I'm afraid there's little of that here now," Jason said regretfully. "The kilns have always been in the southeast corner of the lower city. Now that the temple and Herod's palace have been built just above, they thought the smoke would spoil the beautiful stonework."

"Yes, most potters were ordered to move. It was very hard on them," added his wife.

Benjamin's face fell. It seemed there was no end to the disappointments he must face.

"Why don't you try Ain Karim?" Jason said after a moment's thought. "Zachariah, John's father, was a potter there. That's where John was born."

At that name Benjamin was all attention.

"He worked for the priest Abiel," Jason continued, seeing Benjamin's interest. "Abiel died recently, but his son Shemaiah carries on the business. His course is on duty at the temple this week. I can ask him if he needs a helper."

"Please do!" Benjamin answered earnestly, hardly daring to hope *something* might turn out right.

Hearing Benjamin was a friend of Zachariah's son John, Shemaiah agreed to give him a trial and a place to stay. When the day came for Benjamin's departure, Jason was sorry to see him go, for he had helped the elderly couple in many ways.

"Come and stay with us for the next Passover, Benjamin," he said as they were leaving.

"Thank you, I'd like to, I've never been to one," he confessed. "At Qumran they were against anything done at the temple. I'd like to see for myself."

On the way to Ain Karim, Benjamin asked Shemaiah if any of the village people were followers of Jesus of Nazareth or had been baptized by John.

"Most of us heard the Baptizer once or twice, and of course we were impressed. Some were baptized, I believe. But almost all are priestly families, and we have to be careful. Ever since that evil Herod had all the babies murdered, most families have been afraid to get involved in anything out of the ordinary. After hearing what happened to the Baptizer, it seems we were wise. But I remember his father—he was a good man."

"He must have been, if his son took after him at all," Benjamin said eagerly.

Shemaiah gave him a sharp glance. "I hope you are not planning to do any proselytizing. We don't need any more trouble."

"No, no," Benjamin assured him. "I've never been a preacher. John is dead and I've no time for Jesus of Nazareth. All I want is an honest day's work and to learn a bit more about the temple and synagogue."

Shortly after, Shemaiah pointed out Zachariah's old home. "I don't think you'd get much of a welcome there," he warned. "Zoma, a cousin, took possession after his death, when nothing more was heard of Elizabeth and the baby. His wife, Abigail, went completely crazy after her two grandsons were killed by Herod's soldiers with the other babies. A granddaughter and her family live there now, but I doubt they'll want to hear anything about John."

Benjamin fumed inwardly at the thought that anyone would not want to acknowledge the prophet, but knew he must try and fit into this new situation for a time, at least.

As the days passed, Benjamin found it hard to adjust to living in a village community, away from his lifelong companions. But Shemaiah and his family were kind, and Benjamin enjoyed making a greater variety of vessels compared to those required at Qumran.

Soon he made quite a name for his work, and Shemaiah invited him to stay permanently. But inwardly he still suffered from that numbness that had beset him after Joanna's reply to his request for Ruth.

The months passed quietly and at last the great annual Passover festival approached. During Passover tens of thousands of animals would be offered as sacrifices by the million residents and pilgrims who flocked to the temple.

Benjamin traveled to Jerusalem with others from the village and arrived to find Jason quite agitated.

"Jesus was at the temple early yesterday and drove out the animals and moneychangers, just as he did at the beginning. He doesn't seem to realize how angry this makes the high priests. They are *really* upset this time!"

Benjamin's heart beat faster. If Jesus was here, then many of his disciples would be, too! He was still determined not to be bewitched by Jesus, but he longed to see his old friends again. He decided to spend all the time he could in the temple courtyard watching for them.

"All this on top of Lazarus coming back to life is just too much for them," Jason continued.

"*What* did you say?"

"You must have met Lazarus. He was the neighbor in Bethany to my brother Eleazer. They belonged to the community for years."

"I remember. Lazarus was one of the first to be baptized."

"Well, he was never strong, and recently got worse and died. In fact he'd been buried four days. Then Jesus came along and *called him out of the grave!* He walked out, perfectly well!"

"I can't believe that!"

"The doctor *said* he was dead, and he was shut in the tomb all that time without food and drink."

Benjamin remained obstinately silent, but it struck him as strange to be upset at someone raised from death.

At the temple next morning to his great joy he saw Justus and Nathan.

"The Lord bless thee and keep thee!"

"Why, Benjamin! I didn't recognize you in those fine clothes!" Justus embraced him joyfully, followed by Nathan.

"Do you live here? Tell us what you are doing," they asked eargerly.

Benjamin told them briefly, then rather reluctantly asked what Nathan had done since they parted.

"We went straight to the Master. When we told him of John's death he was very sad and suggested we go across the lake for a time of quiet and prayer. He said John was truly a burning, shining light that had led many to the kingdom—"

"He was certainly that," Benjamin agreed.

"But he added that his own works were an even greater testimony that God had sent him," he said. "Crowds followed us round the lake on foot, begging for teaching, and they stayed a very long time. The Master fed over five thousand people from just two little fish and five small bread loaves! It was incredible!"

Benjamin was silent, so Justus continued. "Another thing that has kept us busy is preaching and healing in the villages. You remember we were on our first assignment when we met you in Samaria. It's a wonderful, yet humbling experience to be used by God in that way."

"Do you baptize with the Spirit and fire?"

"No, Benjamin. Can't you forget about that?" Justus chided gently. "It must still be to come. But hundreds of people came to meet the Master as we approached Jerusalem this time. They waved palm branches shouting 'Hosanna to the son of David! Blessed is the kingdom that is coming!' So we believe he will become the king soon. These are exciting days!"

Again Benjamin was silent.

"Did you hear about my family's former neighbor, Lazarus? He was brought back to life."

"Yes, Jason told me."

"Their whole village is still talking about it! We're all staying up there, it's quieter than here, and safer, considering the growing opposition of the religious leaders. We must be on our way now," Nathan concluded, "but we are here all week, so we will see you again. We often pray for you and wish you would join us."

Benjamin watched them go with an aching heart. It all sounded so good and yet Jesus still had not fulfilled John's prophecy. Unless that happened he would never believe!

Benjamin enjoyed the privilege of sharing the Passover lamb with a family, as Jason's two sons and their children all joined them for the historic feast. It was late when it was over, but Benjamin was assured they could all sleep later in the morning.

He was awakened early, however, by a strange noise in the street outside. At first it was the sound of many sandaled feet and murmuring voices, but then he began to distinguish a rhythmic shout, "Crucify him, crucify him!"

As the meaning of the words penetrated, curiosity and horror jarred him fully awake. He had never seen a crucifixion and felt ashamed at the urge to go view it. Yet, after a few moments he could lie still no longer. Throwing on his outer robe and sandals, he hastily went out.

The main procession was already out of sight down the narrow street, but there was no doubt as to its direction. Everyone was headed one way and others were joining from nearby houses.

Benjamin overtook many and soon made out the glint of Roman helmets ahead and an occasional spear flashing in the early sunlight.

"What's happening?" he asked a young fellow in the crowd.

"Three prisoners are to be crucified."

"Who are they?"

"Two robbers, I don't know their names. And Jesus of Nazareth."

"What?"

"Yes, he's causing trouble everywhere. He'll make the Romans come down on us all. He must be gotten rid of for the benefit of everyone. They're on their way to Golgotha."

Benjamin was stunned. Should he go back and tell Jason? Yet as people hurried past he felt compelled to join them. Again he quickened his pace until he was in sight of the guards and their prisoners. Two of the prisoners were strong-looking men who carried, without much difficulty, the wooden beams on which they would be hung.

The center figure was different. A tangle of huge thorns was twisted around his head, causing blood to stream down face and hair so that he could hardly see where he was going.

The bare shoulders and back were also badly torn from a recent flogging and every movement of the heavy beam across them was agony. He was slowing the procession now, and when one or two lashes unavailed to hurry him, the centurion ordered a dark-skinned bystander to carry the beam.

THE LAMB IS SACRIFICED

Benjamin was still trying to get a proper glimpse of the face, but it was impossible with all the blood and matted hair. He could only tell the face was badly bruised and swollen.

Benjamin's pace slackened. He had seen enough. He'd been right all along. This was obviously no king of Israel. He couldn't see a single disciple in the crowd and felt great sympathy for them now. Obviously they must have discovered their mistake and left him. He would go tell Jason.

Making his way back against the crowd, however, Benjamin couldn't help feeling this was terribly unjust treatment for one who had healed the sick. And if Jesus couldn't help himself now, he could never have saved John, either.

Jason and his family were up now, and they were horrified at the news.

"I knew it, I knew it!" Jason moaned, his head in his hands. "The hierarchy here won't suffer any rival influence. Yet he's such a *good* man. We really believed he was Messiah!"

The morning meal was heavy with grief. Afterward Jason and his sons had to leave for duty at the temple. Benjamin decided to go with them.

The place was strangely quiet for the middle of such an important feast, and people could be seen whispering together, some with sorrow, some with anger on their faces, about the crucifixion of Jesus.

At noon, a strange darkness descended over the city. No one could explain it, because the day had been bright and clear just moments before. Many people grew fearful of an earthquake or other calamity. Some sought shelter within the temple courtyard's walls. Others hurried back to their homes.

Benjamin shared their anxiety, but Jason was busy in the priests' quarters, and Benjamin felt terribly alone as he watched the frenzied coming and going. He suddenly became conscious of a strange jolt that seemed to come from the area of the temple itself, so he moved up with some others to the men's courtyard. There he saw many priests hurrying about.

Jason spied him and came running over. "A terrible thing has happened," he whispered. "The great curtain shutting off the Holy of Holies has been ripped apart from top to bottom. I don't know when I'll be able to leave, so don't wait for me."

Shortly after, the darkness lifted as mysteriously as it had come. Despite his skepticism about Jesus, Benjamin felt an urge to go to the place of crucifixion and see what had happened there.

He hurried out through a gate in the city wall. From there he could look across at the strange configuration on the white hillside opposite: three dark caves in its face that gave the appearance of a human skull.

Above, he could make out three wooden crosses outlined against the sky, so he took the winding path up the hill to the flat area at the top. A crowd of people was still there, drawn by the lure of a grisley spectacle. Around the execution crosses the guards stood or squatted, while some of the chief priests looked on, a satisfied smirk on their faces. Farther away, Benjamin saw a small group of women, obviously weeping behind their veils.

Suddenly his eyes were riveted there. Surely one was Lady Joanna! And the figure beside her must be Ruth. He caught his breath, wondering if Ruth was not yet married. If the women were here, then the disciples must be too, he reasoned, but he searched the crowd in vain.

As Benjamin approached, the Roman guards and their centurion were expressing amazement that Jesus seemed to be dead already. One of the soldiers was ordered to stab his side with a spear, and when he did blood and water poured out, but the body did not move.

Benjamin had no doubt now that Jesus was dead, and they would all have to stop believing he was the Messiah. He moved closer to greet Joanna and find out where she was staying.

He moved over slowly, approaching from the rear.

"Excuse me . . . Lady Joanna?"

"Benjamin! Oh, how *could* they do this to him!" Her tears came afresh. "Yet somehow he knew it would happen."

"How could he?" Benjamin said.

"I don't know. The Master kept warning us, but we couldn't believe it then."

"But *why?*"

"I can't explain, because I don't understand myself. I have been certain he was the Messiah and I still refuse to believe otherwise, but now—what happens after this, we have no idea. We are just waiting to see what they do with . . . the body. We *must* give him a worthy burial." Tears flowed again.

There seemed no point in waiting longer, so Benjamin put his question: "Where are you staying?"

"With a believer named John Mark, and his mother, Mary. She has a large upper room for guests and has kept it for the Master's followers. His mother came and is with us, but most of the men stayed in Bethany, thinking it would be safer." She sighed. "The house is two streets north of Caiaphas' palace, then turn left, and it's the house on the corner."

Benjamin thanked her, then glanced at Ruth, who was comforting one of the weeping women. He felt sure that since she was here she was not yet married. But what good did that do him if they persisted in their obviously misguided belief Jesus was the Messiah John predicted?

As he made his way back to Jason's house, some words John had had them memorize from the prophecy of Isaiah suddenly shot through Benjamin's mind and seemed to dance on the paving stones as he walked.

"He was bruised for our iniquities. . . . The Lord has laid on him the iniquity of us all. . . . He poured out his soul unto death and was numbered with the transgressors. . . . His visage was marred more than any man. . . ."

As these words bombarded his brain, Benjamin shivered as he thought back to the scene he had just witnessed. Its similarity with these prophecies was uncanny. He tried to thrust them from his mind, only to have other words of his beloved master fill their place: "Behold the Lamb of God, which takes away the sin of the world."

Benjamin shook his head in puzzled despair. It was all beyond his comprehension. He just knew this Jesus was dead, as his master John was. This was the end of everything they had both proclaimed. The Qumran Brothers were probably right after all. Ought he to think of returning there? Then he grimaced at the memory of Zimri. No, he couldn't face that. And he must not forget the directions to that house. Surely they would all soon come to their senses and see that he was right.

30

The Prophecy Comes True

Benjamin had planned to stay over the Sabbath with Jason's family, but they were so overcome with grief that he decided to remain an extra day.

That morning, their relatives Cleopas and Mary stopped in on their way back to Emmaus, and Mary had a wild story about having gone with Joanna and some of the other women to Jesus' grave with spices. There they had found the tomb empty and had seen an angel who told them Jesus was risen and alive.

Cleopas didn't believe this and said none of the other men did, either. Benjamin's heart sank. How long would these women cling to their foolish hope? He would just have to wait until they were forced to admit that Jesus was really dead and gone. With discouraged steps, he returned to Ain Karim.

A few weeks later, Benjamin sat totally absorbed one early afternoon in the water pot he was fashioning with his powerful hands. His sole satisfaction now was seeing the completed rows of beautiful jars and other vessels he was able to produce. Only in working did he seem able to deaden the despair gnawing at his mind.

Shemaiah came into the workroom, having just returned from a visit to Jerusalem.

"I see you haven't wasted any time." He smiled as he looked at the row of jars "You know, Benjamin, I've been thinking. You are assured of a steady income now with this fine work. Why don't you get married?"

Benjamin gave a start that jerked the rim of his pot badly out of shape.

"I was brought up in the Qumran community. They never marry," he snapped. Even as he said the words he felt a hypocrite, knowing in his heart he still hoped to be able to marry Ruth when she gave up her foolish belief in Jesus as the Messiah.

"But you left there a long time ago, and you aren't following their dietary laws," Shemaiah said. "Why not think about it? I heard that Zachariah's old home will be vacant soon, the husband there has just got a permanent job at the temple. I thought you might have enjoyed living there. But it's too big for one person."

Benjamin's slow brain began to consider these unexpected possibilities, but he felt unable to think clearly.

"I—I just don't know what to say," he finally blurted out. "Give me a few days to think about it. I don't see why I shouldn't have the house anyway," he ended more belligerently. Then after a moment he asked, "I suppose you haven't heard any more about Jesus of Nazareth?"

"He wasn't mentioned in the temple. I did hear someone say his followers have all returned to Galilee, although at first there were rumors that various people had seen him alive again."

So, it was as he had expected, and Ruth would be there, too. *Surely* she and Joanna would be willing to listen to reason some day. Benjamin started his wheel again as Shemaiah turned to leave and began remolding the damaged water jar. As he carefully set it down on the self with others waiting to be baked, he heard voices in the street asking if he lived there.

Benjamin straightened abruptly, excitement coursing through him, and a moment later Justus and Nathan stood in the doorway. They joyfully embraced, and Benjamin pointed them to a bench.

"We can't stay long," Justus began, "but we've just had some wonderful news which made us think of you at once, so we came to tell you."

"You traveled all the way from Galilee just to see me?"

"No, we were up there to see Messiah, but then he told us to return to Jerusalem and meet him on the Mount of Olives. He made an important announcement."

"But he's *dead*. I *saw* the soldier spear him!"

"He was, but no longer! He returned to life on the third day. We have seen him a number of times. Why won't you believe us?"

Nathan asked. "Anyway, we all went to meet him at the Mount of Olives, and what do you think, Benjamin? He told us to stay in Jerusalem and wait for what the Father promised. He told us that John baptized with water, but that we shall be baptized with the Holy Spirit not many days hence. Benjamin, don't you see, it's coming true at last!"

Benjamin just stared at them.

"Benjamin, we don't know how it will happen, but we are sure it will and we want you there to see it." Justus looked him right in the eye. "I know our dear John would want you there, too. Plan to come to Jerusalem for the Feast of Pentecost next week. I think it will happen then."

"Yes, and you can stay with my cousin Jason. I asked him on the way down," added Nathan. "*Do* say you will come."

Looking into their eager faces, Benjamin was deeply moved, though he had no confidence in what they had told him. It would just be one more disappointment, he believed, but he couldn't resist their entreaties, especially after what Justus had said about John.

"All right, I'll come. It will be good to see everyone again," he added, not daring to ask specifically if the women would be there, too.

Justus and Nathan arrived back in time for the evening prayers. More than one hundred believers were now meeting daily for prayer since the meeting on the Mount of Olives. At that time Jesus had disappeared up in the clouds after telling them they were to be his witnesses throughout the world. They had been disappointed when he told them it was not for them to know when the kingdom would be established, but at least they had the encouragement that his own brothers had now become believers.

Simon Peter, ever the man of action, soon felt they should be doing more than praying. After the meeting that night he stood up and said that if they were to go out preaching again, they should choose a replacement for the traitor, Judas Iscariot, who had committed suicide shortly after the crucifixion.

"What about the Master's brother, James?" someone had suggested.

"But he hasn't been through all we have. He has a lot to learn yet," objected John.

Peter agreed. "It was the Baptizer who really started it all. We in the eleven were all baptized through his preaching, and began our change of life then. So we'll make it a condition that the new man also started with John, continued through with the Lord, and witnessed his resurrection."

There was general agreement. "All right, put forward two names. Then we'll cast lots to see which one the Lord chooses," Peter announced.

After some murmured discussion, a name was called by one group.

"We suggest Joseph Barsabbas Justus."

Justus slowly stood up with a look of concern.

"I appreciate this great honor," he began, "but I believe I am not the one to have a place in the twelve. It is true I was with John from the very beginning of his call. But as you know, I am from a priestly family and have been a scribe and member of the strict Qumran sect. These things leave their mark. I believe the Master chose no one with these qualifications among the twelve for a reason. This is a new day, a new covenant, when he chooses to use his great power through ordinary men . . . and women. The day of a priesthood is over, I believe."

Peter looked a little puzzled, as if not quite following this reasoning. "Well, we can leave the Almighty to decide that," he said brusquely. "Another name?"

"Matthias," came from a different corner.

"Very good. Matthew Levi, come and write these names on two stones."

Matthew came forward and carefully wrote out the two names on round stones, then dropped them into an empty jug.

"Let us pray," Peter's voice boomed out. "Lord, you know all hearts, make clear which one of these two you have chosen to take the ministry and apostleship from which Judas turned aside."

He lifted the container with the stones in it, shook it well, and allowed one to fall out. He and Matthew bent to examine it, then Peter cleared his throat.

"The name of the new apostle is Matthias. Let us commend him to the Lord."

Afterward Justus warmly congratulated Matthias and was a little surprised at the sense of relief he felt at not being appointed to this office he once coveted. Could it be, he wondered, that John's words, "He must increase and I must decrease" were being worked out in his life by his new Master?

Jason and Benjamin, who had followed his friends to Jerusalem a few days later, had just finished breakfast one morning when they heard a strange roar, somewhat like a hurricane. Yet the trees in sight of the house were motionless.

"It seems to come from that direction," Jason said, looking up the street. "Let's go see."

Others were coming out of their houses fearing an earthquake, and they followed them. Soon they caught sight of Peter running down the steps of John Mark's house, the other believers behind him. At once they began talking to those they met.

Nathan quickly saw Benjamin and ran to meet him.

"Benjamin!" he exclaimed, "it's happened! Just as John said! The Holy Spirit came into our room as we were all praying and filled our hearts, and fire came down upon each of our heads, yet we were not burned! Now we are suddenly able to speak to all these people in their own languages to witness to the grace of God. Benjamin, you must believe now, you *must*!" He seized Benjamin's hands in his intense longing.

His old comrade looked into his face, and suddenly knew he spoke the truth. Benjamin found his resistance melting away, his mind convinced at last. Jesus *was* the Lamb of God, and the baptizer with the Spirit and fire. Hallelujah! He in turn gripped Nathan and tears of joy poured down his cheeks.

"Listen! Peter's shouting something, let's go hear." Nathan pulled Benjamin with him to the end of the street, which opened into a small square. There stood Peter, the eleven beside him, addressing a considerable crowd. Farther down the street, other believers were still talking to individuals, but they gradually motioned them to go listen to Peter.

"These are not drunk, as you suppose," he was saying. "This is what was spoken by the prophet Joel: . . . 'In the last days, says God, I will pour out My Spirit on all flesh; Your sons and your daughters shall prophesy. . . .'"

Nathan and Benjamin grinned at each other. "That's what Justus read to us in the old days," Nathan whispered.

"Yes," agreed Benjamin. Suddenly his new job was tinged with remorse. *Why* had he been so stubborn and not believed like all the rest? He could have seen Messiah and had the joy of serving him. And he had missed the baptism of fire, too. But why had that prophecy been fulfilled so late?

He turned to see Justus hurrying toward him, a smile of joy on his face.

"You really believe now, Benjamin, I can see," he greeted him.

"Yes, thank God! What a fool I've been! But Justus, why was the fulfillment of the prophecy delayed so long?"

Justus thought a moment. "I don't know. Maybe we had to know the Master first, and have faith in him, and realize our own helplessness to do things in our own wisdom and strength. Also there wasn't the same need for the Spirit while Jesus was with us in person."

"But why then was it delayed even after his resurrection?"

"Perhaps that gave time for the authorities to forget him and leave his disciples in peace, giving them time to pray and realize their complete dependence on him. Also, of course, it needed a great feast like this, with people in the city from many nationalities, far and wide, for the greatest impact to be made on the world in the shortest time. God's ways are indeed beyond our understanding. We can only praise his great name, and thank him it *has* happened."

Justus moved on, and Benjamin tried to pick up the thread of Peter's discourse again.

"This Jesus God has raised up, of which we are all witnesses," he was saying triumphantly. ". . . having received from the Father the promise of the Holy Spirit. . . ."

Benjamin was amazed at the power of this young fisherman who had seemed a rather unstable character in the early days of discipleship under John. The crowd had grown now to several thousand, and the people were deeply moved.

Again Peter's voice rang out clearly, "Repent, and let everyone of you be baptized in the name of Jesus Christ for the remission of sins. . . ."

The same old message, Benjamin thought, then noticed the new title, Jesus *Christ*. That must be the seal of John's prophecy that he was the Coming One, the Anointed.

"For the promise is to you and to your children," Peter continued, "and to all who are afar off."

Those words caused a new thought to flash into Benjamin's

mind. So God must approve of children, and therefore of marriage! He forgot Peter and eagerly looked down the street. After a fruitless search, he turned to look behind. In a distant doorway he was positive he could see Ruth talking to three women who were listening intently. Now he must search for Joanna! Finally he caught sight of her as a woman she was talking to moved away. Benjamin immediately approached at a rapid pace, sure now what her answer would be to his request for Ruth.

"That's wonderful, Benjamin," Joanna said when he told her his great news. "And I know Ruth will be delighted to hear it, too. She has prayed for you so often. I gave her and Gad their freedom after my husband's death, but she chose to stay with me and has been like a real daughter. I shall miss her very much. But let us go find her."

Benjamin was suddenly tongue-tied as they approached, and it was Joanna who told Ruth the good news of his belief and of his wish to marry her.

"I've been so *stupid*," he stammered. "I don't know why I couldn't see it before. Now it seems I really *know* the Messiah in my heart, and I promise you we will follow him together, and I will do my best to care for you.

"I have no fear of that," Ruth answered gently, "after seeing how you cared for John. It was your love and devotion to him, I think, that blinded you to anything else. But are you quite *sure* now that marriage is the right thing for us? John would not have approved, would he?"

"No, at least not before," Benjamin admitted. "But now I think the Holy Spirit would have opened his eyes as he has mine," he continued with growing assurance. "When you offered to help John escape from Sebaste at the risk of your life, he began to see women in a new light. I could tell. His whole purpose was to prepare the way for Messiah, and now I want to serve *him* with all my heart and life."

"Then we can do that together," Ruth said happily.